Broken SERIES
BOOK FOUR

Broken love

NEW YORK TIMES & USA TODAY BESTSELLING AUTHOR
KELLY ELLIOTT

This is a work of fiction. Names, characters, places, brands, media, and incidents are either the product of the author's imagination or are used fictitiously. The author acknowledges the trademarked status and trademark owners of various products referenced in this work of fiction, which have been used without permission. The publication/use of these trademarks is not authorized, associated with, or sponsored by the trademark owners.

Copyright © 2016 by Kelly Elliott
Published by K. Elliott Enterprises

Cover design by Sara Eirew Photographer
Cover photo by Shannon Cain
http://photographybyshannoncain.com
Editing by Nichole Strauss
Interior Designer: Julie Titus with JT Formatting

All rights reserved. Without limiting the rights under copyright reserved above, no part of this publication may be reproduced, stored in or introduced into a retrieval system, or transmitted, in any form, or by any means (electronic, mechanical, photocopying, recording, or otherwise) without the prior written permission of the above copyright owner of this book.

First Edition: April 2016
Library of Congress Cataloging-in-Publication Data
Broken Love (Broken Series, Book 4) – 1st ed
ISBN-13: 978-1943633135

For exclusive releases and giveaways signup for Kelly's newsletter at
www.kellyelliottauthor.com

This book is dedicated to Danielle Sanchez.
If it weren't for you *Broken Love* would have never come about. Thank you for helping me bring Ava and Ryder to life. Oh yeah, and thank goodness you remember my characters better than I do.

#BestPublicistEver

This book is for anyone who has ever been broken. Never give up and always remember love heals all who are broken.

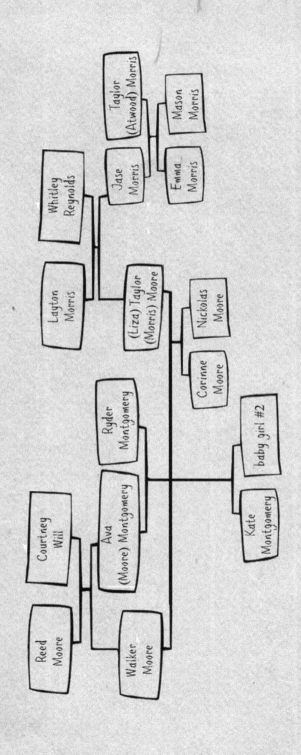

One

Ava

Nothing about my relationship with Johnny was normal. We met and fell in love immediately. He asked me to marry him on our two-month anniversary, and I said yes. My mother cried, and my father lectured me for three hours straight. He kept repeating, "This isn't normal, Ava."

What was normal anyway?

According to my father, knowing someone at least six months before agreeing to marry him or her was normal. I, of course, disagreed and let my whirlwind relationship with Johnny totally blind me of what I couldn't see before my very eyes.

As I stood in front of four different cakes, I couldn't help but glance around the bakery. Johnny and I were having a small wedding, held at his parents' country club in Austin. His mother had insisted we not elope, which was exactly what we had both wanted to do.

Turning my attention to Johnny, I watched as he talked to the young redhead who had been helping us.

"So, have you narrowed it down?" she asked, as she smiled brightly at Johnny and barely acknowledged I was there.

With a shrug of his shoulders, Johnny turned to me and said, "Ava, could I possibly talk to you outside for a moment?"

I gave Johnny a slight smile as I nodded my head. "Of course."

Johnny placed his hand on my lower back and guided me out of the bakery. I frowned as I thought how his hand on my lower back should cause my stomach to dip. At least that is how it was for the girls in the romance books I read. The touch of his hand on my body should ignite my body in flames.

Ha! I'd never experienced those feelings before in my entire life. There was a reason it was called fiction.

As we stepped out of the bakery, I flashed him a smile as I decided maybe what we needed was some afternoon delight. Placing my hand on his chest, I licked my lips and purred, "I know something else I'd rather be tasting."

Johnny looked away as he stared down the street with an empty look in his eyes. "Ava, I need to talk to you."

My smile faded as I instantly gnawed on my lower lip. His voice was serious and I had a terrible feeling he was about to say something that was going to prove my father right.

"Okay, right now or after we pick out a cake?"

Johnny looked into my eyes and shook his head. "I need to be honest with you, Ava."

My heart sank as I held my breath involuntarily before finding the air to speak again. "Honesty is always nice."

As he closed his eyes, I fought to hold back the tears I knew were about to fall.

"There's someone else. I didn't mean for it to happen, but it did. She's amazing and she makes me feel alive."

Anger quickly raced through my body as I took a step back. "Is that so? Kind of like how I made you feel alive? Or does she make you feel alive in some other kind of way?"

Shaking his head, Johnny let out a sigh. "I've known Lisa almost my whole life. We ran into each other about a month ago and well, things just sparked between us."

I placed my hand over my stomach and let out a moan. "Oh. My. God. You've been cheating on me?"

"No! Well, I mean it wasn't like I did it on purpose. We fell in love, Ava, and I can't deny how I feel about her. I've only slept with her twice."

My mouth dropped open as I stared at him with a blank expression. "Are you kidding me right now? Are you really that big of a dick that you would actually tell me you've only slept with her *twice*? Is that somehow supposed to make me feel better, you dickhead?"

Johnny glanced around as he took me by the arm and started walking toward his Audi. I hated that car. I hated him. I hated that my father had been right.

"I would have thought you'd be happy that I told you this before we got married."

Holy freaking hell.

What did I ever see in this jerk?

Letting out a chuckle, I nodded. "No, you're right. Better you told me before I went off and married you and God forbid had a child with you."

"Ava, you have to admit this was all rushed. We got caught up in the whole romance side of things and lost focus on reality."

"Reality? You think I've lost focus on reality? You know what's real, Johnny?"

He lifted his hand and gently placed it on the side of my face. His thumb moved ever so slow as his eyes softened. "The pain you're feeling right now, Ava. I know this hurts, but baby, you're going to find someone else."

He did not. No. He. Did. Not.

"You got one part of that right. Pain. But it's not the pain I'm feeling, it's the pain you're about to feel, you asshole."

I lifted my knee and hit him right in the balls. I hadn't seen a guy go down on one knee since I accidentally hit Walker in the balls with a golf club.

Johnny doubled over as he cried out in pain.

"Have a happy life with Lisa."

Turning on my heels, I walked away quickly. Not sure whether I should cry or scream, I pulled out my phone and dialed the one person I knew would understand.

My mother.

"Hey, baby girl. How did the cake tasting go? Did you pick out a cake?"

Pressing my lips together, I tried to figure out how to deliver the blow. "No. But I did kick Johnny in the balls out on the sidewalk in front of the bakery."

Silence.

"You remember that time I hit Walker with the golf club?"

"Yes," my mother said slowly.

"Picture that. He went down on one knee pretty damn fast."

"What happened?"

Rolling my eyes, I wiped the tears away. "He met someone else. Someone who made him feel alive. He had sex with her, Mom. The bastard cheated on me. I hate him."

"Oh, sweetheart. I'm so sorry this has happened to you. Baby, why don't you head on home and spend a few days with us. I know your father would love to have you home."

Laughing, I shook my head and said, "Oh, I'm sure he would. The second he sees me he's going to say I told you so."

"He would not, Ava Moore. Your father loves you and cares about you."

Closing my eyes tightly, I whispered, "I know."

Before I had a chance to open my eyes, I slammed into someone. My eyes flew open as my phone flew out of my hand and I let out a curse word.

"Shit!"

I had been stopped dead in my tracks. Dropping down, I reached for my phone and for the papers I'd just caused this man to drop. As I lifted my eyes, I sucked in a breath of air.

Beautiful hazel eyes stared into my blue. "I-I'm so sorry," I said as I handed him a few pieces of paper.

The smile that spread across his face caused the earth to shake. Okay, not really, but it felt like it. I almost fell back onto my ass as I tried to contain the crazy feeling that zipped through my body when his hand brushed lightly across mine.

"I wasn't looking where I was going," I said, as he helped me into a standing position.

The beautiful mystery man pinned me with his stare. My eyes roamed his perfect face. He was slightly tan, but I couldn't tell if that was from the sun or his genes. His dark hair had that perfect messy look to it as he ran his hand through it and laughed.

"You don't say? It's not every day I run into a beautiful lady. I believe my day has officially been made."

His voice sounded like an angel.

Okay, so I don't really know what an angel would sound like, but if I could imagine it, I'd say this guy had it down. It was soft, yet masculine. Sexy, yet compassionate.

"I'm glad," I whispered.

He lifted his eyebrows and tilted his head as his eyes landed on my lips. "Glad you ran into me?"

My cell phone began ringing in my hand as I lifted it up to see it was my mother. Shit! I'd forgotten she was on the line. Giving him an awkward smile, I said, "No! Well, yes. No wait, I'm glad your day has been made … by me running into you."

Oh dear God, Ava. Stop talking. Lifting my phone, I grinned and said, "It's my mom."

"May I at least get your name?"

My teeth sunk down into my lip as I let out a soft chuckle. "Ava."

Mystery man's eyes lit up as he gave me a slight nod, followed by the sexiest wink I'd ever seen. He lifted his hand to my chin and forced my eyes to his. If I hadn't been acutely aware of every single action he made, I'd have missed his thumb move lightly over my bottom lip.

"The pleasure was most defiantly mine, Ava."

The stupid goofy grin on my face was evident as he chuckled, dropped his hand, and began walking off as I stood there in a stupor.

My phone rang again as I hit answer and whispered, "Hello?"

"Ava, are you okay? What happened?"

I shook my head to clear my thoughts as I glanced over my shoulder at my mystery man walking away from me. Getting a grip on myself, I headed toward my car. I was so thankful I had suggested meeting Johnny at the bakery.

"Sorry, Mom. I accidentally ran into someone. Hey, I think I'm going to do what you said. I need a few days of fresh country air. Besides, I can work from anywhere."

I could practically hear my mother jumping. "Oh good! When are you coming?"

"Today. I just need to go to my place and pack a bag."

"Okay, sweetheart. Be careful driving, and we'll see you in a few hours. Oh, I'll make your favorite dinner!"

Reaching my car, I turned around again. I wasn't sure why. Maybe I was hoping my mystery man would be standing there.

"Sounds great, Mom. I'll let you know when I'm on my way. I love you, Mom."

"I love you too, Ava. We'll have you forgetting Johnny in no time."

Slipping into the driver's seat, I started my car and said, "Johnny who?"

Two

Ava

Rushing into my condo, I felt my phone buzz. My mother had been coddling me ever since I went back home and spent two days with my parents in Llano.

I rolled my eyes and let out a sigh as I swiped across my phone and breathed out. "Hey, Mom. I'm fine. I'm still alive, and no I haven't cried once. It's been almost three weeks. I'm so beyond over it."

"Ha ha. You can't be mad at me for wanting to make sure my baby girl is doing okay."

With a loud thud, the bags that were in my hand landed on the floor. "I'm more than fine, Mom. I'm going out tonight with friends and we're going to have a good time."

"Don't drink and drive."

"Mom, I live in a condo in downtown Austin. I walk everywhere."

I could hear her frustrated sigh so I decided to play nice. "But, I promise I won't drink too much."

"Good. Remember, your father has that thing tomorrow about the ranch and he really wants you, Walker, and Liza to be there."

"I'll be there. I swear!"

"Have fun tonight, sweetheart, and be careful and remember … don't drink too much."

I couldn't help but smile. I knew my parents loved me and just worried. It had to be hard letting their little girl move to Austin and start a new life.

"Mom, I hardly drink anyway. I'll call you tomorrow before I leave to head home. Love you! Bye!"

"Bye, sweetie."

I pushed out a fast breath of air as I glanced around my room. My eyes caught the teal cocktail dress hanging up on my closet door. "Hello, beautiful," I said as I grabbed the dress from the satin hanger and headed to my bathroom. I'd had my eyes on this dress since it first came into Mon Amour, the boutique I worked at as a manager. I also worked for Maurice Parker, one of the top wedding dress designers in the country. I'd met him while in Paris and he hired me practically on the spot. Designing was my number one desire and what I wanted to do.

Slipping the dress on, I pulled my hair up and wrapped it around a few times, making a somewhat elegant, yet kind of sloppy, bun on the top of my head.

Maroon 5's song "Animals" blared over my phone. I headed back into my room and picked my phone up.

"Hey, Jay."

"Back at ya, babe! Are you ready to get your party on? It's not every day we celebrate the fact that I'm giving my va-jay-jay to one man."

With a soft chuckle, I slipped on my heels and leaned in toward the mirror to check my makeup one more time. "Yes, I'm ready. Are you here?"

"Fixin' to pull up, so hurry your ass up. My last night of freedom is upon us."

Grabbing my clutch, I headed out of my condo, locking it behind me. "You aren't even getting married for another two weeks, Jay."

"Doesn't matter. Tonight is the last night all my girls will be able to get together before I'm taken off the market."

"Um … you're already off the market."

Jay sighed. "Details, Ava. Why are you always stuck on the details?"

"Oh shit, I'm going to lose you. Getting in the elevator."

"Ava!"

I hit End on my phone and chuckled.

Looking over to my left, I noticed the guy who lived on the floor above me. He glanced at me and smiled. "You look beautiful this evening. Hot date?"

I let out a nervous laugh as I shook my head. "Nah. I'm not dating anyone right now."

His smile grew bigger.

"Girls' night. One of my best friends is getting married in a couple of weeks."

"Ah, let the trouble begin."

Deciding I wanted to be naughty, I looked over my shoulder as I stepped out of the elevator and said, "Here's hoping."

By the time I made it outside, Jay was pulled up and waiting for me. "Night, Harry!" I shouted at the doorman as I attempted to run over to Jay's convertible in five-inch heels.

Slipping into her car, I grabbed a scarf and wrapped it around my head. Jay drove with the top down every single day. Even if it rained, she put it down.

"Holy kittens on a cracker, you look hot!"

I laughed as I turned my head to face her. Her jet black hair was pulled up in a ponytail and she had on her signature red lipstick. "You know that doesn't make sense."

"What doesn't?"

"Holy kittens on a cracker. It makes zero sense."

Jay shrugged her shoulders and said, "I don't care. I like it, therefore I use it."

Rolling my eyes, I sighed and said, "Whatever. I need to seriously flirt with at least one man tonight. A little light petting might be fun too."

Jay laughed as she hit the gas and took off on the green light. "That's my Ava! It's so freaking great to have you back!"

Was the room spinning or was I spinning? I couldn't tell as I tried to focus on walking from our table, across the dance floor and to the bathroom.

I've got this. I'm a strong, independent woman. I can make my way to the bathroom.

"Hey, Ava!"

Ugh. I'd know that voice from anywhere. Plastering on a fake smile, I turned and looked at Dee Monroe. My old college roommate. "Dee!" I said as I threw myself into her body.

She hugged me and pushed me back as she gave me a once over. "Holy shit. Look at you looking so hot."

I raised my hand and tried to brush off her comment, but I accidentally hit her in the face.

"Ouch! What the hell, Ava!"

My hands slammed over my face as I started laughing. "I'm so s-sorry!" I busted out laughing as I tried to tell myself to stop. Literally.

"Stop it, Ava! It's not nice to laugh at people!"

Dee looked at me like I was nuts. "What in the hell is wrong with you?"

I pointed to myself and dropped my mouth open as I stared at Dee. "Me? You're asking what's wrong with me?"

Narrowing her eyes at me, she nodded. "I's tell you what's wrong with me. I's don't like you, Dee. Nope." I popped my p so loud it caused my lips to tingle. Dee's mouth slowly dropped open as her eyes widened in horror. Something I'm sure I would do too if I was sober and realized what I had just said.

"You always thought you were so great in college. I's knows better though." Taking my pointer finger, I jammed her in the chest. "You are a drama-filled queen. No wait. You're filled with drama. You're a drama queen."

"I beg your pardon?"

I rolled my eyes. "I know, it's loud in here." I placed my hands around my mouth like a cone and shouted, "You're a bitch, Dee! A drama-loving, dick-humping ... no wait ... dick-sucking, bitch!"

Dee's faced turned red and she looked like she was about to say something when someone ran right into me, knocking me over.

"What in the cookie hell kitten cracker!" I shouted as I landed right on my ass.

I was going to kill the asshole who knocked me down. I attempted to stand up, only to have the room spin on me again and my heels slide out from underneath me.

"Whoa, I got ya."

I knew that voice. My body came to life as I tried to focus on the person helping me up.

"Ava? Shit, are you okay?"

I squeezed my eyes shut and shook my head while I slowly opened them again. Only to find familiar hazel eyes staring down at me.

My head began to pound and I felt sick as I placed my hand over my mouth and said, "Holy shit. It's you."

Three

Ryder

I couldn't believe I had her in my arms. Again. The first time I ran into Ava I tried to ignore how her touch lit a fire in my body. Now, looking at her dressed in a tight short-ass dress with legs to die for ... yeah ... I was happy as hell to see her again.

Letting a smile play across my face, I nodded and said, "It's me all right."

Ava opened her mouth to talk but then slammed her hands over her mouth. I knew what was going to happen next. Taking her by the arm, I shouted, "Hold on, baby, let's get you outside."

Pushing through the crowd, I kicked the door open and quickly led Ava over to the side of the building where she promptly threw up.

All. Over. My. Shoes.

Closing my eyes briefly, I mumbled, "That's fucking disgusting."

"Oh God, I think I'm dying."

Laughing, I pushed a strand of her loose blonde hair behind her head. "Nah, you're just a beautiful woman standing on the side of a building puking her guts out ... onto my shoes."

The look of horror that passed over her face was the cutest damn thing

I'd ever seen. "I'm so sorry, mystery man."

I pulled my head back in surprise and was about to ask her why she called me mystery man when another girl ran up. "Ava! Are you okay?" When she turned and looked at me, she quickly forgot about Ava and smiled. "Well well well, hello there, handsome."

I looked between her and Ava with a blank expression.

"Water," Ava whispered.

The girl spun around and quickly took Ava in her arms. "Oh, sweetie. I told you not to drink those whiskey shots. You don't do hard liquor well."

Looking at me, the girl mouthed, *she doesn't drink much.*

Nodding my head, I said, "Let me go get a bottle of water for her."

Ava's friend winked and then ran her tongue along her lips. "Hurry back."

I wasn't sure how to read the friend, but I could for sure read that Ava had drank way too much.

After returning back outside with a bottle of water, Ava was sitting on a bench while her girlfriend was talking to some guy.

Sitting down next to Ava, I placed my hand on her leg and she jumped. "Hey, um … you know … I's don't even know your name. I's think if I'm gonna dream about you I should have a name with the face."

Smiling, I handed her the water. "Here, drink all of this."

Doing as I said, Ava began downing the water. "Slowly, baby, you'll get sick again."

Ava turned to me with her mouth dropped open as she let her hand fall to her lap, sloshing the water. "My God, I've gots to tell you … that makes me all kinds of hot when you call me baby."

"My name is Ryder."

Ava closed her eyes and mumbled something incoherently before saying, "Even his name is hot."

I looked away until I was sure the flush from my cheeks was gone. "Ava, I think you've had enough for one night. How are you getting home?"

Ava pointed her finger to the other side of her as I looked to see no one standing there. Her friend must have taken off back into the bar.

"There's no one there."

Ava jerked her head too fast and called out, "Whoa, Ryder seriously you don't have to make the whole world spin, okay. Just put me back down."

I tried to hold my laughter back as I leaned in and whispered against her neck, just under her ear. "Trust me, Ava. If you were in my arms, you'd experience a lot more than just being dizzy."

Ava swallowed hard as her body shuddered. "I think I need to lie down."

Standing up, I held my hand out for Ava and led her back into the club. I had to wrap my arm around her waist to keep her walking straight. After fifteen minutes of looking for this so-called friend, I made my way over to my brother, Nate.

"Nate, I ran into a—" Glancing down at Ava, I tried to figure out what I wanted to say. "Um, a friend."

"Uh-huh. She sure is pretty," Nate said as he looked at Ava.

Ava hit Nate in the chest … hard. "Awe … you's is so sneaks."

Nate's eyebrows rose. "Sneaks?"

"She's had a bit too much to drink. I'm going to take her home since I can't find her friend anywhere."

Nate gave me a wink and said, "Right. Well, you have yourself one hell of a good time tonight, you lucky son-of-a-bitch."

Anger began to build in my blood as I shook my head. "It isn't anything like that."

Lifting the glass full of vodka to his lips, he smiled and drank.

Fuck this. I'm getting Ava out of here now.

"See ya tomorrow," I said as I turned to head out of the club.

"Don't be fucking late, Ryder."

By the time I got Ava back to my car, she had thrown up two more times and told me how she had dreamed about me. One dream was graphic and I had to adjust my dick in my pants.

I slipped Ava into the front seat and ran around to the driver's side. Jumping in, I looked at Ava and said, "Where do you … live … fuck."

Ava was passed out with her sweet little mouth hanging open and what appeared to be a small amount of drool starting to form in the corner. It was the cutest damn thing I'd ever seen.

I wasn't sure what to do. Glancing down at her clutch, I felt like a dick for even thinking of opening it, but I had no choice.

"Please don't be like tampons or something in there." My body shook in fear as I took a deep breath and looked into her purse. Living with three older sisters I saw things that could never be un-seen.

The only things she had in there was a tube of lipstick, her phone, and her wallet. Taking her wallet out, I glanced back over to her. She was now snoring and in a deep slumber.

I pulled out her license and typed the address into my GPS. She only lived ten minutes away.

Ava's phone began buzzing so I pulled it out of her purse only to hear Maroon 5's "Animals" playing and the name Jay flashing across the screen. Jealousy raced over my body as I quickly decided to answer it.

"Hello?"

"Um ... wait ... so no ... okay who the fuck is this?"

I instantly recognized the voice. "A friend who cared enough to make sure Ava got home safe."

"What did you just say, homeslice?"

"Did you just call me homeslice?"

"Yes. Yes, I did, motherfucker."

Smiling, I nodded my head. "That seems like more of a normal reaction to a strange man who answered your friend's phone."

I heard a loud bang and then it was quiet. She must have stepped outside. "Listen here, prick eater, you better turn your ass around and bring my best friend back or I'll hurt you. And by hurt you, I mean I'll cut your dick off and make you eat it."

My upper lip snarled as I pulled the phone away from my ear and looked at the sweet girl's picture on the screen. "You'll what?" I asked in utter shock.

"You heard me."

My GPS alerted me that Ava's place was on the right just a half a mile up the road.

"Listen, GI Jane, I'm almost to Ava's house to take her home. If you're that concerned, why don't you head on over here and take care of her."

"Fine, make sure she texts me when she gets into her condo."

"Fine."

"Fine."

"I already said that."

"Dick."

"Night, Jay."

Hitting End, I pulled up and parked then got out of the car and walked up to the valet guy.

"You visiting someone?"

Opening the door, I reached in and picked up Ava. "Yep. She had a little too much to drink."

"Damn, Ava."

The way this guy was looking at her had me all kinds of pissed off. "Um, I'm not sure if I should allow you into the building, sir."

Laughing, I shook my head and began bouncing Ava. "I'm up! I'm awakes."

Ava looked around and smiled when she saw she was in my arms. "I'm dreaming again. Yes." Fist pumping, she turned and looked at the valet guy. "Oh, Ryan you've never graced a dream before."

Clearing my throat, I said, "Ava baby, you're not dreaming and Ryan here won't let me bring you up to your place."

Ava slowly turned and looked at me. "Just because I'm drunk, Ryder, doesn't mean I'm going to have sex with you. I mean, I want to have sex with you."

My eyebrows shot up as I pulled my head back while Ava kept digging herself in deeper. "I think sex with you would be curl toeing. I can only imagine all the ways you'd make me—"

"Okay! Ryan, you going to open the door, dude, or are we both going to have to listen to Ava graphically describe her dreams?"

Ryan frowned as he looked at Ava. When he turned to look at me, he shot me a dirty look.

As he took a step forward, he said, "Enjoy your evening, Ms. Moore, sir."

I knew it was a dick move, but I lifted the left corner of my mouth as I said, "Oh I intend to."

Four

Ava

I pulled the pillow over my head as I moaned.

Jesus, even my internal moan hurt my head.

Dropping the pillow to my side, I slowly sat up and swung my legs over the bed. I glanced down to see I was wearing a T-shirt. Closing my eyes, I buried my face in my hands. "I don't remember anything last night."

Slowly standing, I pushed my feet into my slippers and made my way to the kitchen, shuffling my slippers across the wood floor.

I lifted my arms above my head and stretched as I tried to think of where in the hell my Motrin was. I'd never had such a terrible headache. I couldn't believe I wasn't sick to my stomach.

Opening a cabinet, I pulled the Motrin out and grabbed three. Opening the refrigerator, I grabbed the orange juice. After pouring myself a glass, I turned and leaned against the counter as I popped all three pills into my mouth. The coffee machine was on and there was a fresh pot of coffee going.

I pushed off the counter as I frantically looked around. "Holy shit," I whispered. Had I brought someone home?

"Hello?"

Taking a few steps around the kitchen island, I looked into the living room.

"Hello? Is anyone here?"

Silence.

I closed my eyes and willed myself to remember last night.

"Coffee. What I need is coffee."

It was probably Jay who brought me home and made the coffee. Oh damn, she's gonna be pissed and say I ruined her night.

I grabbed a coffee mug out of my dishwasher and headed over to the coffee pot. I poured a cup and brought it up to my mouth. I would have inhaled it, but I was pretty sure my head would have exploded. The mug was about to reach my lips when I saw a note.

Taking a sip, I picked up the note and focused my hungover eyes on it.

"No. Oh please, God, no."

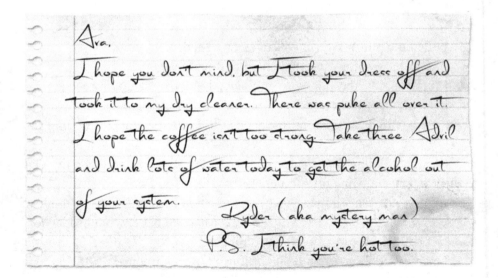

Ava,

I hope you don't mind, but I took your dress off and took it to my dry cleaner. There was puke all over it. I hope the coffee isn't too strong. Take three Advil and drink lots of water today to get the alcohol out of your system.

Ryder (aka mystery man)

P.S. I think you're hot too.

"No!" I screamed and then stopped when the pain pierced my head.

"Oh my God. Oh my God." I spun around and headed to the sofa where I sat down and began rocking back and forth. "Oh shit. It's all coming back. Ryder ran into me. Then I threw up. What happened next?"

I quickly stood up as I placed my hand on my stomach. "I'm going to be sick!" I yelled as I ran through my condo to my bathroom. Dropping to the floor, I wiped my tears away. I always cried when I threw up. Ever since I was little.

Lightly placing my head on the wall behind me, I wondered what all I had said to Ryder. My body slumped as I let out an overly-dramatic sigh. When I finally decided that sitting on the bathroom floor wasn't going to do a damn thing, I stood up and headed into the kitchen.

"Food. Once I eat, I'll feel better and everything will be okay. It's not like I'm ever going to see him again."

"You always talk to yourself?"

I screamed as I spun around to see Jay standing in my doorway. "You! You left me alone."

Jay smiled as she tossed her purse onto the table I had at my front entrance. "Oh trust me, you were not alone. Mr. Hotty McHot Pants was with you. Sounds like you had one hell of a night."

My eyes widened in horror as my heart dropped to my stomach. "W-what? How do you know?"

"Ryder called me from your phone. Said something about having to leave for a meeting or something and he couldn't bear the thought of you waking up all alone. Guess he thought you might be feeling the aftereffects of last night. So tell me, Ava, did Ryder *ride her* last night?"

"What?" I asked confused.

My mouth dropped open as I let her words sink in. Ryder brought me home last night? Yes, I remember that. Don't I?

"Are you sore?" Jay asked as she poured herself a cup of coffee.

Frowning, I said, "Yes, my head is killing me."

"No, I mean between your legs."

"Why in the hell would I be sore between—" Then her words hit me like a brick wall.

Jay smiled but attempted to hide it behind her coffee mug. My eyes darted from side to side as I tried to focus in on my body. "We couldn't have. He wouldn't. What kind of man has sex with a woman who's drunk?"

"Hot guys?"

I shook my head the best I could considering it was pounding in my ears now. "Nope. I'd know if I had sex. I haven't had sex."

"Maybe his dick was small and you can't tell."

I rolled my eyes at Jay. "Do you hear what comes out of your mouth?"

My phone rang and for a moment I panicked it might be Ryder. Seeing Mom flash across the screen, I let out a sigh of relief. "Thank you, Lord Jesus," I whispered.

"Hey, Mom."

"Morning, sweetheart. Are you on your way?"

I glanced up at the clock on my wall. *Shit! I'm late!*

"Yep! I left not too long ago. I'll be there soon."

Jay raised her eyebrow up at me and shook her head.

"Okay, sweetheart. Don't be late; you know how important this is to your father."

"Right! I'm not going to let Daddy down, I swear."

Taking another sip of coffee, I rushed past Jay and headed into my bedroom.

"See you soon!"

"Bye, Mom."

I hit End and turned to Jay. "Help me!"

"I'm on it. First things first. Brush your damn teeth and take a quick shower. You smell like a damn bar."

I pulled down the driveway to my parents' house and floored it.

I'm late. Oh shit, I'm late.

Liza was sitting on the front porch holding my precious little nephew, Nickolas.

I put the car in park and practically ran over to them.

"Let me have him!"

Liza laughed and handed Nickolas to me.

"Hello to you too."

I glanced up and smiled at Liza. "We totally need to do a girls' night. I have so much to tell you about Paris and Italy. Maurice got on Jase's nerves when he spent a couple days with us. I loved it! Of course ever since France, Jase really hasn't been the same."

"I know. He spent some time with a girl there and things didn't end the way he wanted them to. I've tried talking to him about it but he keeps pushing me away."

The front door screen made a small noise when it opened, causing us both to turn and look. My mother placed her hand on her hip and starred at me. "Ava? How long have you been here?"

"Gosh, for a while now."

Liza turned and looked at me with a smirk. "Yep, she's been sitting out here loving on her nephew."

My mother's smile warmed as she walked over and kissed me on the forehead. "Okay, well your father and Layton are with the boys and the gentlemen who are going to help the ranch become certified organic. They're headed back up to Layton and Whit's place and they want us to meet them there."

Walker and Jase were the ones to convince our fathers that it was time to go organic. It was something we all talked about as a family. My father and Layton had been business partners for years, and I loved how involved we all were as a family when it came to the cattle ranch, including me. I'd been known to throw on a pair of jeans and boots and get in there when it came time to doing the dirty stuff.

"So, who exactly are these guys who are going to be helping?"

Motioning for us to get up and follower her to Liza's car, I stood up and smiled down at Nickolas who was sleeping peacefully in my arms.

Liza opened the backseat door as I placed him in his car seat and Liza took over.

"Two guys who started a consulting business helping ranches all over the country who are wanting to go organic. Their father owns a cattle ranch in Montana."

I smiled and said, "Oh, I've always wanted to go to Montana." Snapping my seatbelt in, I laughed. "Can they offer us a tour of their dad's ranch?"

Liza got in the car and started down the driveway. "Yes. As a matter of fact, they offered for all of us to come stay for a weekend and tour the ranch."

"Are y'all going to go?" I asked looking between Liza and my mother who was sitting in the back seat.

My mother nodded. "I think so. Layton thinks it would be a great learning experience, plus it is a hell of a lot cooler up there right now."

Dropping my mouth open, I glared at my mother. "Wait! When are y'all going?"

"Two weeks," Liza said with a giggle.

"What the hell! Y'all are all going to Montana and you didn't even let me know!"

My mother cleared her throat as she adjusted something on Nickolas. "Well, Ava I figured you weren't going to drop everything for a last minute trip."

"To fucking Montana I would!"

"Watch your language," my mother said with a slight grin. She always told me I was her little me and I knew I was. I also liked being compared to my mother. Not only was she beautiful, but smart as hell and sassy to boot.

My arms crossed over my body and I pouted as Liza lost it and laughed full on.

"Oh, stop being a baby, Ava. We just decided this earlier today when your father got the email from Mr. Montgomery. He wants us to come before they start getting colder weather in."

"I'm in!"

"What about your job?" Liza asked.

"It's fine. The owner of the boutique owes me a huge favor, so I can take some time off from there. And I can work anywhere for Maurice with the designs."

My mother smiled big and said, "Well, it looks like we're taking a family vacation to Montana!"

Liza and I both let out soft screams of joy so we didn't wake up Nickolas.

Minutes later we were pulling up and parking in front of Layton and Whitley's house. Whitley came walking out onto the porch and down to the car with a huge smile on her face. "Oh I love when my daughter comes to visit me!"

Liza laughed. "Mom! I see you every day when I come to work!"

Whitley brushed off Liza and headed to me where she pulled me into her arms and hugged me. "I'm talking about my adopted daughter." Pushing me back some, Whitley let her eyes wander all over me and then pulled me back into a hug as she whispered, "You look so beautiful, but your eyes are totally bloodshot."

I let out a chuckle as I whispered back, "Is it that obvious?"

Whitley stepped back and quickly said, "I have eye drops, don't worry."

Laughing, I gave her a friendly push as I headed up to the house.

"Everyone is outside; Jase just started grilling some steaks!" Whitley called from over her shoulder as she scooped Nickolas out of Liza's arms.

Wrapping her arm with mine, my mother and I headed through the house and to the back. "Now, Ava, try to keep your very outspoken thoughts to yourself."

My mouth fell open as I let out a gasp. "Oh my God. What do you think I'm going to do? Offend the little old consultant men, and then they won't want to work for us?"

"Yes. That's exactly what I'm afraid of."

Liza bumped my shoulder as she rushed past me. "Don't worry, Court, when she sees them she'll be too busy wiping the drool from her mouth to even talk."

I rolled my eyes and took off after Liza as she yelped and ran through the kitchen with me hot on her trail.

"This is not the first impression I'm talking about, Ava Moore!" my mother called out as I followed Liza out onto the back porch. Liza immediately took a right turn and I didn't realize how fast I was going. Trying to come to a stop, I hit the stairs and ran down them only to run right into the back of someone, causing their drink to go everywhere.

"Shit!" I shouted as my head throbbed from slamming into what felt like a brick wall. As I put my fingers up to my temple and closed my eyes, I prayed the hangover would just go away.

"Ava?"

I know that voice.

Peeking one eye open, the other one quickly followed as I gasped and said, "Ryder?"

I quickly scanned around only to find everyone staring at both of us, and I couldn't help but notice the stunned expression on my father's face. "You know my daughter, Ryder?"

The smile that spread across Ryder's face spoke volumes.

"Yes, sir, I do."

I could feel all eyes on me as I let out a nervous chuckle. "Well, I mean we're just acquaintances."

Ryder raised his eyebrows as the other extremely hot guy standing next to him coughed and looked at Ryder.

"No, I mean we're more than that." Shaking my head and then moaning from the sheer pain, I held up my hands and said, "No! I mean, we're just friends. New friends. Like I ran into him on the street and knocked all his paperwork out of his hands and then ran into him again—"

Oh Jesus, I'm digging myself into a hole.

"We ran into each other again yesterday when I was attending a meeting at a restaurant in Austin."

The other guy coughed again and glared at Ryder.

My father walked up and kissed me on the cheek as he looked back at Ryder and said, "What a small world."

It appeared Ryder had to force himself to pull his eyes off of me and as he looked at my father and nodded. "Indeed it is."

"Yes, it is for sure," the guy behind Ryder said.

Walker approached and said, "Well, Ryder, since it appears you already know my sister, Nate Montgomery, this is my younger sister, Ava Moore."

I smiled and extended my hand over to Nate. "It's a pleasure to meet you."

Nate smiled back a warm smile and a wink, "The pleasure is all mine. Since you've had the pleasure of getting to know my brother, I guess that means I get to monopolize all your time this afternoon then."

Letting out a nervous and very awkward laugh, I said, "I'm afraid I don't get too excited about talking about cattle and all of that."

Nate tossed his head back and laughed. "Fair enough."

Turning, Nate walked over to Layton as my father continued to stare at me like I had just caused a huge shit storm.

I slowly glanced over and stole a peek at Ryder. He was staring at me too, but he still wore that damn sexy-ass smile. I spun around on my heels and headed over to the safe zone.

The baby. No single hot guy wanted to be anywhere near a baby.

After sitting and chatting with Liza, my mother called out and asked me to help get everything ready to eat. As I stood, I leaned over and glared at Liza. "So when I pop a kid out, does that mean I get to just sit there and hold them while everyone else does all the work?"

Liza grinned and said, "Pretty much."

I worked quick and fast, helping my mother and Whitley get the table all set. Jase brought in all the steaks and set them in the middle of the table as Layton motioned for everyone to take a seat. I wasn't surprised to see Ryder make a beeline and sit right next to me. Jase took the seat to my left and bumped my shoulder as he sat down. I rolled my eyes and quickly reached for the glass of wine I had in front of me.

"How are you feeling today?" Ryder asked in a hushed voice.

"Fine," I mumbled back.

"I heard Bloody Mary's were the thing to drink for a hangover. Did you take the Advil?"

My head turned as I looked at Ryder who was taking a sip of water. The room began spinning as thoughts flooded my mind. The fact that I couldn't remember anything about last night was driving me insane. And the way Ryder's leg was brushing up next to me was driving me even more insane. No man had ever affected me like that before.

Pushing back my chair, I set my napkin down as everyone turned and looked at me. "Excuse us, but I need to speak with Ryder in private."

"Oh shit," Jase and Walker both said at once as I turned and headed out of the dining room.

I could hear Ryder's chair move against the wood floor as he said, "Um, if you'll excuse us."

I pushed the back door open and quickly began walking down the stairs and away from the house. Ryder's footsteps were gaining on me when I felt a jolt of electricity zip through my body and settle right between my legs.

Ryder took me by the arm and turned me around. Before he even had a chance to talk, I began poking him in the chest with my finger.

"How dare you. How dare you take me home and undress me and god knows what else you did when I was passed out. Then for you to just act like nothing happened and whisper things in my ear making me go all crazy ... and ... and ..."

Ryder was staring at me like I had two heads as I continued to fly off the handle.

"And what?" he asked in a sexy as hell voice.

My face flushed. "I just need to know if we had sex last night."

Ryder's eyes widened in horror as he dropped his hand down to his side, causing me to instantly want his touch back. "What? No, we didn't have sex last night. What in the hell, Ava? What kind of a guy do you think I am?"

"Well gosh, Ryder, I have no clue seeing as I've only seen you three times in my entire life and one of those times I was drunk out of my mind."

Ryder pushed his hand through his hair and sighed. "I brought you home, you changed into a T-shirt and passed out in your bed. I slept on the sofa just in case you needed anything during the night. After I made a pot of coffee for you, I got your lousy friend's number off your phone and texted her."

"Lousy friend?" I said as I put my hands on my hips.

"Yes, you heard me right. You were drunk out of your mind all she cared about was having a good time. She couldn't have cared less that I was bringing you home and she certainly didn't try and stop me. So, excuse me for being a gentleman and wanting to make sure you arrived home safely, and that you were okay through the night."

I began chewing on my lower lip. "So, no sex?"

Ryder narrowed his eyes at me and sighed. "No. Besides, you would have felt the aftereffects this morning if we had had sex."

All the air left my lungs as Ryder turned and headed back into the house. I placed my hand over my stomach to calm myself and tried to push his last sentence from my mind.

Five

Ryder

Two Weeks Later

"Ryder, stop pacing the floor. Why are you so nervous?"

I came to a stop and turned to my mother. She was sitting in her favorite rocking chair knitting something for my sister Dani's baby who was due Christmas day.

"I'm not nervous. Why do you think I'm nervous?"

My mother gave me that look. The one that said I knew damn well why she thought I was nervous. "You're pacing. You don't pace … ever."

With a shrug of my shoulders, I sat down and picked up a magazine. "Nah, I'm not nervous. I just want to make sure everything goes well this weekend with Layton Morris and Reed Moore.

"It's going to be amazing. From what your brother said, it's already a done deal."

I let out a curt laugh. "Yeah, well Nate isn't always right, Mom."

"Don't be hating on your brother, Ryder. It is unbecoming of you."

"You're right, that's Nate's way of doing things."

She dropped her knitting in her lap and slowly shook her head and giggled. "Oh, how the two of you used to fight. I'm so glad those days are over."

With a crooked smile, I nodded. "Well, we don't have anything to fight over anymore."

Janet, my parents' housekeeper, walked into the room. "Mr. Montgomery, the guests have arrived."

With a quick jump up, I smiled as I walked up to Janet and kissed her gently on the cheek. She blushed each and every time. "Thank you, Janet."

"Oh, stop that, boy!"

My mother chuckled from behind me as she walked up and laced her arm with mine. Janet had been working for my parents for as long as I could remember. She had been like a second mother to me growing up.

"Janet, darling, would you mind asking MaryLou to get some tea ready and bring it into the parlor?"

With a warm smile, Janet nodded. "Yes, Mrs. Lucy, right away."

I guided my mother out of her sewing room and headed to the front door. "I can't wait to meet this family. I've heard so much about them."

"It's two families, remember, Mom."

Giving me a friendly swat on the arm, my mother said, "I know it's two families. I may be getting older, Ryder, but I'm not that old."

With a toss of my head back, I shook my head. "No ma'am, you are far from it."

As we stepped outside, the first thing I saw was Nate helping Ava with her bag.

That bastard. The way he was smiling at her boiled my blood. Neither one of us brought up Ava after we left Layton's house two weeks ago.

"Welcome! Oh, welcome to the ranch," my mother called out as she headed down the stairs. "There is a baby! Oh, how exciting!"

I couldn't help but smile as my mother took Nickolas out of Liza's arms.

"How did he do on the plane?"

Liza grinned from ear to ear as I walked down the stairs and headed to the back of the second car.

"He did amazing. The perfect baby!" Liza gushed.

"Come, darling, let's you and I make our way into the living room while they get the luggage all situated."

Liza smiled as she glanced over her shoulder toward Ava, who stood there with a stunned expression.

"Ryder, how are you doing?" Reed asked as he reached his hand out for mine.

"I'm doing well, Mr. Moore. I take it your trip up here was good?"

Reed slapped me on the side of my arm and gave me a smile. "Call me Reed. Yes, the trip was great." Taking a look around, Reed shook his head. "Good Lord, this place is breathtaking. I mean to tell you I don't think I've ever seen anything as beautiful as this place."

With a smile, I took in the surroundings. "It is beautiful."

"Why in the world did you want to leave this place?" Walker asked as he walked up next to us and gazed out to the mountains.

"It's only temporary. I'm actually planning on moving back and slowly starting to take over the ranch."

Reed turned and looked at me. "Really? You're not making Texas your home?"

Pursing my lips, I shook my head. "Nah. I love Texas, don't get me wrong, but my heart belongs here in Montana."

I glanced over to see Ava standing there staring at me with a stunned look on her face. She quickly snapped out of it when Nate told Courtney, her mother, to follow him.

Layton walked up with his wife, Whitley. "I think I need a horse and some fresh air," Layton said with a whistle.

I let out a chuckle and motioned for them to follow me. "Let's show y'all to your rooms."

Jase walked next to me as he looked up at the giant house and said, "Damn … the cattle business must be good up here."

"Jase Morris," Whitley said from behind me as I laughed.

"It's not bad, but my father earned most of his money in real estate."

Jase raised an eyebrow. "Really? I can't wait to meet him."

As we headed into the house, Nate, Janet, MaryLou, and myself all showed the Moore and Morris families to their respective rooms.

All but, Walker, Liza, and Whitley, stayed back with my mother and Nickolas. Everyone else set off for the barn. Layton and Reed occupied most of my time with questions about the day-to-day operating of our cattle ranch. Glancing up, I couldn't help but notice how Nate walked further ahead with Ava and Jase.

Monk, who was in charge of my father's stables, stepped out of the barn right as we walked up.

"Ah, there is the man who takes care of this whole place," Nate said as he shook Monk's hand.

"Well, I don't know about this whole place, but the horses and the three stables, yes. That would be me."

"Three? Wow. How many horses do y'all have?" Ava asked as she peeked around Monk's shoulder. I could see her body practically bouncing with excitement.

Monk laughed as his hand went through his hair. "A lot. The Montgomery's own about forty-five horses and about seventy-five more are boarded or here to breed."

"Wow!" Courtney and Ava said at the same time. Nate leaned over and whispered something to Ava, causing her to giggle.

I'm going to pound his face in tonight when he's sleeping.

"Ryder? Did you hear what I asked?"

I shook my head to snap out of it as I looked over to Monk. "No, what was that?"

"Your father requested you show Mr. Moore and Mr. Morris around. I have Juniper, Rascal and Monty all ready for you."

"Oh um … yes! Great. Sounds good. Thanks so much, Monk."

I turned to Reed and Layton and smiled. "My father is an all-work no-play kind of man."

Both men laughed as they headed into the barn. Nate was talking to Jase, so I took the opportunity to make my way over to Ava. "Ms. Moore, this is Trinity Rose. She'll be your horse," Monk said with a tip of his hat.

Ava's hands began to run down Trinity's strong back as she smiled and began talking to her. "Hey there, beautiful girl."

I placed my hand on Trinity's side and gave her a good pat. "Trinity is one of my favorite horses. Gentle, but isn't afraid to let go every now and then."

Ava smiled as she looked back at the horse. "It's good to see you again, Ava."

Without so much as looking in my direction, she nodded. "You too, Ryder."

My heart dropped as I looked down and kicked at some hay in the dirt. "I've got to take your dad and Layton on a little tour of the ranch."

Ava had walked all the way around Trinity before stopping and looking up into my eyes. I wasn't sure what I was seeing in those beautiful blue eyes. Whatever it was … I was captivated by them.

"Have fun with that. Nate offered to show me around."

If felt as if someone had turned on an instant heat wave as my body became ridged. "That so?"

With a tilt of her head and a smile, Ava said, "Yep."

I nodded and took a step back. "Enjoy your ride, Ava."

Her smile faded as I tipped my head and started down to the other end of the barn.

"Hey, Ryder? May I ask you something?"

I stopped and turned back to her. "Of course."

She licked lips and then bit down on her lower lip. "Are you … um … did I hear you say you were moving back up here to Montana?"

"At some point, yeah, I'll be moving back to stay."

Ava nodded slowly. With that, I turned and walked away from her. The further I walked away, the more I cussed at myself for not just pulling her into my arms and telling her I hadn't been able to stop thinking about her for the last two weeks.

Everyone was up and on their horses in no time as I watched Nate and Ava slowly walk off toward the west pasture. Jase and Courtney decided they were going to go with us on the ranch tour.

As I watched Ava ride off on Trinity, a sick feeling passed over me as I tried to push it away. I'd never had a girl affect me like Ava. It seemed my brother felt the same way. If he thought I was going to just roll over and let him take her away from me, he had another thing coming.

For once in my adult life, there was something worth fighting my brother over … and her name was Ava.

Six

Ava

Nate for sure wasn't the type of guy who was at a loss for things to talk about. He talked about everything from growing up in Montana to the new loft apartment he was building in Austin.

"So, you're not planning on moving back to Montana like Ryder?"

Nate let out a roar of laughter. "Hell no. I couldn't wait to get out of here."

With a slight smile, I looked around at the breathtaking views. Mountains were everywhere. "But it's so beautiful here."

"And out in the middle of nowhere. It's different, Ava, if you haven't grown up here. Sure, it's beautiful and most people come up and they're swept away by the views. Try living here."

With a shrug, I let out a sigh. "I don't know. Sometimes I miss living back in Llano."

"You don't like living in Austin?"

Glancing over to Nate, I was taken by how handsome he was. Not as handsome as Ryder, but for sure a *turn your head and change your panties when he flashes you his smile*, kind of handsome. His hair was much lighter than Ryder's, more of a dark blond. He had the same green eyes that

Ryder had, though.

Nate brought his horse to a stop and slid off as I followed. When I walked around the horse, I was met by a huge smile. I slowly searched his face until my eyes landed on his lips. All I could think about was Ryder. He was moving to Montana. When? Why? How could I possibly even think of starting something with someone who I knew would be moving?

"There is a beautiful overlook if you're up for a small hike."

With grin, I said, "Sure. Sounds like fun."

Nate and I hiked up a pretty good size hill and the whole time I kept reassessing my workout regimen. Time to add more cardio, that was for sure. Once we made it to the top, I sucked in a breath and said, "Oh my word. It looks like a picture."

"It's probably one of my favorite places on the ranch. Ryder and I used to come here all the time."

The mention of Ryder's name had my chest dropping. For one brief moment, I had wished it was him who had brought me here and not Nate. But then Ryder had pretty much avoided me ever since I showed up.

"I can see why," I whispered. "It's beyond beautiful."

Nate sat down and began asking me questions about what I did and if I enjoyed Paris and Italy. I was soon lost in an easy conversation with him as we laughed and talked about everything and anything.

Nate pushed out a breath of air and said, "Well, I should take you back. Dad's got a huge dinner planned to welcome you guys. I'm sure you'll want to doll yourself up."

Smirking, I gave him a look. "Doll myself up? Really, did you just say that?"

"Isn't that what girls do?"

The instant Nate reached down and took my hand in his, the moment turned. I wanted to pull it from his hand, yet at the same time, I didn't mind that he had taken it. He was guiding me down the hill and I took it as a kind gesture to help me. He dropped it the moment we got to the flat surface.

"I don't like the phrase *dolled up*."

Nate laughed. "I see that. You about had steam coming from your ears, and I'm pretty sure you foamed at the mouth in your anger."

I have him a quick push and said, "Shut up!"

"I'll race you back."

I turned and pushed Nate as hard as I could and watched him stumble as I took off and jumped up on Trinity. Before I knew it, we were back at the barn. Everyone else had already returned and was getting ready for dinner.

Monk took our horses as Nate and I headed out of the barn. Before I knew what was happening, Nate had me pressed up against the wall, his eyes burning as he searched my face.

"I've been fighting the urge to kiss you all afternoon, Ava."

My eyes widened in horror. *Oh. My. Gosh. What do I do? What do I say?* Was I attracted to Nate? I mean sure, he was good looking and everything, but he didn't affect me like Ryder did. No one had ever affected me like Ryder did.

But Ryder was going to be living in Montana, and I'd be in Texas. How would that work?

Nate moved a little closer as I placed my hands on his chest to stop from coming any closer.

"Um … Nate … I've had a lovely afternoon but—"

His eyebrows rose. "But you're attracted to my brother."

I bit down on my lip. There was no denying I was very attracted to Ryder. He had consumed my thoughts the last two weeks, almost to the point where I was about to ask my father for his number.

Before I had a chance to answer, I felt his presence. It was as if I could sense his eyes on me. Turning to the left, my breath caught as I looked at Ryder standing there with a stunned expression.

Nate followed my stare and moved when I pushed him away from me.

"Ryder," was all I could say as he glared at his brother quickly before replacing his expression with a blank one.

"Mom was looking for you. She didn't want the two of you being late for dinner."

Nate smiled as he began walking toward Ryder. "We were just on our way up."

I pushed off the wall and called out for Ryder as he turned and headed back out of the barn.

"Ryder! Wait!" I took off running, but by the time I rounded the corner, he had taken off on a four-wheeler and was headed back to the main house. Spinning around, I looked at Nate. "He thinks something happened between us."

Nate laughed and shrugged. "He'll get over it."

I reached out and grabbed his arm. "No, you'll tell him nothing happened."

Nate's smile turned wicked. "Sure I will. Let's get to the house before my mother sends out another search party."

My stomach felt sick as I followed Nate back up to the house. The entire time all I saw was the look on Ryder's face as he stood at the end of the barn.

Seven

Ryder

I stood in the mirror and looked at myself as I took in my appearance. Dressed in black jeans, my trusty old cowboy boots, and a white buttoned-down shirt, I looked every bit the part. The good son who still did what his parents asked him to do. Instead of me being the one to show Ava the ranch, I showed Layton and Reed, even though Nate should have been there right alongside me.

He knew I wouldn't let my father down and he took full advantage of the situation.

Bastard.

I pushed my hand through my somewhat still wet hair, and headed down to the living room where everyone was meeting. My father should be making his grand appearance right about now.

With a frustrated sigh, I headed to the bedroom door and threw it open. The more I thought about Nate and Ava and what I walked in on, the more pissed off I got. I should have known she didn't have any interest in me.

As I walked down the main stairwell, I glanced up and blue eyes caught mine. Ava looked beautiful dressed in tan pants and a white blouse.

My eyes traveled her body and back up to her lips that I'd dreamt of kissing a hundred times.

It didn't long for me to catch a glimpse of Nate standing next to Ava. I looked away as I continued to make my way down the stairs. My father was standing next to my mother with his arm wrapped around her waist as they talked to Layton and Whitley. With a smile, I gave him a quick wave as he smiled back. He had been out of town for the last week, so this was the first time I'd seen him.

"There is the man who is going to be running this ranch someday."

Nate huffed as I shot him a *go to hell* look. It wasn't my fault he didn't want anything to do with running the ranch. He enjoyed the traveling and consulting. I didn't. I wanted to be on the back of a horse checking property lines, not sitting in some rancher's living room dressed in a suit.

Layton and Reed both turned and gave me a grin. "Dad, it's good to see you," I said as I shook his hand. "You weren't all waiting for me, were you?"

My mother smiled and gave me a wink. "Yes, but that's okay; I have a surprise for you."

I lifted an eyebrow. "Really? What do you have up your sleeve?"

"Me."

The voice sounded familiar as I looked over my mother's shoulder to see my sister, Jennifer, standing there. I smiled from ear to ear.

"Well, if it isn't my beautiful sister!"

Moving toward them, Dani popped out. "Surprise!"

"Oh my God. It's both of them!" I said as I wrapped my sisters up in my arms. Each of them got a kiss on the cheek. "Dani, you've gotten so much bigger."

Her lower lip jetted out as she nodded her head and rested her hands on her stomach. "I know. Just a few more months."

"Hey there, Ryder."

Turning to look over my shoulder, I saw Destiny. She was my sister Jennifer's best friend, and my ex-girlfriend who cheated on me with my best friend, Roy.

With a quick nod, I gave her a halfhearted smile. "Destiny, how are you?"

Her mouth twitched as she gave me a smile. "I'm doing good. It's good to see you."

Trying to get out of this awkward moment, I caught a glimpse of Ava as she walked by. One quick look showed she was staring at Destiny.

With a bigger smile, I turned to my two sisters and slapped my hands. "Who is going to sandwich me?"

Nate walked up and pushed me to the side. "They want to sandwich me, not you."

"Boys, stop fighting," my mother said as she pointed her finger at me and then Nate.

Before I had a chance to react, Nate made a beeline and sat in between Jennifer and Dani. Destiny was on the other side of Jennifer, so I made my way to the opposite side of the table. Sitting down next to my father, who was at the end, and Jase, who was on my left.

"Jase, how are you liking Montana?" I asked.

"Love it. I was just telling Ava if I didn't love Texas so much, I'd be packing my bags and moving here."

With a laugh, I looked up to see Ava sitting across from Jase. "What about you, Ava? You seemed to be enjoying your afternoon with Nate from the looks of things."

Her mouth opened slightly as her eyes darted down the table to Nate. She flashed him a dirty look and narrowed her eyes at him. Nate chuckled and then leaned over and began talking to Destiny.

Asshole.

Ava looked back to me and was about to say something when my father stood up. "Let me just say what a pleasure it is to have the Morris and Moore families with us here today. I'm excited to know that my sons are, hopefully, leading you down the road to becoming an organic cattle ranch like the one you see here at Montgomery Ranch. For the next three days, our ranch is your ranch."

Holding his glass of wine up, he motioned for everyone to join him in toast. "To organic."

"To organic!" everyone said as glasses clanked together.

Everyone settled into conversations as the food was served. Of course the main dish was steak and potatoes. My father wouldn't have it any other way.

Every now and then I'd glance up and see Ava speaking with Liza, who was sitting next to her, or to my sister, Dani, across the table who was next to her husband, Rich.

Jase and I talked mostly about ranching and cattle. He had some great questions for the conversion and I was excited to answer them. My father chimed in every now and then before his attention would get drawn to another conversation going on.

"So, when are you moving back to Montana, Ryder?"

I glanced up to see Ava staring at me. Waiting for me to answer as if her life depended on it.

"You're moving back home?" Destiny called out as she jumped up and headed over to me.

She leaned down and placed her lips to my ear as I continued to watch Ava. For a moment I thought I saw jealousy cross over her face.

"We need to talk in private."

"Later," I said as I glared at her.

"Fine." With a turn on her heels, Destiny headed back to her seat.

"Lovely girl," Ava whispered.

"She has her moments," I said as I smiled and took a bite of steak. I couldn't deny I liked seeing Ava get bent out of shape a little bit over Destiny. Why she did, I have no clue. She seemed to be pretty happy with Nate pressed up against her.

Shaking the image from my head, I tried to drag in a breath. For some reason, the room felt as if it was closing in on me and I couldn't breathe. Leaning over to my father, I softly said, "Dad, I'll be right back."

A look of concern crossed over his face as he said, "Is everything okay?"

"Yeah, I just need a minute."

Standing quickly, I glanced down to Ava. Her mouth opened as if she was about to say something, but Liza tapped her shoulder and asked her a question. I walked as fast as I could and dragged in a deep breath of air as I stood on the front porch. The evening temperature was quickly dropping as a chill rushed through my body.

I jumped when I felt a hand on my shoulder. "Not now, Destiny. I'm not in the mood to talk to you."

"How about me then?"

The sound of Ava's voice traveled through my body, warming it instantly.

"We should probably make it a new rule not to get up and leave the table to talk," Ava said with a slight chuckle.

I turned and leaned against the porch rail as Ava barely bit down on her lip as she smiled bigger.

"I didn't ask you to come out here, though."

Her smile faded. "No, you didn't. Did Nate talk to you about earlier?"

I tried to swallow the lump in my throat as I looked away. "No. Honestly, Ava, you don't owe me any explanation at all. If you and my brother have hit it off then—" I shook my head and let out a gruff laugh. "Then so be it."

"So that's it? You're just going to go with what you thought you saw and not even give me a chance to explain."

My head jerked back as I stared at her. "Explain what? My brother had you pushed against a wall and I'm pretty sure if I'd have walked in thirty seconds later you would have been kissing him."

Anger flashed across her face as she shook her head. "No, what you would have seen was me pushing your brother away and telling him I was attracted to you ... not him. My hands were on his chest, keeping him from getting closer. I asked him to talk to you about it because I knew that's what you thought."

I let her words sit in my head for a few moments. "You told Nate you're attracted to me?"

Ava pressed her lips together as she lowered her head some and gazed up at me through those long beautiful eyelashes. Her blue eyes were sparkling. "I did tell him that, yes. I also wanted to tell you that I haven't been able to stop thinking about you for the last two weeks. And that I had a stupid count down on my phone, counting the days until I got to see you ... even though I told everyone it was for the trip."

My smile grew bigger as my heartbeat began speeding up. I'd never had a woman make me feel the way Ava made me feel. I wanted her like no one else, yet I wanted to move slowly with her. Savor each and every moment.

"I thought about you too. I dreamt about you, thought about you in the shower, at the gym, while trying to work. Your face and those beautiful blue eyes haunted my every moment."

Ava's mouth parted open as she sucked in a breath ever so slightly. Her chest began to heave a bit more as her breathing picked up. "I've never had anyone say anything like that to me before. My panties are soaking wet now."

My eyes closed as my dick jumped and I let out a soft moan. "I just died."

With a snap of my eyes, my body trembled when Ava's hands touched my chest. Her smile was beyond breathtaking. "There's only one way to make sure you haven't died."

I licked my lips in anticipation of her next words. "W-what's that?"

"Kiss me."

My hands cupped Ava's face as I brought her lips to mine and kissed her. Our tongues moved together in perfect harmony as we both let out a soft moan.

Heaven.

I was in heaven and I never wanted the moment to end.

Pulling my lips back, Ava slowly smiled as she shook her head ever so slightly. "I think I'm going to need more convincing."

With a chuckle, I brushed my lips against hers. "Tell me what I need to do."

Ava's eyes lit with excitement. "There's only one thing I can think of that will fully show me you're one hundred percent still alive."

With a raised eyebrow, I tried to come off as being calm, cool, and collected. But inside, my body was behaving like a sixteen-year-old boy wanting to have sex for the first time. "That is?"

"Make love to me, Ryder."

My heart dropped as I looked into Ava's eyes. "Now?"

With a chuckle, Ava shook her head. "As much as I want to say yes, I think it would be rather rude to disappear from dinner."

"Who cares!" I said as I pulled her body closer to mine, pressing my hard dick against her body. I'd been dreaming for weeks of this woman; I wanted her this instant.

Ava's eyes danced with excitement as she slowly ran her tongue along her teeth. A low growl formed in the back of my throat as I debated dragging her off somewhere.

"Hey, love birds, Mom is getting pissed and you know she means business when she sends the pregnant sister out to get you."

Glancing up, I smiled at my sister. "Tell Mom we'll be right in, Dani."

With a lift of her eyebrow, she gave me that look. "You better get your ass in there."

"One minute is all we need."

Dani gave me a wink before turning and heading back into the house.

I looked back into Ava's beautiful blue eyes. "When?"

"Tonight. After I know my parents are asleep. Something about having sex in the same house as my parents is a bit ... unsettling."

With a smile, I placed my finger on her chin and brought her lips to mine. "I promise they'll be none the wiser."

Ava giggled. "Okay, 'cause if they ever found out, my father would kick your ass."

My smile faded as Ava closed her eyes and made ready for my lips. Swallowing hard, I gave Ava a quick, but soft kiss. "Great. Now I'm going to be freaked out."

With a laugh, Ava grabbed my hand as we walked back into the house together. The second we stepped back into the dining room, all eyes fell on us. I couldn't help but notice Reed glance down to see our hands intertwined. He looked quickly back up at Ava and then me. With a weak smile, I nodded my head and said, "Sorry about that."

"That's twice you and my daughter have gotten up from a dinner table. Anything I need to know?"

Ava squeezed my hand as we headed back to our seats. "No, Daddy. All is fine."

After taking my seat, Jase leaned over and said, "Dude, I love seeing the smile on Ava's face, but you hurt her, I hurt you."

Turning to look at Jase with wide eyes, I whispered, "Point taken." When I looked over to Ava's brother, Walker, he communicated the same damn thing with the look on his face. With a smile, I gave him a nod of acknowledgment and turned back to my father. The look on his face told me I was going to be having a conversation with him later about this as well.

My eyes turned to Ava who was now smiling and talking my sister's ear off. I couldn't help but feel happiness bubbling over. Of course my smile faded when I caught Reed giving me a death stare.

This should be an interesting evening.

Eight

Ava

Dinner dragged on and was followed by drinks in the parlor as Ryder and I stole glances every now and then. Each time my heart would beat a little harder in my chest. The idea of being with him tonight was almost too much to take. My lips still tingled from his kiss. My skin still on fire from where he touched me.

"I'm pretty sure if you keep staring at my brother like that, his pants are going to just fly off at any moment."

Dani stood before me with her hands rested on her belly. "Is it that obvious?" I asked while looking around the room.

"Oh yeah." Dani looked over her shoulder toward her sister, Jennifer, and her friend, Destiny. "You've got Destiny over there in a huff, but I have to admit, it's been fun watching her all evening try to capture my brother's attention."

My eyes narrowed as I stared at Destiny. Her long blonde hair was perfect. Not a strand out of place. Her toned legs told me she most likely ran or at least paid a small fortune for a good trainer at the gym. "Does she live here in Montana?"

Dani took a sip of her water. "Yep. Her father is best friends with my father. He owns the ranch right next to ours. Growing up, I think it was almost expected that Ryder and Destiny were to date. They were the same age, liked the same things, and were good friends."

Jealousy raced through my veins as I tried to not picture Ryder and Destiny together. The thought made me feel sick.

"Don't think too much about it, Ava. Ryder never really was that into Destiny. I think he dated her more to satisfy my father over anything else."

My interest was piqued. "Why did your father want him to date Destiny?"

Dani shrugged as if not giving it much thought. "I dunno. Maybe thinking someday the two ranches would merge or something. Who knows why my father does anything he does. He loves his kids, but he has always put the ranch first before any of us."

Turning to look at Dani, I wanted to ask her more, but decided to let it go. Ryder showed no interest in Destiny, and I knew there was nothing there for me to worry about.

As the evening dragged on, I grew more and more anxious to be alone with Ryder. Images of my dreams replayed in my head. Ryder had been talking most of the evening with Walker and Jase, while my father and Layton spoke with Nate, Sr.

Needing to at least be closer to Ryder, I made my way across the room as Ryder headed toward me. The moment our eyes met, I couldn't help but smile. It felt as if the entire room full of people faded away, leaving just the two of us.

Stopping in front of him, Ryder's smile nearly knocked me off my feet. "Hey," was the only stupid thing I could manage to say.

"Hey, back at ya."

"So, I've been thinking."

Ryder's eyes looked over my body in a hungry way. "About?"

"Tonight."

"What about tonight, Ava?"

The way his voice vibrated throughout my body had me wishing I hadn't made my way over to him. My body was now aching to feel him. To learn every little thing that turned him on. His lips were begging to be nibbled on.

Feeling flushed from my thoughts, I shook my head. "I need some fresh air."

Ryder held his arm out for me as I laced it through his while we made our way through the living room and toward the front door. Once outside, the cool night air hit my face and cooled off my desire some.

Ryder wrapped his arms around me and buried his face into my neck. "I want you so badly, Ava."

My head dropped back to his chest, allowing him easier access to my neck. His lips moved across my skin, leaving a burning trail in their path. "Ryder."

"We have three days before you leave to head back to Texas. I want to spend every minute with you."

Ugh. The reality of our future hit me right in the face. I couldn't forget Ryder was moving to Montana. I was about to sleep with a man who I knew I might not be able to have a future with. That scared the hell out of me.

The night sky caught my attention. It was then I saw how massive the sky was and the amount of stars you could see.

"Wow," I whispered. "Look at the stars."

Ryder chuckled. "Hell, this is nothing. I'll take you somewhere to-morrow night and show you what a true Montana night sky looks like."

A bubbling feeling of excitement filled my chest. "I'd love that."

Turning, I wrapped my arms around his neck. "For now, though, I need you to kiss me."

Ryder's eyes lit up. "My pleasure."

The second his lips touched mine, I was lost in the perfect blissful moment. Ryder moaned softly into my mouth and my stomach clenched with desire as I tightened my arms around his neck. He slowly lifted me off the ground as his hard length pressed against my body.

I wasn't sure how long we kissed for before I felt my feet touch the ground again. Ryder slowly pulled his lips away from mine, and I fought with everything I had not to beg him for more.

His hands cupped my face as our eyes locked. "I've never in my life felt like this, Ava."

My heart dropped in my chest as I pressed my lips together to keep from smiling like an idiot. "Me either," I finally said as I felt my cheeks heat. "I'm so glad we bumped into each other."

Ryder grinned and was about to say something when the front screen door slammed shut. "Ryder. I hate to interrupt you, but I really do need to talk to you."

Looking over Ryder's shoulder, I saw one pissed off Destiny standing there with her hands on her hips. Ryder sighed and dropped his hands to his sides. "Do you mind if I talk to her?"

"Of course not. I'll just head back in."

As I walked past Destiny, she gave me the fakest smile I'd ever seen. I reached for the door and glanced over my shoulder. Ryder was watching me as I walked into the house. I wanted to gag when I heard her start talking. She obviously knew I could still hear her when she busted out with, "Ryder, I've missed you so much."

Walking into the foyer, I made a gagging motion as someone busted out laughing. To my surprise, Jennifer, Ryder's other sister, was standing there looking at me. My face turned red with embarrassment.

"Don't worry about Destiny. Ryder won't even look twice at her. I'm pretty sure everyone in the room tonight could see the way my brother was looking at you."

I swallowed hard and placed my hands on my cheeks to cool my face down. "Well, I um, I'm not really sure how to respond."

Jennifer laughed. "No need to. I have to say, though, I've never seen my brother so caught up in a girl before. Granted I live here and he lives in Texas, so I've never really seen him in a serious relationship before. Oh my God. I'm rambling on and on." Shaking her head, she scrunched her nose up. "Tell me how you met."

"Well um, I had just been dumped at the cake store by my fiancé and was walking down the street on the phone with my mother when we ran into each other."

Jennifer's eyes lit up. "Wow. He broke up with you at the cake store?"

With a wave of my hand, I chuckled. "It was for the best. I quickly realized it wasn't love I was feeling. Especially when I ran into Ryder."

"And it was love at first sight? Did you feel a spark between you? Did your skin feel as if a blaze of fire was moving along it when Ryder touched you?"

I stood there staring at Jennifer with a stunned look on my face. "Ahh—"

She spun around as she wrapped her arms around her body. Stopping, she quickly ran over and took both my hands in her hands. "What did he say to you? Did you exchange numbers?"

"Well no, we didn't. I hadn't even gotten his name. I called him … mystery man."

Jennifer gasped. "No!"

"Yes!" I said with a little bit too much excitement.

"Then what happened?"

Okay, I had to admit, I was getting caught up in her euphoria. "Well … I thought about him for a few days. His amazing eyes were constantly in my dreams."

"Oh, Ryder does have beautiful green eyes."

I nodded. "He does."

"So go on! Go on!" Jennifer said as she hopped a few times.

"I saw him at a club. I was drunk out of my mind and he ran into me again."

"Again? It was destiny!"

Jennifer was really much too caught up in this story and I had to admit, it was fun pulling her along. "Yes. I was drunk, though, and ended up not really remembering anything other than the fact that your brother brought me home and took care of me when I was sick from too many shots."

Her body relaxed as her eyes went dreamy. "Ryder always was the romantic one out of my two brothers."

With a smile, I looked down. "So anyway, being the gentleman that your brother is, he arranged to have my best friend there when I woke. Well much to my surprise, I found out he had stayed all night."

Jennifer slammed her hands over her mouth. "No! Did you … you know?"

I widened my eyes. "I wasn't sure. I figured we had, but I didn't … you know … feel different."

Jennifer looked at me with a lost look on her face. "What?" she asked.

"You know. I didn't *feel* different."

She slowly shook her head. "Oh, I wouldn't know, Ava. I'm a virgin."

Oh. My. God. That explained this whole crazy conversation. Jennifer had to be at least twenty. I was super impressed she had kept her virginity, especially since she was knock-me-over gorgeous. "Oh. Well, at any rate, I had to be at my father's house that day for this huge meeting he was having with two gentlemen from Austin. My father and Layton were talking about going organic."

Jennifer jumped up. "No freaking way! Ryder and Nate?"

With a giggle, I nodded. "Yes! I couldn't believe my eyes when I saw Ryder standing before me. Of course, then I got mad because I thought we had slept together and how could he sleep with a girl so drunk out of her mind."

"Right. Of course, that would be a douche move for sure!"

I glanced through the front window and saw Destiny was still talking to Ryder. Turning back to Jennifer, I gave her a sweet smile. "But your brother is far from being a douche. He simply took care of me while I suffered from taking way too many shots."

Jennifer sighed. "And you have been dating since. How sweet."

I shook my head. "Oh no. We haven't been dating."

With a frown, Jennifer turned her head and looked at me with a stunned expression on her face. "But, the way you look at each other. You were just kissing on the front porch." She let out a confused chuckle. "I'm confused, Ava."

"Don't be. It's not that complicated. We just needed a little push I guess. I think it's safe to say I'm very much interested in your brother."

Placing her hands over her heart, Jennifer sighed loudly. "Oh. My. Gawd. That was the most beautiful love story I've ever heard."

My smile faded. "Well, I think our story is just beginning, at least I hope it is."

"Oh my gawd! That's such a beautiful thing to say, Ava! I'm so happy Ryder has found you. It's like destiny met fate! Oh it's all so perfect."

Now I'm so confused. What is happening?

"It's like watching one of my romance books coming to life before my eyes."

Ahh. It all made sense now. "Jennifer, have you had a chance to talk to my mother yet?"

Shaking her head, Jennifer said, "No. Why?"

I laced my arm in hers as we made our way back into the living and over to my mother.

"Jennifer, this is my mother, Courtney. She's an editor. She loves romance books."

I thought Jennifer was going to leap into my mother's arms. "Oh. My. Gawd!" Jennifer said as she quickly began spitting out book names. One look from my mother and I knew I'd be catching hell later on from her. She loved talking books, but talking to Jennifer would wear her out and she would quickly find my father and say she was ready for bed.

My evil plan of getting my parents up to their room early was working. *Even though I just came up with it two minutes ago.*

Nine

Ryder

I wanted to punch myself in the face as I listened to Destiny tell me how much she deserved a second chance.

I held up my hands to get her to stop talking. "Destiny, stop. Please just stop talking. There was never anything real between us. It was something our fathers wanted. I'm not even living here; I live in Texas!"

With a smile, she placed her finger in her mouth and bit down on it. "But, you're moving home."

I needed to nip this in the bud and quickly. "Destiny, I'm with Ava."

Her eyes widened. "With Ava? As in, you're dating her?"

Were we dating? I mean, hell, we made plans to have sex later. I'd consider that dating.

"Ryder? Are you going to answer me?"

"Yes, Destiny. Ava and I together."

"Exclusive?"

My mouth dropped open as I stared at her.

"Yes, exclusive. Jesus Christ, Destiny," I said as I raked my hand through my hair.

"Destiny, I'm about ready to head on out."

I glanced over to the door and saw my sister, Jennifer. With a smile, I walked past Destiny and kissed my youngest sister on the cheek. "We didn't get a chance to really talk."

Jennifer smiled a smile so wide I couldn't help but chuckle. "It's okay, I got to talk to Ava, who I love by the way! I might love her mother a bit more though and possibly might have scared her some with my book talk."

My sister Jennifer was an English literature major and loved to read. "I'll be sure to let her know you're not crazy."

Hitting me lightly on the chest, Jennifer winked. "Treat her right, Ryder. I can tell she's special."

"Oh gag me," Destiny said as she pushed past my sister and I. "I'm ready to go."

Jennifer rolled her eyes before giving me a hug goodbye. "I'll talk to you tomorrow."

"Sounds good. Be careful driving, Jennifer."

"Will do! Bye, Ryder."

My sister took off like a bolt of lightning and made her way through the house, saying goodbye to everyone. Destiny kissed my parents goodbye and followed Jennifer out the door. One quick look around the room and my eyes caught that smile. Ava stood across the room chatting with my sister Dani and her husband, Rich.

I made my way over to them and heard Dani telling Ava goodnight.

"You're not driving back tonight are you?" I asked as I slid my arm around Ava's waist. I was making it very clear to everyone we were together. I couldn't help but catch Nate's smile as I briefly looked his way. Tomorrow I'd be having a nice little chat with him about the stunt he pulled in the barn today.

"No, we're staying in my old bedroom."

Dani's mouth dropped open with an idea she pretended she had just come up with. If I knew my sister, she'd been cooking it up for a few hours. "Hey, I've got a great idea. Maybe we can go for a hike tomorrow morning, show Ava a little bit of Montana."

"That would be amazing!" Ava said with a grin.

"Perfect. We'll chat more at breakfast. Right now, though, I'm exhausted and this pregnant girl needs to get some sleep." Dani wrapped Ava up in a hug while I shook Rich's hand. "It was wonderful meeting you and your family, Ava. I'm so glad you all decided to come spend a few days here with us."

Ava's face blushed. "It was wonderful meeting you too, Dani. I can't wait to see more of Montana."

Dani turned and gave me a wink. "Sleep good, Ryder."

"Oh don't worry, I'm sure I will."

"Uh-huh. I bet you will."

I wrapped my arm around Ava again as I watched my sister retreating out of the room. "I think I'm going to go say goodnight to everyone. I'm exhausted," Ava said as she looked up at me.

"I won't be too far behind you."

With a sexy smile, Ava leaned up and kissed me on the lips as she whispered, "See you soon."

My dick jumped in my pants at the thought of finally being with her. Trying to keep cool, I spent a few minutes talking to Layton and Jase before excusing myself and heading up to my room. I needed to take a quick shower before Ava came knocking on my door.

I glanced at the clock and sighed. "What is taking her so long?" I said as I scrubbed my hand over my face while I practically put a hole in the rug from pacing.

Reaching for my cell phone, I went to send Ava a text when I realized I didn't even have her number. My heart dropped to the floor. "How in the hell did I not think to get her number?"

I sat down on the edge of the bed and sighed. Maybe she changed her mind. No ... no way did she change her mind. I saw the look in her eyes. She wanted me as much as I wanted her.

The knock on my door was so light, I barely heard it. Jumping up, I practically ran to the door and threw it open. Standing before me was not Ava, but my brother, Nate.

"What the fuck do you want?"

"Nice to see you too, bro. You got a second?"

I quickly glanced down the hall. Ava was four doors down on the left.

"No, I don't have a second."

Nate lifted his brows and wiggled them. "You got a girl in there?"

My head snapped back down to his as I pulled him into my room and shut the door. "No, I don't have a girl in here. What the fuck was that move you tried to put on Ava earlier today?"

Nate laughed. "Well, you weren't making a move, so I figured you weren't interested. I went in for the hit."

Anger filled my veins as I balled my fists. "What did you just say?"

Nate brushed me off with his hands. "Calm down, I get you have a thing for her and she has one for you. I won't make any moves on her again. Can we move on to the bigger problem you have right now?"

I stared at him for a good minute before I spoke. "So you won't try to make any plays on her, am I right?"

"Yes, you're right! Dude, I said I wouldn't hit on Ava again. Even a blind person couldn't have missed how the two of you were eye fucking each other all night."

Feeling satisfied, I smiled. "Fine. What's the bigger problem?"

"Destiny."

I pulled my head back and laughed. "Destiny? Why is she a problem?"

Nate sat down on my bed. "I overheard her telling Dad her father has been pressuring her to marry so he could retire from ranching."

With a shrug of my shoulders, I said, "So. How is that my problem?"

"She told Dad she wasn't over you and started talking to him about combining the ranches if you two were to get married."

I let out a gruff laugh. "Please, I'm not in high school any more, Nate. Dad is not going to try and pressure me into marrying Destiny."

Nate stood up and looked at me with a concerned look on his face. "Listen, when you walked back into the house at dinner holding Ava's hand, it was obvious to everyone the two of you are an item. Tell me you didn't see the look Dad gave you when you sat down."

I had seen it and I knew he was going to want to talk to me about Ava, but never in my wildest dreams did I believe he would be upset by me having a relationship with her.

"I think you're reading too much into this, Nate."

"Fine, then riddle me this, Ryder. How is this relationship going to work between you and Ava?"

"If I need to explain the birds and the bees to you, dude, you're the one with the bigger problem here."

Nate rolled his eyes and sighed in frustration. "I'm talking about when you move back to Montana and she's living in Texas. You and I both know the long distance shit doesn't work out. No matter how much you said you weren't into Destiny, it was the distance which ultimately caused you to break if off with her."

"No, it was me realizing I didn't love her or want a future with her."

"Whatever it was, it didn't work. Dad is going to remind you of that and we both know he wants Parker's ranch, and if that means you marrying his daughter for him to get it, I promise you he's going to push you in that direction."

Taking Nate by the arm, I pushed him toward my door. "I know what I'm doing and I seriously doubt Dad wants anything bad enough to push his kid into doing something he doesn't want to do."

Nate stopped and looked at me with his mouth gaped open. "Do we not share the same father? The same man who made us both miss the state football championship because he wanted our help on the ranch that day."

"I'm done with this conversation. Night, Nate."

I pulled open the door to see Ava standing in the hallway.

"Ava," Nate and I both said at once and a little too loudly.

Closing her eyes, she shook her head as the door across the hall opened. Reed came walking out and asked, "What's going on?"

Ava glared at Nate and then me. "Nothing, Daddy. I was headed down to the kitchen to get something to eat. Ryder and Nate here ran into me as I was walking down the hall."

Reed glanced between all three of us. "Huh. Okay, well don't stay up late, sweetheart."

I couldn't read Ava's eyes. She looked mad, disappointed even. "Don't worry, Dad. I won't be."

Spinning on her heels, she headed downstairs. I wanted nothing more than to follow her, but Reed was burning holes into me with his death stare.

"Well, good meeting, Ryder. Talk to you tomorrow."

With a smile, I nodded my head and smiled. "Yep. Later."

Reed stood there for a few minutes waiting for me to go back into my room. "All right then, night, Reed."

With a grunt, he said goodnight and went back into his room. I stood in the hallway unsure of what to do. When Reed opened his door again and looked out at me, I knew I had to go back into my room.

I shut the door and cursed under my breath. Ava was headed to the kitchen and I was trapped in my own room.

"Fuck."

My phone buzzed on the dresser as I walked over and saw I had a text from Nate.

Nate: High school. Late night meetings in the barn. You catching my drift?

With a smile, I fist bumped and sent my brother a text back.

Me: Thanks dude.

After slipping on a pair of boots, I made my way over to the window and threw it open. I couldn't even count on my hands how many times I climbed out of my window to sneak out.

Leaning out, I looked over to the trees Nate and I used to make our escapes.

Shit. It sure seems a lot higher.

And dangerous.

With a deep breath and a silent prayer, I climbed out the window and reached my foot out for the metal roof. I made my way over to the large group of oak trees. Twisting and turning my way through the trees, it hit me. "This shit was easier at seventeen."

"What are you doing?"

Stopping, I held onto the trunk tighter as I looked down at Ava standing in the yard.

"I'm climbing down a tree."

"I see that. Why are you climbing down a tree?"

Letting out a frustrated sigh, I started carefully making my way down again. "To get to the kitchen, Ava!"

When my feet finally hit the ground, I dropped and kissed the grass. "I made it!" I said in a hushed excited voice.

"Oh yay!" Ava said. "Why didn't you just use the stairs like a normal person?"

"Your dad was watching my door."

Ava placed her hands on her hips. "Is that why you never came to my room?"

Wait. What?

"Me? You were supposed to come to my room."

Ava's mouth dropped open in surprise. "Ryder, the girl never goes to the guy's room!"

"Why not?"

"I don't know … she just doesn't. It should be the guy coming to the girl. You know … like a guy riding up on a white horse and whisking her away and talking all romantic shit and stuff."

"You've been talking to Jennifer, haven't you?"

Ava giggled. "Whatever! I got tired of waiting for you, so I came to your room only to find Nate there."

"He stopped by to talk to me about something."

The light from the full moon lit up Ava's face beautifully. "So, talking to Nate was more important than sneaking to my room and having hot, passionate sex with me?"

I nearly choked on my own spit.

Finally finding my voice, I asked, "Hot sex?"

Ava took a step closer to me. "I believe I said hot, *passionate* sex."

"I can't take it anymore, Ava."

With an innocent smile, she tilted her head and walked up to me. "What can't you take anymore, Ryder?" Her hand moved down and cupped my hard dick. "This?"

With a moan, I dropped my head back. "Why do I feel like a high school kid having sex for the first time?"

My body trembled when Ava's lips moved across my neck. "How many times have you snuck down that tree to be with a girl, Ryder?"

I pulled my head forward and looked directly into Ava's eyes. "The moment I met you, Ava, I forgot every girl I've ever touched, kissed, or had sex with."

Her breathtaking smile caused my world to stop. "You just swooned me, Mr. Montgomery."

"Is that so?"

Ava's hand moved up my body as she placed both hands on my chest.

"I feel your heartbeat," she whispered.

"I want to feel yours, but with your skin touching mine."

Her lips parted slightly as I reached down and picked her up. With a squeal, Ava laughed. "What are you doing?"

"Why were you outside, Ava?"

"W-what?"

"Why were you outside?"

Chewing on her lip, Ava whispered. "I was going to throw little pebbles at your window because I knew my father would be watching your door, and I can't take waiting to be with you a second longer."

My stomach felt like I was on a roller coaster as I stared into her eyes.

"What are you doing to me, Ava?"

Her eyes searched my face. "I could ask you the same thing."

I quickly headed away from the house and toward the barn.

"We're going to the barn? That doesn't seem very romantic for our first time together, Ryder."

"Just wait, Ava Moore. If you want romance, that's what you'll get, buttercup."

Ten

Ava

Did he just call me buttercup? Something about it made my insides melt.

Ryder walked past the barn and continued on walking away from the house. "Um ... I don't know how to tell you this, but you passed the barn."

"We're not going to the barn."

"Are we gonna find a tree or something? That also doesn't seem like a fun first time. I mean, call me old fashion, but I'd at least like to actually lay down when we make love."

Ryder laughed. "Has anyone ever told you that you talk too much? Hush up before someone hears you."

I glanced back at the fading lights of the house. "I'm pretty sure my dad can't hear us this far out. Unless he has me bugged ... which I wouldn't be surprised."

With another chuckle, Ryder shook his head. "We're going to the original house."

"The original house?" That's when I saw the small stone structure. "What is this place?" I asked as Ryder walked up to the large wooden door.

As he set me down, I glanced back over my shoulder. I could barely see the barn in the distance. "I didn't even know this little house was here!"

Ryder reached up and took a key down and opened the door. "You can't really see it through the trees. My grandfather built this house for my grandmother as a wedding present."

The old wooden door creaked open as Ryder took my hand and led me into the darkness. The smell was familiar, and I couldn't help but smile. "It smells like my grandparents' attic," I whispered.

Never letting go of my hand, Ryder walked over to a table where he opened a drawer and took something out. Hitting a match, he lit an oil lamp. The entire room filled with light as I sucked in a surprised breath.

"It's beautiful," I whispered.

The room was probably the size of my living room and bedroom in my condo back in Austin. In the corner was a small kitchen area. A table that could seat two sat across from the kitchen. In the middle of the room was an old antique sofa that was flanked by two small tables that had oil lanterns on them as well. The sofa table that sat in front of the sofa looked fragile, but held a small bouquet of flowers along with a sketchpad.

"Who lives here?" I asked.

"No one really. I'll sometimes stay here when I come to visit if I need some time to myself. It's usually my mother who comes in here. She grew up in this little house and often spends time here."

"Did she put these flowers here?"

Ryder walked up to the flowers and ran his fingers along one of the flowers.

"Yeah, she brings them for my sister, Kate."

"Kate?" I quickly ran through his sisters' names. I knew I had them right. Before I had a chance to ask, Ryder turned and looked at me.

"My sister Kate was the oldest. She loved this little house and always said it was going to be her house someday. Every day she would come after school and sit on the sofa and draw. She wanted to be a designer and would tell us how proud we would all be when her designs were on the runways of Paris."

My heartbeat increased as I instantly felt a connection to Ryder's sister. I was so afraid to ask the next question. "W-what happened to her?"

Dragging in a deep breath, he looked away. "She died the summer before her senior year of high school. She slipped coming down the stairs, hit her head and broke her neck. She died instantly. Her boyfriend was the one who found her."

My hands covered my mouth. "I'm so sorry."

Ryder smiled and nodded. "I didn't bring you hear to tell you a sad story. I brought you here to start a new one."

My chest fluttered. I was feeling so many different emotions. "A new one?"

His hand caressed my face softly as his thumb ran lightly over my skin. "Yeah, buttercup. Our story."

I'd never in my life felt this way, and I was beginning to wonder if this was what love really felt like. There was no way I could possibly be in love with Ryder. There was no doubt there was something amazing between us, but I wasn't ready to say it was love.

"You swooned me again," I whispered.

Ryder's lips moved lightly across mine as he softly spoke. "I'm starting to think this swooning thing is something good."

A moan escaped from my mouth when his hand cupped my breast. "Very, *very* good thing."

The warmth of his body was gone and I instantly missed it. Ryder lifted the oil lamp and held it up, lighting up more of the space. It was then I noticed it was two stories.

"There's an upstairs?"

Ryder smiled. "Yeah, the bedrooms are up there. Only two."

I walked around the small room and took everything in the best I could in the light and current state I was in … which was a complete mess. From the story about his sister, to his utterly beautiful job of sweeping me off my feet. My libido was begging for me to strip down in the middle of the tiny room and beg Ryder to take me.

"Oh Ryder, this is so charming. I'd love to see it during the day."

His arms wrapped around my body as he nestled his face into my neck. "I can arrange for that. Only if you promise to spend the night with me here."

With a smile, I lifted my hand and ran it through his soft hair. "You have no idea how happy you just made me."

He spun me around and looked deeply into my eyes. "Let me make love to you."

My lips pressed together as I fought to talk without my voice cracking. I've never had a guy romance me like this before. I've heard stories about things like this, mainly from my mother when she and her book club would talk about a book they just read and their current book boyfriends, as they called them. A few friends in college would share stories about how romantic their boyfriends were, but no one had ever treated me or talked to me like Ryder did. I thought I had found something different with Johnny, but I was so wrong. I never knew what falling in love was until I met Ryder. The way he made me feel was … magical.

"Please, Ryder. I can't wait any longer. Please."

With my hand in his, he led me up the narrow staircase. On each side there was a door. Ryder turned to the right and led me into a room that was just big enough to hold a full-size bed and two small nightstands. The only other thing in the room was a quilt rack that housed a few quilts on it.

"Everything is clean; my mother thought I might want to stay here."

I nodded my head as I tore up the corner of my lip. *What if I sucked?* I mean, I thought I was pretty good in bed, but I never really thought to ask any of my past boyfriends how they rated me.

Ryder dropped my hand and walked over to a side table. Placing the oil lamp on it, he turned and looked at me.

I frantically began rubbing my hands together as I barely said, "I'm scared."

His face was so beautiful in the light; I felt tears beginning to pool in my eyes. "Why are you scared, Ava?"

With a quick shrug, I shook my head. "What if I'm not any good? Like, I really suck in the sex department and you're so disgusted you have to leave in the middle of it all."

Ryder pulled his T-shirt over his head and tossed to the side. "Nonsense. There is nothing about you I don't love."

Oh. My. God. He said the L word. Do I panic?

No.

Do I say it back?

Hell no! He didn't tell you he loved you, Ava. He said he loved everything about you.

Isn't that the same thing?

No. Totally not the same thing. He's thinking with his little man and that's all. It was a slip of the tongue.

As my mind argued with itself, I watched Ryder remove his boots, and then his belt. One quick push down of his pants and I was gasping for air.

Holy living shit balls. He was for sure not thinking with his little man, because he was far from little.

"I don't think you're going to fit inside of me!" I blurted out without thinking.

Ryder laughed as he took himself in his hand and I had a mini orgasm right there on the spot. "Okay well … you have successfully caused my panties to go wet."

Lifting his eyebrow, he stroked himself slowly as he walked up to me. "Do you want me to undress you, Ava, or do you want to undress yourself?"

This was getting embarrassing. I couldn't pull my eyes from his hand stroking himself. It was the hottest thing I'd ever seen. Forcing myself to move, I quickly undressed myself except for the tan lace panties and matching bra I had on.

"My God, you're the most beautiful woman I have ever laid eyes on."

Swallowing hard, I moved my hand down to his and moaned as my fingers wrapped around his hard dick.

Ryder shook his head and grabbed my hand and pulled it over my head. "Stop. I won't last two minutes with you touching me."

With a wicked smile, I locked onto my lip with my teeth and batted my eyes up at him. "What will you do when you're buried deep inside of me?"

His eyes turned dark and before I knew it, I was on the bed and Ryder was slipping my panties off and burying his face between my legs.

"Oh God!" I screamed out as he did things with his tongue I never knew possible. My orgasm hit me hard as I grabbed his hair and pushed him closer to my body while I called out his name.

His lips covered what felt like every inch of my body before he pushed my bra up and exposed my breasts. His mouth was gentle as he took each nipple in and gave them the attention they had been longing for the last few weeks.

My body twisted around on the bed as Ryder's hands and lips took me to a place I never wanted to leave.

"What about birth control?"

What was he asking me? I was in a euphoria like I'd never known.

"Ava, baby, are you listening to me?"

My eyes opened as I pulled myself together and leaned up on my elbows. "Three step method."

Ryder gave me a confused look. "What?"

"Birth control, condom, pull out."

"You're on birth control?"

I nodded my head as my eyes moved down to his hard throbbing dick. God, I wanted to feel him inside of me. "Please tell me you have a condom."

The look on his face told me did. "Yeah, hold on. Nate hid a box up here a few months ago."

I wanted to ask how many girls he'd brought here to have sex with, but I decided it was best if I didn't know. It only took Ryder about thirty seconds to find the box and grab a handful and throw them on the bed.

"Feeling lucky?" I asked with a wink.

"I haven't had sex in forever and I'm pretty sure making love to you is going to be like nothing I've ever experienced before, so yes … I'm feeling very lucky."

Okay, now he just put the pressure of best experience ever onto my shoulders. "How long is forever?" I asked.

Ugh. Oh my God, Ava! You broke the number one rule. Never ask a guy when the last time he had sex was.

Ryder's eyes met mine. "Over nine months."

"Nine months! Why?"

Giving me a smile that made my insides quiver, he said, "I haven't met anyone I wanted to be with until the day I damn near knocked you over."

Ryder ripped the condom open and slipped it on as he motioned for me to lie back down. He didn't jump right to it, though, like most guys would. He took his sweet time.

Ryder moved his hands over my body like he was worshipping it. I was on fire just from his touch. When his hand moved between my legs, his lips pressed against mine. Our tongues danced in rhythm as Ryder readied my body for him.

Pulling his lips from mine, he kissed softly along my neck and over to my ear where he whispered, "Ava, my sweet Ava," as he pushed himself ever so slowly inside of me. Inch by holy-freaking-hell-he's-huge inch.

My body lifted as I greedily took him in. The feeling was beyond amazing as Ryder buried himself all the way into me and didn't move. Bracing his elbows on the bed, he placed both hands on my face and kissed me ever so softly. Each time, he whispered words against my lips. My body felt like I was on a journey that I prayed would never end. Each dip of my stomach or flutter of my heart was another piece of myself I gave to him.

"Ava, you've more amazing than my dreams."

My fingers moved over his arms as he slowly began to move in and out of my body. "Don't stop, Ryder. Please don't stop."

You would think the first time two people had sex it would be raw and passionate. I had expected it to be that way, but Ryder was a game changer. Nothing would ever be the same again. Everything he did took me by surprise and I loved each and every second of it.

"God, Ava, I'm never going to be the same after this."

I tightly closed my eyes as his spoken words mimicked my own thoughts. I could feel another orgasm building as I opened my eyes and gripped onto his arms tighter. "I'm going to—oh God I'm going to come again!" My breathing increased as my heart sped up. I'd never experienced an orgasm while having sex.

Ryder moved faster and my body began to tremble. "If you come baby, I'm going to come right along with you."

And just like that, my body unleashed the most amazing orgasm of my entire life. Not even a super duper high-powered vibrator ever pulled something like this from me.

I wrapped my legs around him tighter as Ryder called out my name at the exact moment I called out his.

When he finally stopped moving, he stayed inside of me with his forehead leaned against mine, both of us fighting for air as if we had just run a marathon.

I wanted to cry, not because I was hurt, but because of how moved I was at this very moment. *Nothing before or after this night will ever compare to this moment.*

"Ava," Ryder whispered as he kept his forehead to mine.

"Ryder," I breathed back.

"There will never be a moment like this in my life ever again. I want to freeze time so I'll never forget it. You have captured my heart and soul forever."

A single tear rolled slowly down my cheek as I closed my eyes and froze this moment forever in my heart.

Eleven

Ryder

The sun was shining in through the window casting a beautiful glow on Ava's face. I hadn't slept this good in a long time, and I knew it was because I held the woman of my dreams in my arms all night.

Her warm breath softly hit my body as I felt it come to life. "I feel your heart beating."

With a smile, I kissed the top of her head. "It beats only for you."

Lifting her chin and resting it on my chest, her eyes were enticing me to kiss those soft full lips. "Have you been talking to, Jennifer?"

With a chuckle, I pulled her on top of me and looked into her eyes. "How did you sleep, buttercup?"

"I slept amazingly, all thanks to you," she beamed. "I also feel so at peace here in this house. It's strange."

My fingers lazily moved over her back as my eyes fleeted around the room. "Yeah, this place is rather special."

"Ryder?"

Turning to look back at her, I pushed a piece of blonde hair away from her eyes. "Yeah?"

"We never went back up to main house!"

I'm dead. I'm so fucking dead.

I pushed Ava off of me as I headed back down the stairs. "Where are you going?" she called out.

"Getting dressed!" I exclaimed over my shoulder. Quickly finding my clothes, I got dressed as fast as I could.

Ava walked around as if she didn't have a care in the world.

Motioning over to her, I asked, "What are you doing?"

She stopped and gave me a deadpan look. "What do you mean?"

"Ava! Your dad is going to figure out that we spent the night together and then he is going to kill me. Do you realize the severity of the situation?"

With a chortle, she waved me off with her hand and got dressed. We both headed downstairs with me practically pulling her arm out of her socket.

"Hurry, Ava."

With a huff, she replied, "I'm a grown woman. My father has no say in what I can and can't do. If I want to sneak out and have hot sex with the most handsome and romantic man I've ever met … then I'll do it."

My hands dropped to my sides. "You think I'm romantic?"

Her eyes lit up like fire as she ran her tongue over her teeth. "Oh yeah. And handsome, don't forget I said handsome."

My chest heaved as my breathing grew heavier. "You wouldn't think I was very romantic if you knew what I was thinking right now."

"Really?" Ava asked as she walked up to me and placed her hands on my chest. "Try me."

"I want to bend you over that sofa and fuck you from behind."

When her eyes widened and her body trembled, I knew she wanted the same thing. "Now see, I think that is very romantic and hot as hell."

I lifted my brow. "Oh yeah?"

"Yep. But I'm confused as to why we're talking about fucking when we could actually be doing it."

All sense left my brain at that point as my hands cupped her face and I kissed her. Ava quickly began trying to get my pants back off when the door to the house flew open.

"What in the hell are you two doing?"

I pushed Ava back so hard she stumbled and landed on the sofa.

"We're not doing anything!" I shouted as I turned, expecting to see Reed, but instead I was looking at my brother.

"You son-of-a-bitch. Talk about scaring the living piss out of someone!" I shouted at him.

I quickly made my way over to Ava. "I'm so sorry I pushed you. I thought it was your dad."

Ava pushed my hand away and stood as she glared at me before glancing over to Nate. "You better have a damn good excuse for interrupting what you just interrupted."

Nate pulled his head back in a disgusted manner before shaking it off and pointing to me. "Reed is looking for both of you, but especially you, bro. When I realized where you both probably were, I came to warn you."

I swallowed hard as Ava laughed as she slipped on her shoes and pushed passed Nate while heading out the door. "Puh-lease. I'm not afraid of my dad."

My eyes widened as I looked at Nate. He smiled slowly and said, "Dude … you are so dead. I get your truck and the condo in Austin when Reed kills you."

I pulled my boots on and walked up to Nate. With a quick push, Nate stumbled backwards. "Fuck you, Nate."

"This is how you're going to treat me after I came looking for the two of you? I see how you are, bro. I'll remember this."

I rolled my eyes and jogged to catch up to Ava. My fingers laced with hers as she peeked up and smiled her beautiful smile. Her blue eyes sparkled as her hair practically glowed from the sun hitting it.

God how I loved this girl.

Wait. What?

Instantly I stopped walking. "What's wrong?" Ava asked as she gave me a concerned look.

Nate chuckled as he walked by. "He probably just realized this is his walk of death."

Ava slapped Nate on the arm and focused back on me. My heart was pounding and I was positive my face had drained of all color.

"Ryder? Is everything okay? You don't look so good. Do you feel all right?"

I searched her face before looking into her eyes. She looked so content even though there was a hint of worry in there. Her face had a glow to it and I knew it was because of the night we shared together. I felt the same way, and I'd give anything to go back to the little stone house and make love to her all day.

Suddenly becoming acutely aware of my heart pounding in my chest and every breath I took, I let what I thought sink in.

I love her.

Those three words had never made an appearance in my head before like this.

My stomach fluttered like the pansy ass I was, but I didn't care. Everything about this felt right. I'd never experienced this feeling before and it had to be love.

Shouldn't I be scared shitless? Running away would seem like the normal reaction I would think, but all I wanted to do was pull Ava into my arms and tell her how I felt.

Unfortunately, my mouth agreed to do just that before my brain caught up to what my heart was telling my body to do.

"I love you."

Her eyes widened in shock before pooling with tears. She looked confused, yet she smiled the most breathtaking smile ever.

"What did you say?" she whispered.

Nate came rushing up to me and grabbed me by the shoulders, bumping Ava out of the way. "What in the hell did you just say?" He shook his head as he looked at me with dazed look. "You uttered the three words. You. Uttered. The. Three. Words! Take it back! Take it back before it's too late!"

Spinning to Ava, Nate pointed to her. "What did you do to my brother?"

"Me?" she said as she looked between us.

Much to my regret, I stood there still in a state of shock that I had blurted out how I felt about Ava. That wasn't going to give me any swooning points, that's for sure.

"What makes you think I did something?" Ava asked.

Nate turned back to me and slapped me across the face, breaking me out of the trance I was in.

Ava gasped as I yelled, "What in the fuck, dude? You hit me!"

"Snap out of it, Ryder! You can't be in love for fucks sake. You just slept with her. You hardly know each other."

Ava pushed Nate out of the way and stood in front of me. "Ryder," she choked out. "Did you ... um ... did you mean what you said?"

My mouth opened to speak, but nothing would come out. "I ... um ... I ... ahh ..."

"It's the magical pussy effect. That's what this is. I've seen plenty of good men go down because of it."

Snapping my head over to Nate, I narrowed my eyes at him as Ava continued to wait for my answer. Pinning him with a glare, I said, "You're such an asshole, Nate."

"Tell me I'm lying. You can't even answer her right now. It's the classic symptom."

Closing my eyes, I tried to get my thoughts together as Nate continued to run his mouth. When I opened my eyes, I looked back to Ava only to see her eyes filling with doubt.

Oh shit.

"Ava, I—"

"There y'all are!" Liza called out as she walked hand in hand with Walker up to us. Lifting my head, my eyes caught Walker's and I could see the big brother protectiveness coming out loud and clear.

"Ava, dad is looking everywhere for you. When you and Ryder didn't show up for breakfast, the steam was practically coming from his head," Walker said as he shot daggers at me.

"Thanks," Ava said as she turned and started walking away from me.

"Wait, Ava!" I called out as she grabbed Liza and began walking quickly back toward the house.

Walker walked up to me and put his hand on my chest as Nate said, "Oh hell. Here we go. First comes the brother, then it will be the best friend Jase, and the grand finale ... the dad."

If Nate were a few feet closer, I would have punched him just to shut him up.

Walker's jaw tensed as he asked, "What did you do to my sister?"

"I didn't do anything!"

Nate laughed. "Bull shit he didn't. He told her he loved her! Can you believe that shit?"

Walker's eyes softened as he searched my face. "You love my sister?"

"No!" I shouted.

Walker pulled his head back in surprise. "I mean, yes! I mean ... fuck I don't know what I mean! I just blurted it out. I ... I don't know why I said it." My hands pushed through my hair as I let out a frustrated sigh. "No, I do know why I said it. It's just ... I was so overcome with these stupid emotions and I didn't want to say it like that."

Before I knew it, Walker was laughing his ass off. Laughing so much he had tears. Nate and I stood there and stared at him.

"Why is he laughing?" Nate asked in a whispered voice.

With a shrug of my shoulders, I replied, "I have no idea, but I'd much rather him be laughing than looking at me like he wants to kill me."

Lifting his hand, Walker said, "Wait ... oh man. Give me a second."

"I'm glad you find this funny," I responded as I made my way to the house.

Walker wiped his tears away as he walked next to me. "Sorry, dude. It's just the look on your face. It was priceless. You have been bitten by the love bug for sure."

There was that word again. "I need to talk to Ava. She thinks I didn't mean to say I loved her, but I did mean to say it. I just didn't want to say it like that and then when she asked if I meant it I couldn't say it again! I need to tell her I can say it and mean it."

After letting out a long dramatic sigh, Walker slowly shook his head. "I should be really concerned that I understood all of that."

Nate guffawed. "I'm glad you understood it, 'cause I didn't."

"Everyone is waiting up at the house to go for a hike, so unless you want to declare your love for my sister in front of everyone, it will have to wait until after."

Reed was standing outside the house glaring at me as we walked up.

"Yeah, I think I'll wait," I said as I fought the urge to bolt in the opposite direction of where Reed was standing with his arms crossed.

"Just keep walking like you don't see him," Walker said as I snapped my head to look at him.

"W-what?"

Nate laughed as he called out. "Hey, Reed! Look who we found ... Ryder!"

Reed made his way over to us as Walker said, "Good luck, dude."

"Wait. Where are you going?" I demanded as Walker nodded toward his father and made a beeline to the door.

Stopping, I grabbed Nate's arm. "You will never get my truck or condo, you traitor!"

"Ryder, how was your evening?" Reed asked as he stopped in front of me. I was still focused on my brother when he shot me a smirk.

"You're dead to me," I whispered before turning to look at Reed.

"Morning, Reed. It was um … it was … nice?"

Tilting his head, his eyes narrowed as he waited for me to change my response.

"It was … um … fun."

Reed's mouth dropped open as I held up my hands.

"No, no, that's not the word I was looking for."

Ava's father cleared his throat and stated, "Walk with me, Ryder. I think it's time you and I got to know each other a little better."

My eyes widened in horror as I slowly turned and began following Reed toward the barn. *Why the barn? Nothing good could come from going to the barn!*

Glancing over my shoulder, I shot my good-for-nothing brother a pleading look.

With a smile he called out, "You still keep your spare key under that potted plant, right?"

My hand lifted as I gave him the finger while he threw his head back and cackled.

Twelve

Ava

"**S**low down, Ava! Where is the fire?"

He said he loved me. He said he loved me. Oh. My. God.

"Ava? Where in the hell have you been?" my father said as he stomped down the steps of the porch.

"Not now, Dad," I replied. Stopping, I turned and faced my father. "And before you think of going off and doing something stupid, don't. He makes me happy and I … I …" Letting out a sigh, I pointed to him. "Just don't do what I know you're going to do!"

Turning away, I pulled on Liza to follow me. "Wow! Were you about to say you loved Ryder?"

The moment we stepped inside the house, I saw Dani. Walking up to her, I took her hand in my other hand and pulled her along with Liza up to the room I was staying in.

"What's happening? What's going on?" Dani asked. "Slow down! I'm with child and I can't move that fast."

Liza giggled as she replied with, "Not sure, but I think your brother just rocked my sister-in-law's world."

Dani gasped as I rolled my eyes and pushed them both into the room and shut the door. Both of them looked at me with excited expressions.

"So? How was last night?" Dani asked as she covered her mouth like we were in middle school and talking about my first kiss.

"He said he loved me," I blurted out as both of their smiles faded before being replaced with squeals of delight.

Liza and Dani turned to each other and grabbed hands and jumped like twelve-year- olds.

My hands went to my hips as I shot them both a dirty look. "Are we done acting like little girls?"

Liza widened her eyes and took my hands in hers. "Why aren't you happy? Ava ... this is amazing. I mean, it's kind of fast, but oh my gawd!"

Dani shook her head as she looked at me. "What did he do?"

"Nothing. Everything." I buried my face in my hands and screamed into them before dropping them back to my sides.

"Last night was amazing. I felt things I have never in my life felt before, not only physically, but emotionally as well."

"Ew," Liza and Dani said together.

Liza motioned for me to sit down on the bed. "Okay, so you had a wonderful time last night. When did he tell you he loved you?"

I took in a deep breath and tried not to overreact. "Well, when we woke up, Ryder somewhat freaked that we missed breakfast and he was sure my father was going to kill him."

Dani and Liza exchanged glances quickly. "Then I thought I had him talked into a little bit of ... fun ... before we headed back to the house."

Liza wiggled her eyebrows as Dani made a gagging motion. "Ugh ... I'm pregnant and it doesn't take much to make me puke. Move on."

Pressing my lips together to hide my smile, I cleared my dirty thoughts and kept talking. "Well, Nate busted in and said everyone was looking for us so we headed back to the house. Everything else happened so fast ... and I'm so confused. This is all just going so fast."

"Tell us!" Liza exclaimed as I pulled back and snarled my lip at her.

"Okay! Okay! He pulled me to a stop and just said he loved me. Then Nate started on about magical pussies and he wouldn't shut up and Ryder looked stunned and when I asked him if he meant it, he couldn't even form a sentence to talk. Then y'all walked up and I panicked. What if he didn't mean to say it? What if he was caught up in the magic of last night as well and was thinking maybe someday he could love me and he just spit it out?"

Dani sat next to me as she placed her hand on my leg. I could practically feel the warmth coming from her. "If there is one thing I know about my brother, he doesn't ever say anything unless it is coming straight from his heart. You said he just blurted it out?"

With a nod of my head, I felt water pool in my eyes.

"My guess would be he surprised himself by saying it out loud. You said you experienced feelings you'd never felt before, right?"

My teeth sunk into my lip as I fought to stay in control of my emotions while I nodded my head.

"I'm sure my brother felt the same way. It also didn't help that Nate was standing there talking out of his ass, I'm sure."

A snicker slipped from my mouth as replied, "No, it didn't."

Liza put her arm around my shoulders and pulled me close to her. "I'm sure when you questioned him he was stunned, like Dani said. Give him a chance to talk to you before you go jumping to conclusions."

A single tear slipped down my cheek as I wiped it away quickly. "I know. I think the thing that scares me the most is I've fallen in love with him after just one night together."

Dani began sobbing as Liza and looked at her. "Are you okay?" I exclaimed as I jumped up and bent over her.

Dani held her hand up and smiled as she continued to cry. "I'm just so … happy!"

Peeking over to Liza, I gave her a what-the-hell look as she mouthed *pregnancy hormones.*

Ohh … totally made sense now. I remembered Liza going through that with Nickolas.

Taking her sleeve, Dani wiped all the wetness from her face and stood up. "We better get downstairs if we want to head out for a morning hike. By mid-morning I'm exhausted and ready for a nap!"

With a quick grin, I said, "Let me change really quick and I'll meet y'all downstairs."

Liza stood up and stretched. "Man oh man. Nothing like family-weekend drama to wear you out!"

Dani laughed as they made their way over to the bedroom door.

After throwing on some sweatpants, a long sleeve T-shirt and a light jacket, I found my hiking boots and laced them up. Something outside the bedroom window caught my eye as I moved the curtain and sucked in a breath of air.

"Oh ... holy ... shit."

My father and Ryder were walking back from the barn. Leaning in closer to get a better look at Ryder, my head hit the glass.

"Shit!" I yelled out as I strained to see if Ryder was limping or showing any signs of trauma.

Tripping over my untied shoelace, I rushed to get my boots on and ran to the door and threw it open as I waited for Ryder to come up and change.

"Hurry up, son! We've been waiting on you two for the last forty minutes!" Nate Sr. yelled out.

My thumb went to my mouth were I promptly started chewing on my nail. Ryder ran up the steps two at a time and flashed me a smile that took my breath away.

"Hey," he softly spoke as he took me into his arms. "I didn't mean to just blurt that out. I wanted to make that moment special and I wasn't sure if you thought me saying it was too soon or maybe it wasn't romantic enough or—"

I placed my finger over his lips and shook my head. "I love you, too. And it was beyond perfect." I closed my eyes and frowned before opening them again and saying, "No ... it would have been perfect had Nate not been there."

Ryder grinned as he dipped me back and kissed me fast and hard on the lips. "I need to change. I'll meet you downstairs."

My stomach felt like I was on a roller coaster as I returned his smile and nodded. "Kay," was all I managed to get out as Ryder lifted me quickly. Slapping my ass, he headed to his room.

"Wait!" I called out. "What did my father say to you?"

Ryder turned and walked backwards. "That if I hurt you in any way, or have sex with you ever again while he is within a five-mile radius, he will kill me. That's all."

With a shrug, I said, "Oh good! Well, not good that he would kill you, but good that he didn't try to kill you already."

Ryder stopped at his door and then dashed in while I practically skipped down the stairs.

I finally met my prince charming. *I can't wait to tell my mother!*

"It's so incredibly beautiful up here," Jase said as he walked behind me.

"I agree. I've never seen the sky look so clear or so blue."

Liza and Walker brought up the rear, and I knew it was because they wanted to steal a kiss or two along the way. I couldn't blame them. It was rare for them to not have little Nickolas with them.

"We're almost to the top. The view is like nothing you've ever seen," Ryder called out as he looked back at me.

My heart raced with excitement as I continued heading up the trail.

"You get you some action last night?" Jase whispered from behind me.

Stopping, I hit him on the chest. "Seriously? Stop acting like a child."

He lifted his eyebrows and replied, "I'll take that as a yes you did. No wonder your dad was in an uproar this morning."

"I'm not talking to you about this, Jase."

Jase roared with laughter as he walked by and headed closer to Ryder.

Oh. Great. That little bastard lived to make my life hell. *Always has.*

"Don't you dare even utter a single word to him, Jase Morris!" I called out as my foot slipped and I lost my balance.

The moment I felt my ankle roll and pop, I knew this wasn't going to turn out good. The snapping feeling was followed by a shooting pain up my leg that caused me to lose my balance even more. The only thing I heard was my name being called out as I fell to the ground and down a small hill. I thought everything was going to be okay until I picked up a bit of speed and my lower leg hit a boulder. The pain hit me instantly as everything began to spin and I felt sick to my stomach.

"Son-of-a-bitch!" I yelled out as I saw Ryder sliding to a stop and bending over me.

"Ava! Where are you hurt?"

Squeezing my eyes shut, I whimpered. "My leg. Hurts like hell."

"We've got to get her down from here and to the hospital," Walker said as my eyes snapped open.

"What? No! Just give me a few seconds to let the pain go away."

Ryder and Walker looked at each other before Ryder turned back to me. "Baby, your leg is broken; the pain isn't going to go away."

Swallowing hard, the pain felt a thousand times worse than it had five seconds ago.

"W-what?"

Jase stood behind Ryder and Walker. "This is my fault! Shit! Ava, I was just playing around."

"My ankle rolled, and something snapped."

I heard my mother and father calling out my name as I turned my attention to Ryder. "Please tell me it's not broken. I can't look."

Ryder's eyes filled with worry. "Don't look, but I can't tell you it's not broken. It clearly looks broken."

Snarling my lip, I replied with, "Shit."

Well that didn't make me feel any better and only made me want to look at my leg. Taking a quick glance, I saw my leg bent in a way it should not be bent.

"Oh no," I whispered as I felt lightheaded.

Reaching out for anyone I could find, all I could manage to say was, "Gonna ... pass ...out."

Ryder carefully picked me up and started back down the trail as I buried my face into his chest.

"I've got you," Ryder kept repeating every five minutes or so as Walker and Jase led the way down the trail.

Grabbing onto Ryder's jacket, I pleaded, "Please, you be the one to take me to the hospital, okay?"

Ryder held onto me tighter as his voice cracked. "I promise."

The pain was getting so unbearable, I prayed like hell I would just pass out.

"Walker, Jase, and I will take her in my truck. Reed, Courtney, you can follow us," Ryder called out as I felt him walking faster. Peeking my eyes open, I thanked God we were finally off the trail.

"I'll call them, Ryder, and let them know you're on your way!" Lucy called out.

Ryder gently placed me in the backseat of his truck as he ran to the other side and jumped in with me as Walker got behind the wheel.

"Just follow Dani and Rich," Ryder ordered Walker.

"Is Dani okay?" I asked lifting my head to look out the front window.

"She's fine, buttercup. That trail is nothing to her, even being pregnant."

The feel of Ryder's hand brushing against my forehead was calming.

I felt myself slipping into sleep as the pain finally faded away.

"Never going hiking again," I whispered as sleep took over.

Thirteen

Ryder

I paced across the tile floor as I waited along with everyone else in the waiting room.

"Ryder, please stop pacing and sit down next to me."

I glanced over toward my mother and gave her a faint smile. "I can't sit down, Mom."

"How about a cup of coffee then?" Dani said as she placed her hand on my arm.

My eyes looked up at the clock on the white wall. It had been almost two hours since they brought Ava back for surgery.

"Nah, the doctor might come out."

I caught a glimpse of Reed watching me. After our little talk this morning, everything had been perfect. I told him the truth, that I cared very deeply for his daughter and I was going to do everything in my power to make her happy. His only concern was me moving to Montana. A problem I had chosen to ignore for the time being.

Dani sighed. "Fine, Rich and I are going to get some coffee; will you drink it if I bring you one?"

I absentmindedly nodded my head. Before turning to leave, Dani leaned in closer to me and whispered, "Don't get upset, but I saw Dad talking to Destiny a little bit ago."

My head snapped over to my father who was currently talking to Layton. "What? Where?"

"She was here; you know she does charity work for the hospital. I overheard her telling dad how much she missed you and wished you would give her another chance. She brought up the two families merging."

My heart jumped to my throat. "What did he say?" I asked in a hushed voice.

Dani's grin spread from one side of her face to the other. "He told her it was time for her to move on ... that you and Ava were together now and it would be best if Destiny accepted that the two of you were never going to work out."

My eyes about popped out of my head. "No shit? Dad told her that?"

Scrunching up her nose and nodding her head quickly, my sister rubbed her swollen belly. "Yep! Looks like our father knows true love when he sees it."

I narrowed my eyes as I searched her face. There was no way I was getting into that with her now.

"Well, that certainly makes things a hell of a lot easier on me."

Dani patted my chest and winked. "I thought that might cheer you up some! I'm going to get that coffee now."

Rolling my neck, I headed over to a chair and sat down as I watched my father intently. I had to admit I was stunned he wasn't going to push the whole family merger thing with me again. Especially since he knew I was moving back here. Relief instantly flooded though my body as he glanced my way and smiled. With a smile back, I made a note to myself to talk to him about Destiny and the future of our ranches. I had an idea on how we could make a merger happen and it sure as hell didn't involve me having to get married to Destiny.

The doors opened and a doctor dressed in surgical scrubs walked out. Reed and Courtney jumped up when the he called out Ava's name.

"We're her parents," Courtney said as he walked up to them. Liza and Walker were next to them, along with Jase. I stood back with Layton, Whitley, and my parents.

"I'm Doctor Monroe. Has anyone talked to you yet since they brought her in for surgery?"

Reed shook his head. "The ER doctor just told us she had fractured the tibia and fibula. He said she would need surgery."

The doctor shook his head. "Yes, it was a severe but clean break of both bones so everything went back together nicely and are secured with a plate and screws. She also had a small fracture of her ankle, but I'm not worried about that at all. It will be more painful than anything and should heal up fine."

Courtney covered her mouth as Reed said, "She has a broken leg *and* ankle?"

"I'm afraid so. Healing for those breaks will take six to eight weeks, and I'm going to recommend physical therapy as well since she will be off that leg for a good amount of time."

My stomach recoiled at the thought of Ava being in such pain.

Reed reached his hand out to the doctor. "Thank you so much for taking such good care of her. When will we be able to see her?"

"She should be out of recovery in about an hour and a half or so."

As the doctor walked away, I stopped him. "Doctor Monroe, may I ask another question?"

He stopped and looked at me. "You are?"

"Um, Ava's boyfriend."

Damn, that sounded good.

"What is it, son?"

I glanced over to Reed before turning back to the doctor. "Ava was only here for a long weekend; she's originally from Texas. What about traveling?"

"I would think she might want to delay heading back for a least a few days. Just the traveling alone would be rather uncomfortable."

My mother walked up to Courtney and Reed and gave them a warm smile. "You know Ava is more than welcome to stay at the house for as long as she needs to. Plus, we have two housekeepers, MaryLou and Janet. They will be able to help her with getting around."

"I'll be there as well," I replied.

Doctor Monroe shook my hand and said, "Give me a shout if you have any concerns. The nurse will make sure you have my cell number when Ms. Moore is released."

With a firm handshake, I replied, "Thank you, I appreciate it."

"Let's all go get something to eat while we wait for Ava to get to her room," my mother stated as she looked at Nate. "Text Dani and Rich and let them know what's going on. We'll go to the Post Oak Café down the road."

I wasn't surprised at all my mother took over. Ever since my sister Kate died, whenever there was a crisis, she seemed to jump into action. Because she couldn't help Kate, she tried to make up for it in any way she could.

"Food sounds amazing right now," Courtney said with a smile.

Everyone made their way to the elevator as I stayed back. "Ryder? You coming?" Nate asked.

"Yeah, I'll meet you guys there. I have something to take care of."

Nate nodded and followed everyone down the hall while I pulled out my cell phone and started making calls.

I sat in the corner of Ava's room while Courtney and Reed were on either side of her bed. When they brought her up from the recovery room, they had just given her a strong dose of pain med's which put her to sleep almost instantly the nurse said.

"She's waking up," Courtney said as I stood up. Ava looked at her mother and smiled.

"Hey, Mom. What's up?"

Courtney let out a chortle and said, "Hi, sweetheart. How are you feeling?"

Turning her head, Ava looked at her dad. "I feel like a train hit me. Oh hey, Dad."

Reed pushed a strand of hair away from Ava's eyes as he gently spoke to her. "Hey there. Are you in a lot of pain?"

Ava let out a dry laugh. "I'm feeling okay. I'd feel better if Ryder was here."

Reed glanced over his shoulder at me and smiled. "He is here."

Walking up to the side of her bed, I leaned over and gently kissed her lips. "Hey," I whispered as her eyes lit up.

"Thank you for carrying me down the trail. It was very swoon-worthy of you."

"The apple doesn't fall far from the tree," Reed said as I stole a glance in his direction. He smiled at Courtney and then gave me a head pop and said, "We'll talk later."

With a chuckle, I nodded and turned back to Ava, giving her a warm smile.

"So, how bad?" she asked.

I peeked up to Courtney as she motioned for me to talk.

Clearing my throat, I answered, "Well, to start with you have a small fracture in your ankle."

Ava scrunched her nose up. "Ouch."

"That's not the bad part."

"My leg?"

"You broke both the tibia and fibula."

Ava frowned. "That explains the pain when my ankle twisted. I think that's why I lost my balance and fell."

Courtney sighed. "I'm so sorry, sweetheart, that you're going through this."

Ava gave her a weak smile. "For now it's okay, but I'm not so sure how I'll feel when the pain meds wear off."

Reed chuckled and stood next to Courtney. "There's another problem."

"Another problem? Like three broken bones isn't enough!" Ava exclaimed.

Reed stole a glance in my direction before focusing back on Ava. "I don't think you'll be flying back to Texas with us tomorrow."

"Oh."

I couldn't help the small smile that spread across my face when Ava grinned and looked at me.

"So, I'll have to stay here? In Montana?"

Reed cleared his throat and flashed me a dirty look that caused my face to drop.

"Only for a few days, until you feel like you can fly home," Reed said.

Ava stole a glimpse my way before staring down at her hands. "How long will I be in the hospital?"

"They're talking about releasing you tomorrow. Lucy and Nate Sr. offered to let us stay as long as we wanted and—"

Snapping her head up, Ava practically cried out, "No!"

Courtney's eyes widened in surprise.

It was obvious the stronger pain meds were wearing off because Ava was now moving about and grimacing with each movement. "I mean, really Mom, you don't have to delay your flight because of a broken leg."

"Well, I mean, Ava, you're my daughter and I'm leaving you behind with a broken leg *and* ankle? I've already talked it over with your father and he's going to go ahead and fly back with everyone, and I'll stay behind to help you out until you're ready to come back home."

Ava's eyes closed and I knew she wanted a few moments alone with her parents. "Do you need the nurse, buttercup?" I asked.

Her head slowly nodded as I excused myself and left the room to find the nurse. I loved that Courtney wanted to stay and help her daughter, but I prayed like hell Ava talked her out of it.

Fourteen

Ava

O h flippin' shit balls. The last twenty-four hours I had been trying to dream up some excuse to stay in Montana a few days longer, but never did I dream I would have broken my leg and ankle to accomplish that goal.

The moment my mother mentioned staying in Montana, I felt the claustrophobia setting in. I loved my mother, but she babied me and I was a grown woman. Plus, this was the perfect excuse to spend more time with Ryder … alone.

I closed my eyes and tried to adjust myself. The pain in my leg felt like it was getting worse, along with the headache I was getting.

"Do you need the nurse, buttercup?"

God. I. Love. Him.

Ryder had to have seen the way I lit up when I was told I had to stay behind. Then how quickly that joy was sucked out of the room by my sweet mother offering to stay behind.

Ugh. This is not going to be fun.

I slowly nodded my head.

"Reed, Courtney, I'll leave you both to spend a few minutes alone with Ava while I search for the nurse."

Yep. This cowboy was a keeper.

When the door shut, I felt my mother running the back of her hand down my cheek. Smiling at her warm touch, I prayed like hell her feelings were not about to be hurt.

My head turned to the side as I opened my eyes and looked into her blue eyes.

"Mom, you know I love you so very much."

Her smile melted my heart and made it ache all at once.

"But …"

My father made a growl sound and said, "Here it comes."

Narrowing my eyes at him, I turned back to her. "But, I really don't think you should stay. I promise I'm going to be fine, and the moment I fly back home you can come and pick me up and I'll stay out at the ranch with y'all."

Her chin trembled as she reached for my father's hand. "You … you don't want me to stay and help you? Who's going to help you, Ava? You're with strangers."

I gave her a thoughtful look. "I'm not with strangers. Ryder is here."

My mother rolled her eyes. "Please, Ava. You barely know him or his family, and you're willing to stay here and let them care for you?"

The tears building in my eyes were hard to contain as I felt wetness cover my cheeks. "I thought you, of all people, would understand."

I turned and looked out the window as I tried to compose myself.

"Court, maybe now is not the best time to be talking about this. Let's leave Ava be for a bit so she can rest."

I sniffled like a five-year-old as I wiped my snot across the back of my hand. Thank God Ryder wasn't here.

"Do you love him?" she whispered.

Pressing my lips together, I took in both of my parents' expressions. My mother's was hopeful, my father's angry.

Forcing the words to come out without crying, I replied, "Yes. I've never felt like this with anyone before."

"You broke your leg on purpose, didn't you!" my father demanded.

Pinching my brows together, my mouth dropped open. "Seriously? Do you not know me at all, Dad?"

With a slight tap on his stomach, my mother shushed my father. "Reed Moore, you be quiet!"

Her eyes softened as she took my hand in hers. "Oh, Ava. Will this work? I mean, he's going to be moving to Montana and you're in Austin and … and … the whole thing with Johnny happening not long ago."

I squeezed her hand and gave her a reassuring smile. "We are taking this one day at a time. All I know is Ryder makes me feel so special. So happy. I just want the chance to see where this goes, Mom. And you staying behind and trying to take care of my every need is not going to help things any. I'll only stay until I feel up to traveling, and then I'll fly back home with Ryder."

My father swallowed hard as he wrapped his arm around my mother. "Our baby girl is growing up, and why in the hell she rushes into relationships I'll never know."

I let out a titter as I rolled my eyes at him. "Very funny."

"I want you to know I'm not happy about this, but I understand. You're my baby and I just want to take care of you."

My heart felt torn. In a way, I wanted my mother to take care of me, but I also wanted to take this time and spend it with Ryder. We both threw out the *I love you* so quickly, I needed to make sure it wasn't because of the amazing night we spent together. I'd been down this road before and not that long ago. I knew in my heart I'd never felt this way before; I just needed to be sure.

"Well, what better way to find out if Ryder and I belong together than to have him thrown into a situation where he is taking care of me."

My mother grinned as my father moaned. "Oh hell. What am I going to do with you, Ava Grace Moore?"

With a shrug, I flashed him a smile. "There is one thing y'all can do."

"What is it, darling?" my mother said as she held my hand in hers.

With a pained expression, I murmured, "Find out why Ryder is taking so long with that nurse. My leg and ankle are throbbing!"

My heart was pounding in my chest as Ryder pulled down the long drive-way that led to his parents' house.

When he turned off the main road, I glanced his way. "Where are you going?"

He smiled big and my stomach jumped when I saw the dimple pop out on the side of his face. Stealing a peek my way, he chuckled. "You didn't really think I was going to have you stay in my parents' house, did you?"

"Um ... I thought that was the plan."

Ryder reached for my hand and kissed the back of it softly. "The only good thing that came out of your fall was that we get to spend more time together ... alone."

My heart skipped a beat.

The old stone house.

"I'm staying in the old stone house?"

The jovial smile on his face said it all. "*We're* staying in the old stone house, and I'm going to take care of you."

Pressing my lips together tightly, I attempted to hide how happy I was. Clearing my throat, I tried to act like a grown woman who was not internally fist pumping at the idea of spending so much time with Ryder. "What about your job? You can't just up and leave everything to stay here and babysit me. I really was only going to stay a few days to heal up and then I planned on heading home."

Bringing the car to a stop, Ryder turned to face me. His eyes were soft, yet filled with something I found myself longing to see each and every day. Passion. Concern. Love.

"This whole weekend ... hell, this whole last month has been a whirlwind. I've felt things for you I've never felt with any other girl."

Chewing on my lip, I nodded and stated, "I feel the same way."

"Would I love for you to have stayed with me without breaking your leg and ankle, yes. Most certainly, yes."

My hand covered my mouth as I giggled.

"But, you're here with me and I want to take this time to really get to know one another, Ava. I don't want you to think I just threw it out there when I said I loved you. I really feel something so deep within my heart for you, and I want to explore that more."

"So do I, Ryder. I rushed into my last relationship because I thought I was in love. With you it's so different. It's exciting, romantic, and scary all rolled up into these emotions I'm not familiar with."

I looked down at my hands wringing together in my lap. "But … I don't know how it's going to go for us."

Looking up through my eyelashes, I saw him nod his head. "The distance thing."

"Yeah. The distance thing. I would never in a million years ask you to walk away from your dreams."

Ryder pushed a piece of hair behind my ear before running his fingers softly down my cheek. "I would never ask you to leave the life you've worked so hard for either. Please believe that."

"I do."

"Then let's just take this day by day. Nate is fine working on his own with the company, and believe me, my father couldn't be happier that one of his sons is home to work on the ranch. We can stay here as long as you want."

My cheeks felt as if they were burning I was smiling so big. "It's kind of like our own little private hideaway in the mountains."

Ryder's eyes danced with excitement as he searched my face. "It's my version of heaven."

Jesus, he is perfect in every way.

"Come on, let's get you inside. I had MaryLou take care of a few things for me to get everything ready for when you got out of the hospital."

Ryder jumped out of his truck and ran to my side. Opening the door, he carefully helped me out. "Was there a sidewalk here the other day?" I asked as I tried to balance myself with the crutches.

"Nope. I had them put it in yesterday. It doesn't go all the way to the main house, but it does go to the barn."

Dropping my mouth open, my eyes widened as I gave him a stupefied look. "W-what?" I shook my head to get my thoughts together.

"You put in a sidewalk … just for … me?"

With a smile that made me weak in the knees, he reached down and picked me up into his arms, eliciting a small yelp from my lips. The temperature had dropped significantly in just a few days. The cool, crisp air felt good on my face as I buried it into Ryder's chest.

He carried me toward the charming old homestead as the smell of pine invaded my senses. Lifting my head, I saw beautiful flakes begin falling from the gray sky. "It's snowing!" I exclaimed, as a light dusting of white quickly covered every surface.

"First snow of the season!" Ryder said as he opened the door and walked in. One look and I gasped out loud at the sight before me. If I thought outside looked beautiful, it was nothing compared to the inside of the cabin.

Ryder shut the door with his foot and gently set me down.

My heart had never beat so hard in my chest. "W-when did you do this?"

His arm wrapped around my waist as he kissed the top of my head. "I made a few phone calls."

I peeked up at him with a bemused smile. "A few calls? Ryder, you did more than make a few calls."

I scanned the entire house and took in all the white lights hanging from the ceiling. The furniture had been moved around to make room for a queen bed that had been placed in the corner near the fireplace that had a fire already roaring.

On the other side of the fireplace, the old writing desk that was upstairs was set up with my laptop, sketch paper and everything I needed to work.

"You have a very nice boss at Amour Boutique. She said not to worry; your job would be waiting for you when you got back."

Oh my. He's too perfect. He thought to call my job!

"And Maurice was more than thrilled to know you would be laid up in little stone house in Montana for a few weeks."

A few weeks. Maybe breaking my leg was a good thing after all! Alone in a romantic old home with Ryder every day. Yes. Please.

"He sent over some ideas he wanted you to begin working on."

"What? He did?"

Ryder smiled. "Yeah, he said something about he could feel your creativity about to flow. He wants you to … damn, what did he say?"

He glanced up toward the ceiling in thought before snapping his fingers and pointing at me. "He wants you to *l'impressionner*."

My ovaries *just* exploded. "Impress him," I whispered. "You know French?"

"A little," he said with a wicked smile.

I wrapped my arms around him and gazed into his eyes. "I never want to leave. I want to stay in this little house with you forever."

His lips pressed against mine in a passionate kiss as I moaned into his mouth. When he pulled slightly back, he whispered, "I can arrange that."

Fifteen

Ryder

Two weeks had passed since Ava had broken her leg and ankle. I was stunned at how well she was getting around. Life had been absolutely blissful. I don't think I've ever taken such pleasure in making anyone orgasm like I had Ava. Exploring her body had become my new favorite past time. The last few days we had gotten rather experimental to say the least when she begged me to make love to her.

"Ryder, how are you doing today?"

Spinning around, I saw Destiny standing at the entrance to the barn.

"Hey, Destiny. I'm doing great. Yourself?"

She shrugged and made her way in. "Oh, I guess I'm doing okay. Been trying to get a few things taken care of around the place, but you know how that is. It's a lot of work."

With a chuckle, I nodded and turned back to brushing my mother's paint, Lucky.

"Are you looking for Dad?"

"No, I was actually looking for you. Is um … is Ava still here?"

I paused for a moment before continuing to brush the horse. "Yep. I don't think she is planning on leaving any time soon."

"Really?" she asked in a surprised tone. "Doesn't she have commitments she needs to get back to in Austin? Or you, for that matter? I didn't think you were planning on staying in Montana for so long."

"I wasn't going to stay this long, but it's nothing Nate can't handle. Besides, he's going to be handling it full time soon enough."

She stopped right next to me and leaned against the stall door. "Rumor has it you're playing house with your new *friend*."

I dropped my hand and looked her way. "Ava is much more than a *friend*."

Rolling her eyes, she looked away and mumbled, "Whatever," as I went back to brushing the horse.

"Do you remember all the fun times we had in this barn?"

"Were you needing something, Destiny? If so, maybe you should just get on with it."

Before I knew what was happening, she had her body pressed against mine with her arms wrapped around my neck as she tried to kiss me.

I grabbed her arms and pulled them down as I pushed her away. "What in the fuck are you doing?"

Her eyes looked pleading. "Come on, Ryder. Ava is locked away in that house and she'll never know. You know you want me. I see it in your eyes and the way you look at me. Remember how many times we fucked in here? God, the thought of it makes me so horny."

My mouth dropped as I stood there staring at her in disbelief as her hand moved over her body.

"Have you lost your damn mind? If you think for one moment I would ever cheat on Ava, you have another thing coming. I love her and nothing is going to change that."

Destiny laughed. "You love her? Didn't you just start dating her? No one falls in love that fast. Not even a helpless romantic fool like you."

"I feel sorry for you. You really never have felt love, have you?"

"Fuck you, Ryder."

"You already have." Turning away from her, I looked back over my shoulder. "And if my memory serves me right, it was my best friend Roy you fucked in here, not me."

With a huff, she stormed off and out of the barn, passing my mother without so much as saying a word.

Mom stopped and said, "Why hello there, Destiny."

After she blew past her, mom turned to me and winked. "I take it she made a pass at you and got turned down."

With a surprised look, I asked, "How did you know?"

Shaking her head, she chuckled and said, "Because I'm a woman, and I know how vile some of us can be. Jealousy does terrible things to people."

Walking up to me, she kissed me on the cheek and then handed me a basket.

"What's this?"

"A picnic basket."

With a frown, I shook my head. "No, I know what it is, what's it for?"

"It's for you to take Ava lunch. With as much as you have been working the last few days around here, I'm sure she is going out of her mind in that tiny house all alone. I thought about inviting her up to the house tomorrow for lunch."

With a smile, I said, "She would love that, I'm sure. She's really getting around pretty good, I have to say."

"So, with Thanksgiving next week, I dare say Ava will be joining us?"

Setting the basket down, I put all the grooming supplies back in the tack room. "If that's okay with you?"

"Of course it is!" she exclaimed. "I really am found of her, Ryder. I see how happy you both make each other, but I must admit, I was worried."

"Oh? Worried about what?"

"The two of you living together so quickly. Her being stuck in that small house twenty-four seven. According to your sister, it's the most romantic thing she's ever seen."

I couldn't help but let out a laugh. "Jennifer would think that." Reaching for the basket, we walked together out of the barn. "But you have nothing to worry about, Mom. Everything is going great with us."

She remained silent as we walked out of the barn. "So tell me, Ryder. How are you going to feel when Ava has to go back to reality? When your two worlds are separated by the paths you have both taken?"

My chest felt tight as I stopped walking and faced her. "I guess we'll deal with that when the time comes. For right now, we're living in the moment and isn't that what you've always said to do?"

With a smile, she nodded. "Throwing my words back in my face, are you?"

"I learned from the best," I said with a wink.

She waved me off with her hands as she said, "Go bring that sweet girl some food and let her know I'd love for her to join me for lunch tomorrow."

Reaching down, I kissed her cheek lightly. "I will."

The short walk to the stone house had my stomach in knots. There was going to come a time when Ava and I would have to face reality. But for now, I was going to lose myself in the world we knew at the moment.

"I'm stuffed," Ava said as she leaned back and sighed. "I swear I think your mother is trying to put weight on me with the amount of food she keeps sending over."

With a chuckle, I nodded. "She's worried you're bored."

"Oh my gosh, are you kidding me? This morning I finished a design I had been working on and it was amazing to have full concentration on it."

I gathered up the paper plates and brought them over to the trash. One thing my mother believed in was making things simple. Thank God for that.

"Have you sent it to Maurice?"

She gave me a wide smile. "Yep. And he loved it! I'm not sure if he'll use it, but he had very good things to say about it!"

I couldn't help but feel her excitement. "I'm glad he liked it."

Standing, she nodded her head. "Me too. I hate to say it … but breaking my leg might have been the best thing to ever happen to me."

I broke out into a full smile. "And why is that?"

She made her way over to me and wrapped her arms around my neck. "Well, first off, I'm living in a terribly romantic stone house with the most handsome man I've ever laid eyes on."

"Go on," I prompted as my hand moved down to cup her sweet, tight ass.

"Second, sex with this handsome man is beyond amazing."

With a wider grin, I winked. "He is rather good."

Ava held her laughter back as she said, "Yes he is."

I lifted my brow and asked, "And is there a third reason?"

Her eyes danced with passion as I pulled her closer to me. "I can't explain it, but I feel like I'm at home here. Like something about this old house brings out something in me."

I pulled my head back and looked into her beautiful blue eyes. "Really?"

She nodded her head. "Let's just say I'm thinking it's really too soon for me to be traveling. It's probably a good idea for me to stay at least until I get my cast off."

I don't think I'd ever felt so happy in my life. My hand laced though Ava's hair as I pulled her lips to mine and kissed her. It didn't take long for things to heat up and we soon were lost in each other.

As I held Ava in my arms after we made love, I couldn't help but feel the same way she did. There was something about this old stone house. It was almost as if I could feel it in the very core of my body. The more time we spent together, the more I realized I wasn't going to be able to live without Ava in my life.

Sixteen

Ava

Ryder had gotten up early and headed out to do some work on the ranch, giving me a chance to finish up a design Maurice asked me to fix up. It was a new designer he had brought on full time in his store in Paris. I knew had I taken him up on his offer to work for him full time, my wedding gowns would be among top designers who graced the catwalks.

Tomorrow was Thanksgiving and it had been almost a month since I had broken my leg and set up camp in the old stone house. This morning's conversation with my mother didn't go at all like I planned.

"Your father is ready to fly up there and drag you back to Texas."

With a chuckle, I shook my head. "I know I've stayed longer than we planned, but it's worked out really well. Ryder and I have gotten to know so much about each other. Plus I've gotten to know Lucy and Nate Sr. Not to mention Dani is teaching me how to knit."

"Knit?"

"Don't sound so surprised, Mom. I'm making her a blanket for the baby."

The silence over the phone was almost too much to bear. "I'm coming home soon."

"When?"

"After Thanksgiving."

My mother let out a frustrated sigh. "Ava! Thanksgiving is tomorrow and that is a very vague answer!"

Pressing my lips together, I held back my laughter. "Well, ya know it's almost been a month; I could just stay here and go to the doctor for my six-week checkup."

"Christmas. I demand you be back home by Christmas."

My mouth dropped open. "You demand it? Mom, I'm a grown woman, you can't demand anything of me. Besides, I like it here. I feel ... at peace here. Although sometimes I swear this old house is haunted ... it sometimes feels like I'm living in a romance novel."

I could hear her taking in a calming breath. "I, for one, can certainly see the romantic side to all of this, Ava, but sometimes you have to go with reality over a romantic dream. I also understand I can't demand you come home, but it's hard for me knowing another family is taking care of my baby. It should be me taking care of you."

And there lies the real problem.

"Mom, no one on this planet could ever replace you. It's just a part of me is almost afraid to come home. I know it's childish, but the moment I set foot on that plane, it's reality and the fact that at some point in the future Ryder and I will be living thousands of miles apart from each other. Please just give me more time. I have the perfect excuse to be here right now. Let me explore this road."

I could hear her sniffle and it broke my heart. "He's going to steal you from me ... I just know it."

Quickly wiping a tear from my face, I tried to make my laugh sound sincere. "Nonsense! No one is stealing anyone."

I was positive my mother didn't believe that statement any more than I did.

Making my way into the kitchen, I leaned the crutches against the wall and took the boiling water off the stove. Pouring it over my tea bag, I let it seep while I peeked around the house.

"Today I shall explore every single corner of you," I said as I smiled.

Yesterday I had tried to make it upstairs when Ryder came home and caught me half way up the stairs. I soon realized I had made a mistake when I got stuck half way up the steep narrow staircase. We both agreed if I wanted to explore, I should start downstairs.

Taking the cup of tea, I held it in my hand while I used my other arm to hold the crutch. It had taken me some time at first, but I quickly figured out a good way to get around the little house.

I set the tea down on the table and looked around. The old antique furniture in the house was beautiful. I fully intended on looking over the writing desk better, but that would be saved for another day.

"Okay, I say we start with the bookshelf. Who knows what amazing books we can find."

I had gotten into the habit of talking to myself ... or at least that's what I thought in the beginning. I had the strangest feeling I wasn't alone. Ryder said I was getting cabin fever, but I swore I felt a presence. Call me crazy, but I knew I wasn't alone.

I slowly made my way to the bookshelf and smiled as I looked at it. Books from floor to ceiling filled the two bookshelves, with one each flanking the fireplace. Old knickknacks also took up space on the shelves, along with a few old family pictures. The old writing desk was pushed up in the corner and to the right of the fireplace. The view out the window was breathtaking and one I could certainly get used to. Ryder said it had been that way when his sister Kate used to spend time here in the house.

I walked up and reached to pull out a book but screamed when I heard a loud crash. Turning, I saw a picture frame had fallen off the shelf and landed on the desk.

"Holy living shit balls. That scared the piss out of me!"

I used the furniture to make my way over to the desk. My drawing pad was sitting neatly on the side table, waiting patiently for me to get back to work. I didn't have to turn in my design to Maurice until next week, so I had plenty of time to play and explore.

By the time I got to the desk, I felt exhausted. "Jesus," I panted out. "I need to move around more. I'm out of shape."

I lifted the picture and gasped when I saw it. "Kate," I whispered as I looked into her deep blue eyes. Lifting my gaze, I scanned all the other pictures of Ryder's family. Most were of his great-grandparents, his grandparents and his father. There were a few of all the kids, but this seemed to be the only picture of Kate.

"That's weird. I wonder if Lucy put this here after ..."

I stopped talking when I felt a chill come over my body. The glass in the picture frame cracked as I lightly ran my finger along the pattern. I couldn't help but feel like the picture was calling out to me. Almost as if Kate was trying to tell me something.

Closing my eyes, I took in a deep breath.

"So, this is all new to me. I'm not really even sure if you're here, Kate. If you are, please don't make things fall at night. I'm just saying, I have a weak bladder and if you don't want to scare your brother away from me by me peeing in the bed, let's just come to that understanding now shall we?"

I peeked my eyes open and glanced around. "Hello? Anyone here?"

Good lord. I'm talking to pretend ghosts now. Maybe I do need to get out of this house.

Pushing out a breath, I let out a giggle. "I've officially gone insane."

Placing the picture on the desk again, I turned to head back to the table and to the bookshelf but something caught my eye. The sunlight was hitting the picture frame and casting the light onto a book. Reaching up, I pulled it out and gasped.

Montgomery Family Bible

"Oh my word ... this is beautiful."

The leather Bible was old and in delicate shape. I carefully opened it to see the front pages filled out with births and marriages.

My heartbeat began beating faster as I carefully closed it and made my way over to the couch. Slowly sitting down, I set the Bible on the table and cautiously opened it again. This time, I ran my finger over the faded writing.

Robert Montgomery – Hampshire 1890

Candice Montgomery – Hampshire 1892

Katherine Montgomery – Hampshire 1893

"Holy. Shit," I mumbled as I tried to read the next name but couldn't make it out.

My head snapped up as I looked around. "How cool is this!"

When I glanced back down to the Bible, I saw a piece of paper sticking out and turned to the page that held it.

It was an old letter folded up neatly. I ever so carefully unfolded it and started to read it.

My Dearest Lizzy,

I hope that you can forgive my treacherous behavior last night. In my haste to prove to my family of our love, I made a decision that will forever alter both our worlds.

I fear I have caused you undo stress and will never forgive myself if you have changed your mind.

You must alert me at once of your decision on my proposal.

Yours forever,

Robert

I read the letter three times before folding it back up tucking it into the page where I found it.

What did he do? What was the decision he made? Did Lizzy accept his proposal? Was that the same Robert as in the Bible? Who was Lizzy?

My mind raced as I carefully turned each page. I was stunned to find another letter … this one much more recent.

As I read it, my heart dropped and tears formed in my eyes. It was clear who had written it.

Dear Lynn,

    How is Ohio treating you? I miss you so much! You wouldn't believe what I've read in Lizzy's journal. Robert and her had a scandalous love affair! HAHA! At least during their time it was. A love so strong that neither family, money, title, nor time could keep them apart. I think I've found it with Jackson. He makes me feel so alive and I love him so.

    My parents would not be happy to know Jackson and I had been making love in the old stone house. It will be our secret, as I know *you wouldn't tell a soul! I could start my own scandal if my parents found out.*

I miss you! Write me back. I haven't been feeling so great this summer. I wish you were here.

Write back and tell me when you're coming to visit.

Anyway, back to drawing. Love you and miss you bestie!

Love always,

Kate

My hands dropped to my lap as I held the letter.

Kate.

She must not have had a chance to mail the letter to her best friend before she passed away.

I placed the letter on the table and began going through the Bible in hopes of finding another letter or something from either Robert or Kate. After no luck, I turned and glanced back over to the shelf.

"There has to be a journal somewhere."

I stood and made my way back over to investigate. Glancing down to Kate's picture on the desk, my eyes moved across the desk as I took it in. Leaning over, I looked at the old piece of furniture.

"I wonder if it's like Grandma's old desk," I mumbled to myself as I reached under to find a button that might open a secret drawer. When I felt it, I smiled wide. Holy hell … could it have been really that easy?

"Bingo. If all these old pieces had secret compartments how was anything kept secret?"

The excitement in finding an old journal had my hands shaking. Scandalous love affairs! *Wait until I tell Mom about this. She'll eat it up.*

I tried my best to bend over more to watch where the drawer opened. Hitting the button, a small drawer at the bottom of the desk opened. Reaching down, I took out a package that had been neatly wrapped in a piece of burlap.

Shutting the drawer, I stood and looked at the treasure I had in my hands. I'd never been so excited in my life to figure out what I had stumbled upon.

As I made my way back to the sofa, I tried to settle my breathing down. This kind of thing only happened in books where you found old Bibles and journals. "Let's see what kind of trouble the Robert and Lizzy were up to."

The fabric fell to the side easily as I gasped at what was in my hands. It wasn't an old journal from Lizzy. My fingers lightly moved across the journal owner's name.

Kate Montgomery.

Seventeen

Ryder

"Ow is Ava feeling?" Nate asked.

"Better. She's getting around more and I actually think she loves that little house."

Nate frowned. "Wouldn't she be more comfortable in the main house, Ryder? I mean, I get the whole idea of wanting to be alone, but she's stuck in basically one giant room. She has to be bored."

"I've asked her if she wanted to move up to the main house and she said she loves where she is."

Nate shrugged. "It's probably the pain pills keeping her looped up."

With a roll of my eyes, I followed him into the kitchen. "So, how are things going back in Austin?"

"Good. I think I've got this whole thing down of you not being around. We got the McMurphy Ranch in New Mexico. They are ready to sign up for consulting on going organic. All in all, I think I'm pretty good at this without you, bro."

Grabbing a beer from the refrigerator, I popped the cap off and took a drink.

"What about you? Liking life on the ranch? Working your ass off from sunup to sundown to please dear old Dad."

My smile grew as I watched my father walk into the kitchen; his eyes were already burning a hole into Nate.

"Don't know how you do it ... I like city life so much better. No getting up at the crack of dawn, no freezing-cold Montana weather. The endless pussy alone is enough to make me never want to mend a fucking fence again in my life."

This just kept getting better.

"Endless pussy, huh?"

Nate grabbed himself a beer. "Hell yes. You do remember those days before you turned into a pansy ass, right? What is it about this mountain air that turns Montgomery men into being pussy whipped?"

He turned and came to a stop the moment he saw our father. "Hey, Dad." You could see panic filling his eyes and he did the only thing he knew to do. He blurted out his good news. "I got the McMurphy Ranch in New Mexico."

Rolling my eyes, I shook my head. My father had always known Nate was never going to stay in Montana. When I moved to Austin, I knew he was upset. He couldn't figure out why we had to move to a big city when most of our job was traveling to cattle ranches to convince them to go organic.

My father took in a deep breath and slowly let it out. "Nate, I knew early on you were going to be one of ... *those* kids."

"Those kids?" Nate asked.

"Yes ... the kind who were never going to be happy following in their parents' footsteps. The kind who would move to the city for better ... opportunities if you will."

"You have to admit, there are more girls in the city than there are here," Nate spit out quickly.

Holding up his hand, my father shook his head. "I can't argue with you there, but some day, son, when you've exhausted yourself, you're going to regret those words ever came out of your mouth because your brother here will have inherited everything."

I let out a laugh as Nate shot me a dirty look. "So, I'm going to be cut out because I don't want to ride around on a horse all day and check fences, feed cows, and all that fun stuff I did growing up. I'm working for the family, Dad, just in a different way."

"I know that … but don't put your brother down for wanting to follow his heart. I'm proud of you both, no matter what roads you travel down. Now as far as being pussy whipped…"

Nate pointed to me. "That was all geared toward Ryder."

My father lifted his eyebrows and nodded. "I thought so."

The moment I walked into the house, Ava jumped up … well at least she tried to the best she could.

"Oh my gosh, you won't believe what I found! The picture fell and the light pointed me to the Bible!"

"The Bible?" I asked with a confused look on my face.

"Yes! The Bible. I'm pretty sure someone's spirit is here in this house and they helped me to find it all. After I found The Bible, I found the letters and then the secret door. I haven't found Lizzy's journal yet so I'm pretty sure Kate either hid it or your mother found it and put it somewhere. Oh and do you have any idea where Kate's drawings are? I really don't want to ask your mother, because I'm not sure how she would feel if she knew I was looking for them."

Ava placed her hands on her hips and looked up. "Although, I wonder if she told your mom about the journal seeing as she hid her journal. But then again, she wouldn't want your mom finding out she slept with Jackson upstairs."

My mouth dropped. "What?"

"I'm curious if the spirit is Lizzy or Kate's."

Spirit? What in the hell? She took too many pills!

Holding my hands up, I shook my head. "Wait. What in the hell are you talking about?"

Ava stared at me like I had grown two heads. "What's wrong?"

Maybe Nate was right. Ava needed out of this house.

I shook my head as something hit me. "Did you say Kate slept with Jackson in this house?"

She nodded her head. "Yes! Oh my goodness … they had the most romantic relationship. I think your sister knew something wasn't right with her health though."

Turning, I headed over to the table and pulled out a chair and sank down into it. "Ava ... give me a second to come to terms that my sister had sex in this house. God please don't tell me where. I don't think I could bear it."

She tilted her head as she looked at me. "Seriously, Ryder? Your sister was spending time with her boyfriend here and you honestly didn't think anything was happening?"

I scrubbed my hands down my face. "I would rather not think of any of my sisters having sex, thank you very much."

She grabbed her crutches and made her way over to me where she sat on my lap. "I hate to break it to you, babe, but you know how Dani is expecting a baby?"

"Ugh ... yes I know, Ava, but that doesn't mean I like to talk about it."

She wrapped her arms around my neck and kissed me lightly on the lips.

"So what is this about a Bible and journal? What in the world have you been up to today?"

With a smile that spread from ear to ear, she replied, "I've been exploring."

"I see that. You found the family Bible, I take it. It's been somewhat of a hunt for my mother to find it. She hasn't been able to find it in years."

"Did she know about Robert and Lizzy?"

"Yeah, they were our great-great-grandparents."

She squirmed in my lap, causing my dick to start coming up.

"How exciting!"

"If you say so," I said as I lifted my hips to her.

I could see the excitement dancing in Ava's eyes. Maybe this was what she needed, an adventure of some sort to go on.

"I take it Robert had a higher level of class than Lizzy?"

"Yep. He was some kind of Earl. My mother said Lizzy was a ladies maid."

Ava gasped and placed her hand over her heart. "He fell in love with the maid?"

Letting out a chuckle, I nodded. "Yep. Do you want me to ask my mom what all she has on them? I know she did some serious research."

Her eyes grew wider. "Yes! Oh my gosh, do you think she would mind?"

"No, she'd love to talk to you about it I'm sure. She was obsessed with it for the longest time."

She chewed on her lip and asked, "Did Kate also research it?"

"Not that I'm aware of. I think my mom found something years ago that led her on her search. Why?"

Ava pulled out a small book and held it. My sister Kate's name was etched into the leather book.

"Is that?"

"Kate's journal. I've been reading it ever since I found it. I have to tell you something and I know you're going to think I'm insane, but I feel so connected to your sister. We are alike in so many ways it's unreal."

I couldn't help the smile that moved over my face. "You remind me a lot of Kate. Your love of drawing and fashion, mostly. She had the same desire and passion that you do. I have no doubt the two of you would have been the best of friends."

Ava's warm smile made my chest tightened. "I'm sure your family misses her so much."

"Yeah, we do."

"Do you know if your mom kept Kate's sketch books?"

With a shrug of my shoulders, I replied, "I'm sure she did. Kate's room has pretty much been left untouched. They're probably in there."

The look on Ava's face made my heart feel light. If this meant she'd stay longer in Montana, I'd do whatever I could to help her on her little adventure.

Eighteen

Ava

There was no way I could hold my excitement in when Ryder mentioned Kate's sketch books were probably in her room. Of course, the last thing I wanted to do was go asking her parents if I could take a peek in their daughter's room.

"I see your wheels spinning. You want to look in Kate's room?"

Chewing on the corner of my lip, I nodded. "But I would never want to do something your mother wouldn't approve of."

Ryder smiled. "Mom goes into Kate's room a lot; I think she talks with her in there."

"She should really come here," I mumbled under my breath.

His expression fell as he looked at me with a questioning look. "Huh?"

I waved my hand as if to brush off what I said. "Nothing. I'm going to guess your mom hasn't ever found Kate's journal. I'm also going to guess she doesn't know the family Bible was here, especially since I found a letter Kate wrote to her best friend in Ohio."

"Lynn?"

"Yep. In the letter she mentions sleeping with Jackson in the house."

"Yeah, let's not share that with Mom. But, I'm sure she would love to know you found the family Bible. She's been searching for it ever since Kate passed away."

"It's been here all the time," I said as I pointed over to the bookshelf. "Surely she's seen it."

Ryder frowned.

"What's wrong?" I asked.

His eyes narrowed as he said, "I've looked at those books hundreds of times and I've never once seen the Bible. Was it hidden behind another book?"

I stood as Ryder helped me get over to where I found the book.

"Nope. It was right here. This picture of Kate fell and the sunlight hit it just right to where it was shining on the Bible."

Ryder's face turned white as a ghost. "That's kind of creepy."

With a giggle, I hit him lightly on the chest. "Don't tell me you believe in ghosts?"

"Considering that picture of Kate has been in our family room since it was taken and now it's out here ... I'm beginning to believe in ghosts."

My smile faded as my heart dropped. I knew I wasn't going crazy. "Oh. That is creepy," I whispered.

Jennifer leaned over and bumped my shoulder. "So, Ryder tells me you've stumbled onto our sister's journal."

Nodding my head, I peeked over to Lucy. "I have."

I could tell by the smile on her face, she was just as curious as I was when I first stumbled upon it.

"So ... does she talk about Jackson in it?"

I nodded.

Jennifer gasped. "Oh my God! What does she say?"

"Well, she talks about when they first started dating, and how they—" Taking another peek around the table, I looked back at Jennifer. "How should I say this? Progressed in their relationship. I haven't gotten too far into it."

Her lips pressed together as she made a disgusted face. "Gross. Don't ever show it to me or I might gag."

I let out a soft chuckle as I glanced around the table. "So, I have to ask, would your mom mind if I went and looked around Kate's room? I was hoping to find her sketch pads."

"Oh, they're in the stone house."

I gasped and looked at her. "What? They've been in the house the entire time?"

"Yeah, I think they are in the upstairs bedroom closet. I'm not sure if you know this or not, but Kate used to spend hours in that old house. She said she felt at peace there and more creative. Almost all of her drawings were done in that house."

A warm feeling washed over me as I smiled and said, "I feel the same way."

"At first my parents didn't mind, but the more time she spent out there, the more worried my mother became."

"Why?"

Jennifer stole a glance to her mother before looking back at me. "If you say I told you, I swear I'll deny it."

Oh, this just got good. Family gossip.

I crossed my heart and said, "Promise."

Jennifer bit her lower lip before blowing out a deep breath and saying, "Kate believed the house was haunted by our great-great-grandmother."

"Lizzy?"

Pulling her head back in surprise, she said, "Yeah. How did you know about Lizzy?"

"I found your family Bible with a letter Robert wrote to Lizzy."

"You found the family Bible? Holy crap. Mom is going to freak!"

"I was going to talk to her about it after dinner. I know Ryder said she had already done some family research."

"Oh, she is going to be your best friend forever. Ever since Kate passed away my mother has been searching for the Bible. She was on a mad mission for a while. She swore our grandmother hid it before she passed away."

"Why?"

Jennifer shrugged. "She didn't like Mom at all."

"That's terrible."

Jennifer chuckled. "Yep. Mom said our grandmother made her life a living hell."

"Who wants dessert?"

Jennifer and I both looked up to see Lucy and Nate Sr. both standing with pies in each hand.

With a low moan, I shook my head. "I'm sure I've gained ten pounds since I broke my leg."

"At least you're not pregnant like Dani."

We both turned and looked at Dani who wore a beautiful smile. "She looks beautiful though," I said.

"Yeah, she really does." Jennifer sighed. "I hope I find love some-day."

With a grin, I bumped her shoulder. "You will. Just be patient."

Jennifer rolled her eyes and pushed out a frustrated breath. For some-one as romantic as she was, I found it hard to believe she hadn't been swept off her feet yet.

After everyone ate dessert and helped clean up the table, it was time to head into the family room for what Nate described as four hours of sure torment and hell. Jennifer and Ryder started pulling out games as my mouth dropped open.

"Games?"

"I told you ... four hours of torment and hell."

"I hate board games," I whispered.

"You are spending Thanksgiving with the wrong family then, sweet-heart. It's tradition. Stuff your face full of food and then play game after game of stupid nonsense until you're so sick of it all, you would pay to have someone kill you. When what we could be doing is sitting our ass on the couch watching football."

With a huge grin on my face, I turned to Nate. "I have a way of get-ting us out of game night."

His eyebrows rose. "Really? If you can make that happen, I will owe you big time."

"So, what you're really saying is you will owe me a favor. Anything I ask for you'll have to do it."

Nate pinched his eyebrows together as he looked at me. "I can easily accept this offer because you have no clue how powerful game night is on Thanksgiving in the Montgomery house. You cannot win at this one, my sweet newbie."

I reached my hand out and said, "The only way to find out is to shake on it."

Nate laughed and took my hand.

"Deal. If you can somehow make the heavens open up and swallow up all the board games and leave me in peace to watch football ... I'll owe you whatever your little heart desires."

With a grin, I turned to Lucy, who was instructing Dani's husband Rich on how to set up the card table.

"Lucy, did Ryder tell you I found the Montgomery family Bible to-day?"

Everyone stopped moving as all eyes turned to me. Lucy's eyes widened as she stared at me with a disbelieving look on her face.

I could feel Nate's eyes burning a hole into me as he leaned in closer to me. "You little sneaky bitch," Nate whispered.

With a jab in his side, I smiled bigger.

"Where did you find it, Ava?" Lucy gasped.

"On the bookshelf in the stone house."

Lucy's head snapped over to Ryder. "Did you see it?"

He nodded and said, "Yep."

Lifting her hands in the air, Lucy called out, "Game night is cancelled. Ava and I are going on a little history lesson."

"Thank God!" everyone called out as Ryder started laughing while making his way over to me.

"I'm not sure what you just did, but you've obviously made the rest of the family very happy with game night being called off."

"You don't like it either?"

Ryder shook his head. "Hell no. Kate came up with game night and we all hated it. Ever since she passed away, Mom has been insistent on it and none of us have the heart to tell her no."

My heart ached for Lucy. I couldn't imagine what it must have been like for her to lose her daughter. "No one will be mad I had a part in her calling it off will they?"

Ryder flashed me his signature melt-my-panties smile. "Are you kidding? You've probably moved up to hero level in everyone's eyes. Especially Nate's." Ryder turned to look at Nate. "The bastard already has the football game on. I'm sure we'll see his hand slip into his pants and a cold beer in the other hand in no time."

"Gross," I mumbled as I turned away from Nate.

Lucy walked up to me and clapped her hands. "Shall we head to the house?"

Excitement bubbled up once again. "Yes!"

As we made our way back to the stone house, Ryder pulled me back. "You're not showing her Kate's journal, are you?"

My eyes landed on Lucy as I shook my head. "I don't think Kate ever had any intentions of your mom reading her journal. There are some very personal and private things in there."

With a nod of his head, Ryder said, "I think for now you keep that find to yourself."

Even though a part of me felt so guilty for holding something back that was Lucy's daughters, I agreed as we continued to follow Lucy who was now walking in record time.

The moment I handed her the Bible, I could see the happiness on her face, especially when she found the letter Robert had written to Lizzy.

"And this letter was in the Bible?" Lucy asked with a confused expression.

"Yes. I assumed you had seen it before."

She shook her head. "No, I had found Lizzy's journal years ago in their house in Helena. That's how I knew about Lizzy."

"So, Robert and Lizzy were your great-great-grandparents?"

Ryder shrugged, "Great-great ... great-great-great ... what difference does it make?"

I playfully hit him on the chest. "A lot!"

Her head snapped up and she flashed me a wide grin. "When you're moving around a bit more, we'll head in and I'll show you the house. It is a beautiful Victorian house Robert had built when Lizzy and he came over to America."

"Why did he pick Montana?" I asked as Lucy took a picture of Robert's letter.

"I would think the gold in the area. At the time they came here, the area was growing in population. The railroad and gold were big money makers and Robert invested in both. He needed to; he walked away from his birth right in England so he only had the money his mother had given him to start a future."

"Who owns the house now?"

Lucy looked at me like I had grown two heads. "We do. It's been in the family ever since it was built."

My mind was spinning. Where did Kate find the letter and why didn't she give it to her mother? In her own journal she writes about keeping a secret. Whose secret? Her's or Lizzy's? Whatever the hell it was why did Kate keep this letter away from her mom? Maybe the secret was in the old house?

Ryder walked up to me and placed his mouth to my ear. "I already see your mind working. We'll visit the house tomorrow if you feel up for the drive."

I wanted to squeal in delight I was so happy.

After showing Lucy where I found the Bible, and explaining Kate's picture, she stood there staring at the bookshelf. "I must have brought Kate's picture here, but how in the world did I miss the Bible?"

"Maybe Kate had it and placed it on the shelf. Sometimes when we're searching so hard for something, we easily pass it over. The spine doesn't even have any wording on it."

Lucy nodded. "It would appear to be just another book ... but ... I wonder why Kate would have had the Bible?"

Ryder let out a chuckle. "Maybe she was wanting to research the family also."

Lucy slowly shook her head. "You know, now that you mention it, she did ask me a lot of questions about Lizzy and Robert. She seemed to be interested in my thoughts about them running off together." Lucy smiled weakly.

Ryder and I both chortled as we watched Lucy look over the Bible.

"Well, now that I've got this back in my hands, I can get to work on trying to figure out the rest of these names." Lucy took the Bible and headed back to the main house to research the other names. I could hardly make out the handwriting, but she seemed to be able to.

The moment the door shut, I turned to Ryder and said, "I need to go upstairs and find Kate's sketch pads."

"Now?"

My heart was pounding so loud in my chest, I was sure Ryder could hear it. For some reason, I was desperate to find her work. Desperate to know more about her ... and her connection to Lizzy.

What I didn't know was how much my life was going to change when I found the things I was looking for.

Nineteen

Ryder

Opening the door, I smiled when I saw Nate standing there. "I hope you know getting this key away from our mother was damn near impossible."

I patted him on the back as he walked in. "But not impossible."

"No, nothing is impossible if you put your mind to it … and lie."

I let out a chuckle. "What did you tell her?"

"That I was meeting an old friend in Helena and *she* was interested in old Victorian houses. Just the idea that I might meet and settle down with a girl here in Montana was enough for her to hand me the keys no questions asked."

Laughing, I shook my head as Nate looked around. "Where is your evil girlfriend who tricked me into promising her my life? Mom would be so upset if she knew she wasn't the one showing Ava the house."

Rolling my eyes, I said, "That was your own stupidity to make the bet with her. And she's upstairs with her head buried in Kate's old sketches and Mom will never find out."

He flopped down onto the sofa and kicked his feet up. "Don't you think it's crazy Ava is a designer and that is what Kate wanted to be."

With a shrug of my shoulders, I replied, "It's a coincidence that's for sure."

"And wedding dresses. You don't find that a little ... weird?" he asked lifting his eyebrow in question.

The moment we found the sketches, I could see it in Ava's eyes how thrilled she was. When she opened the last sketchbook Kate had been working in, Ava gasped and stared at it. I finally just let her be as she poured over the books.

"I know Ava was thrilled to find Kate's designs. Especially the stuff she was working on before she died. She kept going on and on about how talented Kate was and for being so young."

Nate looked away. "I don't understand why she had to die when she had such a full life ahead of her."

I nodded but didn't speak. Kate's death had taken a toll on all of us. Dani and Jennifer, especially. The three of them had always been so close. Kate had always liked her alone time in the old house, but when the three of them got together it was endless laughter and romantic daydreaming.

We sat there for a few moments as we looked around. Our sister had died in this house, but for some reason it never really hit me until this very moment. "Why do you think this house meant so much to her?"

Nate shook his head. "I don't know. She said she felt like she was more creative here. Like it was her secret garden or something."

I nodded my head. "Ava says the same thing. She also keeps talking about how she feels like there is a presence here in the house."

"Creepy. I've never felt comfortable in this house and I'm not really sure why."

"Ryder?" Ava called out from up behind us. When we both turned to see her sliding down the stairs on her ass.

"What in the hell are you doing?" Nate asked with a snicker.

I jumped up and ran over to her, taking the sketchbooks from her hands and handing them to Nate. "Why didn't you tell me you were ready to come down?"

With the sweetest smile ever, she scrunched up her nose and said, "Well, you were talking to Nate and I didn't want to interrupt."

Once I got her standing, she looked to Nate as he smiled and asked, "So? Are we headed to Helena?"

I could tell my brother was enjoying this little adventure probably as much as Ava, even though he would never admit it. That, or he knew a girl in the city and was planning on hooking up with her tonight since we would be staying overnight.

"Yes! I'm so ready, but first I have to show you both something your sister was working on." She took one of the sketchbooks and put it on the table, opening it to the last drawing.

"She seemed to have a thing for gowns and wedding dresses. This dress, though ... I can't even form the words in my head. I have to show you for you to understand. Nate, will you hand me that pad over there?"

Nate spun around and walked over to the desk and picked up the color pencils I had on the sketchpad. When he looked at the wedding dress, he lifted his eyebrows. "Wow ... Ava, is this your design?"

Her cheeks turned red as she took the pad. "It's mine, yes. Ever since I got to the house, I've never felt so creative and I couldn't wait to start on my own designs after I finished up what Maurice had sent me. I truly felt like I could really step outside my normal thing, and by normal I mean the limits to which Maurice lets me step. But after a few days in the house, I started to picture this dress in my mind. I started it a week ago in my spare time. When I saw what Kate had been working on ... well ... needless to say I was stunned by the similarities to which her and I design."

Placing her drawing down next to Kate's, I could believe my eyes. "Here, y'all take a look for yourselves."

"Wow," I whispered as I took both gowns in. Clearly Kate hadn't finished hers, and Ava was almost done with her design.

Nate leaned in closer. "If I didn't know any better I'd ... I'd say ..."

"They're the same design?" Ava asked.

Nate's eyes caught mine before he looked at Ava. "Or they were designed by the same designer."

Ava smiled. "I know. I won't deny that it feels like I feel her presence. At first I thought it was silly and I was only feeling that way because she died in the house, but now after seeing this. I'm not really sure what to say anymore."

I cleared my throat and shook my head. "Wait. I mean I think this is all easily explained. Ava, you said yourself you needed some time to just design with no restrictions and pressures from the outside world. Don't you think maybe your designing is just a reflection of that and merely a coincidence and that's all?"

Her eyes looked sad, and I wasn't sure if it was because I doubted her or if she honestly believed me. "Probably. But I still find it all very crazy weird that it's so similar."

"I agree with Ava. Kate's dress looks almost identical to Ava's."

Pushing my hand through my hair, I looked around the house. "Maybe you picked up a magazine or a book that Kate looked at as well and saw the same dress."

She pinched her eyebrows together and shot me a dirty look. "I think I know my job well enough to know I don't unintentionally put someone else's work into my own."

I held up my hands in defense. I could see that pushed Ava to the edge. "I'm sorry ... I guess it is a little strange how similar they both are."

When I reached over, I began thumbing through some of Ava's designs and my heart dropped. The last time I had sat in this very room with Kate, she had shown me some dresses she had designed. She said she was going to bring back the style our great-great-grandmother Lizzy wore. Ava's sketches were eerily similar to those drawings as well. "Are you going for an older look with these?" I asked as I turned the pages back about four. The gowns almost seemed like they were from the early nineteen hundreds.

With a weak grin, she tilted her head and said, "I'm not sure. It was something I was feeling at the time, so I was mostly playing around." With a deep breath in, she grinned bigger and said, "Maybe we should get a move on if we're heading to Helena."

My heart felt heavy as I watched Ava glance at the designs and then shut the books. I'd seen my sister Kate get lost in the world of her own, the last thing I wanted to see was Ava do the same. I'd help her with this little adventure, but as soon as we got back, I was going to suggest moving into the main house and out of the stone house.

I wasn't sure how much longer Ava would be staying here in Montana, and as greedy as it sounded, I didn't want to share her with some romance story of Robert and Lizzy. I wanted her to myself, but at what cost would that come?

Twenty

Ava

The forty-minute drive into Helena wasn't nearly as bad as I thought with Ryder's truck being plenty big for my stupid broken leg.

"This is it," Ryder said with a huge smile as he pulled into the driveway of a beautiful Queen Ann Victorian house.

My heart was racing. I hadn't had any time to read more of Kate's journal because I was consumed with her drawings, so I wasn't really even sure what I was looking for. Kate's secret might not have had anything to do with Robert and Lizzy. But now that we were here, I couldn't wait to see the inside of the house.

"Oh. My. Word," I gasped. "This house is amazing!"

"Wait until you see the inside," Ryder said as he parked and took my hand. Turning to him, I shook my head in wonder.

"Why is no one living in this house?"

With a shrug, he said, "Don't know."

Nate pulled up behind us and quickly jumped out to try and beat Ryder to opening the truck door and helping me out. I couldn't believe it when they got into a pushing match right there in the driveway.

"Seriously? Are the two of you twelve?"

Ryder acted as if he was going to leave it be, but turned suddenly and tackled Nate to the ground. As they rolled around in the snow in the middle of probably one of the most prestigious neighborhoods in Helena, I managed to get out of the truck and get my own crutches. I wasn't about to try to walk as I wasn't sure if there was ice on the sidewalk.

"Stop putting snow down my pants, you asshole!" Nate yelled out as I waited for the two of them to grow up.

"I see some things never change."

Turning to my right, I saw a woman my age walking up. She had blonde hair that was pulled up into a French twist. Even though it was freezing outside, she was without a coat. Her pencil skirt and tight blue blouse showed off her curvy body as she stood in I swear ten-inch heels. With a smile on her face, she reached out her hand to me. "Vanessa Emerson. I live next door."

What? How in the hell does someone my age afford to live in this neighborhood? "You own the house next door?" I blurted out.

She must have caught my stunned expression because she chuckled and said, "Let me rephrase that. I live with my parents ... next door."

"Ava Moore, and I'm sorry for the stunned expression, it was rude."

With a bigger smile, she simply said, "No worries."

Vanessa glanced over to Ryder and Nate and shook her head. "You'd think they would be too old to do this."

Putting her fingers up to her mouth, she whistled so loud I was sure I would hear ringing in my ears for the next two weeks.

"Holy shit balls!" I said.

Ryder and Nate immediately stopped and turned to see who whistled. When they both saw Vanessa they began pushing each other to stand up first.

Once they stood up, they both shouted, "Vanessa!"

"I see the two of you haven't changed much."

I'd never seen Nate move as fast as he did. "Hey how have you been?" he asked, engulfing Vanessa in a hug.

When Ryder followed suit, I wasn't sure how to take the way it made me feel. I'd never been a jealous type of person, but for some reason I didn't like something about this whole Vanessa thing.

"Vanessa, you look amazing! Are you still working for Judge Walter?" Nate asked.

"Yes I am and loving every minute of it. How long are you boys in town for? I'm sure my mom and dad would love to have you over for dinner."

Nate spoke up first. "Just tonight."

"Well then how about I see if they are free."

Ryder shook his head, "Oh no, Vanessa don't do that. No need to bother your parents."

I stood there like an idiot ... not to mention I was freezing my ass off.

"Sorry to break up your little reunion here ... but this Texas girl is cold."

All three of them looked my way. It only took Ryder a second to realize I had been standing there waiting before he quickly rushed over to help me navigate up to the house."

"Shit! Ava, I'm so sorry, sweetheart."

"Sweetheart?" Vanessa asked as I stole a peek.

"Sorry, Vanessa. Ava, this is Vanessa, an old friend of the family. Vanessa, this is Ava Moore."

I wasn't sure why it hurt that he hadn't elaborated on me being his girlfriend since he felt the need to say Vanessa was an old friend.

"I've got it, Ryder," I snapped when I made it up to the front door.

His expression was one of confusion, but I didn't care.

"Um ... let me get the door unlocked. Nate had the caretaker come over and turn everything on so the house will be warm."

It was childish for me to be having an attitude, but right now I didn't care.

The door opened and my eyes widened in surprise. The sight before me had my skin tingling with just the idea of staying in this house.

"Oh wow."

"It's beautiful, isn't it?" Vanessa said walking into the foyer and making herself right at home. "Mr. and Mrs. Montgomery had it fully restored to how it would have been when it was first built. Right down to the original colors and wallpaper. The furniture is all original to the house as well."

What in the hell? Did I ask for a guided tour?

Vanessa made her way into the living room and spun around. "Isn't it amazing? I'd do anything to live in this house."

"I bet," I mumbled under my breath.

Vanessa tilted her head and looked at me as Ryder asked, "What was that, Ava?"

"Nothing. Nothing at all. I'm enjoying our little guided tour."

My eyes wandered the room in delight. The wainscot on the living room walls was beautiful and continued up the elegant wood stairs. At the first landing was an amazing stain glass window that I was dying to know if it was original, but I'd rather gash my eyes out than ask Vanessa.

"If we make our way into the dining room, you'll really see some beautiful architecture."

Nate followed Vanessa like he was a lost puppy and she was the key to finding his way home. Ryder went to follow but remembered me and stopped to help me. When he put his arm out I snapped at him. "I'm fine. Go one with them ... it's clear I'm holding you back."

Ryder pulled his head back in surprise and was about to say something when the tour guide called out for him. "Ryder! Come on, and bring Ava with you."

Thank goodness the house wasn't full of furniture so I was able to make my way around fine.

"I love the coffered ceilings in here," Vanessa gushed as Ryder and Nate both looked up like they had never seen them before.

Ugh.

"Over here is the sitting room. Parker got the fire going for you in this room only."

"Parker?" I asked.

"Caretaker," Ryder said with a slight smile.

I couldn't help but notice how Vanessa was looking at Ryder as Nate did everything in his power to get her attention.

"Let's head into the kitchen, shall we?" Vanessa said as both men followed after her.

"I'm sorry ... whose house is this?" I asked as all three of them stopped and looked at me. Vanessa's smile faded as Nate let out a chuckle and Ryder cleared his throat.

Vanessa stood a bit taller as she said, "Excuse me, I'm so sorry. That was so rude of me to barge in like that and take over. I volunteer doing historical home tours and when I saw how excited you were seeing the house,

I figured I'd give a better tour than the boys, but forgive me." She slightly shook her head as she looked at me.

"I'm sorry ... how exactly do you know Ryder and Nate?"

Oh, you bitch. The gloves just came off.

Ryder stepped up next to me. It was in that moment he realized he had never said who I was, but only gave my name. "Oh sorry, Vanessa, Ava is my girlfriend."

"For now," I mumbled as I made my way past all three of them and stepped into one of the most amazing kitchens I'd ever seen.

The cabinets were the same color as the rest of the wood in the house. The light-colored granite offset the darker cabinets perfectly.

"Beautiful," I whispered as Ryder walked up next to me.

"Ava, is something wrong? Why are you mad at me?"

Looking into his eyes, I could see he was confused, but if he didn't realize how he had acted when Ms. Fancy Pants showed up, then that was his fault.

Vanessa walked in and sighed. "Couldn't you see yourself baking in this kitchen, Ava?"

With a fake smile, I turned her way. "Yep."

"Now upstairs are six bedrooms and two bathrooms. Every light fixture in the house is turn-of-the-century original to the house."

Nate walked up next to me and leaned in close as he asked, "Would you like me to shut her off now?"

"Please," I whispered.

Nate clapped his hands together, getting Vanessa's attention. "So, Vanessa, I'm sure Ava is pretty exhausted from the trip here and is probably ready to rest."

Pulling her head back and wearing the fakest concerned look I'd ever seen, she asked, "The forty-minute drive got you tired? Well ... country life must not agree with you."

I opened my mouth to say something when Ryder seemed to finally snap out of his Vanessa-daze.

"Um ... Vanessa, it was really great seeing you, but if you don't mind we'd probably like to get settled in. We have a lot of things to take care of."

She looked hurt as her eyes bounced from me to Ryder. "Right, of course. Dinner tonight?"

"Not for me," I quickly said. Looking over to Ryder, I flashed him a smirk. "But please, don't let me keep you from catching up with an old friend."

I could see Ryder was not pleased with me and I could have cared less.

Vanessa jumped just enough to make her breasts bounce as I turned away and rolled my eyes. "Oh good! Can I count on you boys for dinner?"

"As much fun as that would be, I'm going to have to pass as well. This trip was for Ava."

Disappointment was laced in Vanessa's voice as she said, "I see. Well, it was great seeing you again and I hope to see you before you leave." Turning to me, she held her hand out. "Ava, it was nice meeting you."

With a forced smile, I nodded my head. "It was a pleasure meeting you."

"I'll walk you out, Vanessa," Nate said as he motioned for her to head out of the kitchen first. She turned to kiss Ryder on the cheek, but he was smart enough to avoid it.

With a deep breath in and out, Vanessa nodded. "Good seeing you."

Ryder turned and stared at me intently. "I'm sorry if you got the impression that I—"

Leaning over on my crutches, I held up my hand. "Please don't. I acted like a child and let jealousy take over. I think I'm tired."

Ryder's crooked smile had my stomach dropping as he walked up and placed his hand on the side of my face. "I swear there is nothing there."

My eyes threatened to build with tears for some unknown reason. "I'm tired. Can you please help me upstairs to a bedroom?"

Pulling his head back, Ryder asked, "You don't want to explore the house?"

"Not right now."

"O-okay. Let me help you up the steps and we'll stay in the room I always stay in. There's a queen-size bed in there."

"Sounds good."

We didn't utter a single word as I slowly made my way up the stairs.

Twenty-One

Ryder

"**Y**ou look like you just lost your dog, dude."

With a frustrated sigh, I dropped onto the sofa and glared at Nate.

"Ava's pissed at me."

With a gruff laugh, Nate replied, "I don't blame her. Dude, you introduced her like she was an acquaintance and not your girlfriend. Then you let Vanessa take over and give us a damn tour of our own house."

"Fuck you, Nate. You didn't stop her either."

Nate shrugged. "I was looking at her ass ... you on the other hand were not paying any attention to your crippled girlfriend."

Scrubbing my hands down my face, I let out a moan. "Fucking hell. I was just surprised to see Vanessa. I have no feelings for her what so ever."

"You used to. Matter of fact, didn't the two of you have sex in your —"

Reaching for a pillow, I threw it and hit Nate on the side of the head. "Shut the fuck up, you asshole!"

Nate shot the pillow back at me. "Hey, it's not my fault you ignored Ava."

"I didn't ignore her!"

Nate raised his eyebrows and gave me a stern look. "Really? I'm pretty sure you did. I was the one who had to turn Vanessa off and get her on her way. Not you."

I dropped back against the back of the sofa and sighed. "Why am I such a fuck up? I'd do anything for Ava and I let one stupid moment mess it up."

"You're not smooth with the ladies, bro."

Lifting my head, I glared at my brother. "And you are?"

Nate flashed me a smile and said, "Of course I am. See, if that had been me I'd have played it much cooler. Now we both know you were probably slightly freaked out because two women that you've had sex with were both standing next to each other. One clearly wants back in your pants, and to her that is the ticket to this beautiful home she desperately loves."

Rolling my eyes, I moaned again and dropped my head back.

"The other clearly loves you and doesn't give a rat's ass how much money you have and is perfectly content living in a cramped-up, old, damp stone house. When faced with the challenge of which one do you give your utmost attention too … you chose poorly."

"I didn't give Vanessa all of my attention. Was I expecting to see her … no, I wasn't. It was a shock I'll admit it, and I obviously handled it all wrong because now Ava is upstairs and not the least bit interested in why we came here."

Nate pushed out a breath and stood. "Sorry, dude. That really sucks for you. I hope you've got some kind of plan on making this up to her."

"Plan?"

Narrowing his eyes, Nate tsked. "Yeah, Ryder. A plan to *swoon* her as Jennifer would say. You've got some serious ass kissing to do my friend."

Burying my face in my hands, I mumbled, "I'm such an idiot."

"And with that I bid you adieu."

My hands dropped as I watched my brother head to the front door. "Where are you going?"

He looked over his shoulder and smirked, "To live the single life."

After he left, I pulled my phone out and texted Jennifer.

Me: I messed up and need to swoon Ava

Jennifer: What did you do? Something bad?

Me: I don't think so. Apparently she thinks I gave Vanessa Emerson the wrong kind of attention.

Jennifer: Huh. Did you?

Oh for Christ's sake. Is she going to start on me as well?

Me: I was shocked to see her and yes, I might have been stumbling on what I was doing.

Jennifer: Do you have feelings for Vanessa still?

"It was a one-night stand!"

Hitting Jennifer's number, I walked into the kitchen.

"That's not a good sign you called me when I asked that."

"No I don't, Jennifer. I love Ava."

There was silence for a few moments before she asked, "Do you see your future with Ava?"

"Of course I do. I couldn't imagine my life without her in it."

"Perfect answer! Where is she?"

Closing my eyes, I shook my head. "Upstairs lying down."

"Oh … she must be upset with you. I know how much she was look-ing forward to going to the house."

"You're not making me feel any better, Jennifer."

With a giggle, she said, "Make her a fabulous lunch. Take it up to her on one of the serving trays. Go to the greenhouse too; I know they keep fresh flowers in there. Pick a few and put them in a small vase."

"Where are the vases?" I asked as I looked in the refrigerator.

No food. Great.

"In the butler's pantry on the lower left side."

"There's no food, Jennifer."

"Shit! I didn't think about that. Let me go over this in my head for a moment."

My sister Jennifer lived in Helena and worked for a law firm down-town.

"I've got it. I'll order it from one of my favorite places to eat. All you have to do is take it out of the boxes and put it on the plates. Can you do that without messing up or will we need to worry about Vanessa wanting to help?"

"What?

"Ava just sent me a text … asking about Vanessa."

My heart stopped. "W-what did she ask?

"She asked if Vanessa is always so willing to help you with things. She said Vanessa gave y'all a tour? Holy hell, Ryder! It's your house; why would you let Vanessa come in and take over?"

"I know the error of my ways, Jennifer. Just tell her Vanessa is of no concern and for her not to worry."

"Oh I already did … I told her Vanessa is a little tramp who would do anything to get into your pants or Nate's because she is a money-hungry whore."

My mouth fell to the ground as I stopped dead in my tracks on my way out to the greenhouse.

"Wow … I don't think I've ever heard you talk like that."

"Hold on!" Jennifer said as she began ordering food on another line.

Opening the door to the greenhouse, I smiled as I looked at all the flowers. Reaching for some flower clippers, I cut three purple flowers that I had no clue of what they were. All I knew was they reminded me of Ava.

I set the clippers back down and made my way back to the house, securing the greenhouse door behind me.

"Okay, your food will be there in thirty minutes."

With a grin on my face, I began my search for a vase. "I owe you, Jennifer."

"Yes. Yes you do. And Ryder?"

The whole bottom left cabinet was filled with all different sized vases. Reaching in, I grabbed a smaller one and placed the flowers inside of it.

"Yeah?"

"I really like Ava. Please don't do anything to hurt her."

My entire world felt as if it had stopped. "Do you really think she was hurt by that? I mean, I didn't say or do anything. I honestly didn't think it was a big deal for Vanessa to be in the house."

"Let's put it this way. If you showed up at Ava's place and a guy she grew up with showed up and Ava gushed all over him and then allowed that guy to go into Ava's apartment and show you all around … how would that make you feel?"

I closed my eyes and shook my head. "I don't understand women."

"Ryder! Be honest. Would you like it?"

Filling the vase up with water, I thought about it. "No, I don't guess I would like it."

"Okay. There ya go. That's how Ava felt because I know men and I'm sure both you and Nate gave Vanessa that googly eye thing guys do when a pretty girl shows up."

"Googly eye thing?" I asked.

"Yes. Flirting."

"I didn't flirt with her!"

With a frustrated sigh, Jennifer whispered, "Just make it up to her with this lunch. I've got to go! Love you."

The line went dead as I pulled my cell out to look at it. "I wasn't flirting!"

Sinking down onto the island stool, I blew out a frustrated breath. "Lord, help me to better understand women. Please!"

I walked around the house while I waited for the food. Stepping into the sitting room, I walked over to the small library in the corner. New and old books were mixed together in no real layout. I wasn't sure what I was searching for. Maybe a tell-all book on how not to fuck up with the woman you loved.

The old desk in the corner was original to the house. I sat down and pulled out a drawer. The only thing in the drawer was a box. Pulling it out, I slowly took the rubber band off and opened the note attached to it.

> Mrs. Montgomery,
> I stumbled upon this box
> while in the attic. It appears
> to be letters between
> Robert Montgomery and
> Lizzy Baker Montgomery.
> G

Frowning, I looked at the signature and wondered who G was.

When I opened the box, it was filled with letters. Surely my mother had seen these already.

I opened one letter and began reading it.

My Dearest Lizzy,

Will you ever forgive me? I didn't want to dance with her, I promise you that. Mother was insistent and my hands were tied. You know I only have eyes for you. Please do not ignore me. The pain of knowing you're upset with me is too great to bear.

Yours truly,

Robert

I folded up the letter and put it in the box. "I feel ya, dude. Nice to see women haven't changed in over a hundred years."

The doorbell rang and I jumped up, setting the box on the desk as I made my way to the front door.

When I opened it, I was stunned to see two women standing before me with brown bags in each of their arms.

"We're here with your delivery from Fusion Grill."

Opening the door to let them in, I smiled and said, "Awesome! Follow me to the kitchen."

Each one of them put a bag on the counter and began unpacking it.

"We have two BLTA's with french fries and two bowls of tortilla soup."

My stomach picked that moment to growl. "Sounds good. What do I owe you?"

"It's already been paid for, sir."

Reaching for my wallet, I took out a two twenty's and handed each girl one.

"Thank you so very much, sir."

"No problem. Thank you, ladies. Let me show you out."

By the time I got the plates made up, I was sure Ava had to have cooled down.

At least I prayed with every stair I took that was the case.

Twenty-Two

Ava

After Ryder had helped me up the stairs and into the most beautiful room I'd ever seen, I settled in and listened to the crackling of the fire he had made. I was so mad at myself for acting like a child. I had no reason to be jealous and really Ryder didn't do anything wrong but be shocked by an old friend. Regardless of if something had happened between them or not, it was the past and I needed to leave it there.

Kate's journal sat on my lap as I opened it up and read the next entry.

June 2

Jackson stopped by today and we went for a long walk. It was nice to spend time with him alone. When we're in school each of us is pulled in so many different directions.

I don't think Ryder likes Jackson all that much. Or he's just playing the big brother role. At any rate, if he knew what was going on, he would really not like Jackson.

He took the news of me being pregnant pretty well. We're both scared and not sure how to tell our parents. I'm only six weeks along from what the doctor said. I still have time to figure things out. At least I know Jackson is right there with me. He told me he loved me more than I could ever imagine.

I love him too. And I'll love our baby.

I dropped my hands to my lap and stared straight ahead.

"Oh, holy shit. The secret had nothing to do with Lizzy and everything to do with Kate."

The knock on the door caused me to jump as I quickly shut the journal and slid it under the pillow.

"Hey," Ryder said softly as he walked in carrying a tray full of food. I'd never seen anyone walk so slow and with so much concentration.

"Hey, did you make that?" I asked as I licked my lips.

Ryder didn't utter a word until he set it down on the table at the end of the bed. With a sigh of relief, he glanced up at me and grinned from ear to ear. "It's probably cold because it took me so long to climb the stairs. And hell no, I didn't make it. Jennifer ordered it when I called her for help in figuring out what to do to make up for being such an asshole earlier."

I couldn't help but laugh. "You were moving pretty slow, I don't care if it's cold, and you weren't the one being an asshole. I was too and I'm sorry."

"Let's just say we both played a small role and move on?"

With a nod of my head, I said, "Sounds good to me. I'm starving! What did she send us?"

Ryder took his food off and placed it on the table then carefully picked up the tray and brought it over to me. "I'll eat mine over here."

"Yummy. This looks so good. I hadn't realized how hungry I was until I saw it."

Ryder chuckled. "Same here."

Picking up the sandwich, I took a bite and moaned in sweet relief. "I never thought a BLT would taste so good."

With a head bob, Ryder agreed.

My mind was racing as I tried to process what I had just read in Kate's journal. Clearly Ryder had no idea about the pregnancy with how he reacted to her saying she had sex with Jackson.

"So, Dani's baby will be the first baby, huh?"

His eyes lifted as he looked at me. "First baby?"

"Yeah, you know … first grandbaby for your mom and dad."

He narrowed his eyes and thought for a moment. "Unless Nate's fathered a few kids we don't know about."

Letting out a chuckle, I shook my head and ate some soup. "That's mean, Ryder."

"The scary part is I'm not kidding."

With a roll of my eyes, I kept eating.

"What about Jennifer? No desire to have kids?"

His eyes lifted to mine again. "Not that I'm aware of, but I doubt she would talk to me about that. Ava, you're kind of freaking me out with this baby talk. Is there something I should know?"

"No! God no. I'm curious that's all. I'm sure your mom and dad are excited, and I was just … curious."

"Well, as far as I'm aware, Dani's is indeed the first grandbaby on the way."

I smiled and took another bite of the BLT.

"This room is beautiful."

Ryder looked around as he took another bite and nodded. When he was finished chewing, he turned back to me. "This house is actually going to one of the kids when they get married."

That peeked my interest. "Really? Who?"

"Well, it was Dani's first pick, but she had no desire for it. Jennifer's already said she doesn't want it, so it comes down to me or Nate."

Everything made such sense. Vanessa is after the house and the only way to get the house is … marry Nate or Ryder.

"How will it be decided?" I asked.

"Whoever gets married first."

I swallowed hard. "Married first?"

Ryder smiled bigger and winked. "It's pretty safe to say I've got this one in the bag."

My stomach felt like I was on a roller coaster. "In the bag?" I croaked out.

"Yep. Hell will freeze over before Nate Montgomery ever marries a woman and settles down. I'm sure to beat him to the altar."

Disappointment swept through my body like lightning as I quickly looked down at my soup. How silly of me to even get my hopes up like that. Ryder and I barely just started dating.

I forced a chuckle out. "Probably."

We finished eating the rest of lunch in silence. I couldn't stop thinking about Kate being pregnant. Of course the idea of Ryder marrying anyone but me about had me feeling sick and I had to force myself to eat.

"Ava? Are you even listening to me?"

My head snapped up as I looked into Ryder's beautiful hazel eyes. "I'm sorry … what were you saying?"

"So what do you think?"

"About?"

"The house, silly. Do you like it?"

Trying to clear the lump from my throat, I swung my legs around the edge of the bed as Ryder helped me to stand up.

"Yes. It's beautiful and I can't wait to see more."

I'd never seen Ryder's eyes twinkle like they were. It was almost as if someone was shining a light on them.

"Could you ever see yourself living here?"

Without even thinking, I blurted out my answer. "Yes!"

His hands cupped my face as he brushed his lips across mine. "Good, because you're the only woman I could see living in this house."

He pulled me closer as he deepened the kiss. My arms wrapped around his neck as I let the moment take control.

When he pulled back slightly he rested his head against mine as I spoke the only word I could manage. "Ryder."

"That was my very poor attempt at asking you to marry me, Ava."

My head pulled back as my eyes widened in shock.

Holy shit balls.

"I wouldn't say that was a poor attempt. It was the most romantic thing ever," I said in a breathy voice.

He softly chuckled as he kissed the tip of my nose. "So?"

"So?" I asked.

"How long are you going to make me wait for your answer?"

I was positive I hadn't smiled this much in weeks as I got lost in his eyes.

"Yes. Nothing would make me happier than marrying you."

"Even if that meant staying here in Montana?"

I chewed on my lip for a few quick seconds as I let it all soak in. "I can design from anywhere."

Ryder grinned wide as I felt my eyes begin to water up. Wrapping his arms around me, he lifted me as he pressed his lips to mine.

He broke the kiss just enough to softly say, "I love you, Ava Moore. I love you so much."

I'd never felt like this before. My heart felt as if it was going to explode in my chest.

"I love you too, Ryder. More than you'll ever know."

Another quick engagement.

My father is going to kill me ... but once my mother finds out I'm going to be living in Montana ... she might kill me first.

Twenty-Three

Ryder

December

"**R**yder, you look like you lost a puppy or something."

Glancing up, I smiled at my mother. "Missing Ava."

She grinned as she put some cookies into the oven. "Have you talked to her today?"

"Yeah, first thing this morning. She was going to tell her folks today about the engagement."

My mother stopped what she was doing and smiled. "I still can't believe you're getting married."

Nate walked in and threw his gym bag on the floor while reaching into the refrigerator for a water. "It's one and done from here out. Poor bastard."

With her hands on her hips, our mother shot daggers at Nate. "Nate Montgomery, do not talk like that in my house. You were not raised in a barn so why do you think you can drop your stuff right here in the middle of the floor? And don't be jealous of your brother."

With his mouth dropped open, Nate stared at her before throwing his head back and laughing. "Jealous? Oh please, Mom. The last thing I am of

Ryder is jealous."

"Really?" she asked lifting her eyebrow. "Seems to me you've been in a funk since the engagement."

Taking a long drink of his water, he shrugged. "It's only because now I won't get the house in Helena and I was really hoping to sell that bitch off."

My mother's eyes widened in horror. "Nate, you would never do such a thing."

He winked and kissed her on the cheek. "Well, I guess we'll never know since Ryder beat me to the altar."

"I'm not there yet," I said.

He looked up and thought for a moment. "That's true. Maybe if we invite Vanessa to hang out, I might have another shot at the house."

"Shut the fuck up, you asshole."

"Ryder!" my mother shouted. "Do not use that language in my house!"

"He started it by bringing up Vanessa." Pointing to Nate, he smirked as he crossed his arms over his chest. "You know not to bring her up."

"Why? I thought there was nothing there."

"There isn't!"

"Ryder. Why are you getting so upset?" my mother asked.

Nate chuckled and responded in a jacked up version of a lovey-dovey voice, "I know why. His love bug left him all alone and he's sad."

Walking up to Nate, my mother smacked him across the back of the head. "Knock it off. Christmas is in a few days and I'd really like it if we had no bickering."

"Like that's ever going to happen," my father mumbled. Tossing his keys onto the table, he kissed my mother softly on the lips. "Hello, sweetheart. How was your day?"

"It's been good. Even better now that you're here."

"Oh, for the love of Christ. That's disgusting!"

My father turned to look at Nate. "It's always good having you home, Nate. Always good."

Laughing, I stood and followed my father to his office.

"So, how did the meeting go?"

Sitting in his chair, he sighed and shook his head. "Not as well as I wanted. Seems Chuck thinks he can sell for higher than his place his worth."

"He's determined not to keep it?"

He shook his head. "He won't even give his daughter a chance to learn the ropes and try to run it."

With a halfhearted laugh, I pushed my hand through my hair. "Well, I honestly find it hard to believe Destiny truly wants to run that ranch, Dad. I think what she wanted was to marry a rancher who would run it for her and allow her to keep her beloved acres. Do I think she could run it? Yes, if she put her mind to it."

"Most likely. When I first got there and she asked how everyone was, I told her you were engaged to be married. I thought she was going to fall apart before my eyes and her father didn't act much better."

"So, he would rather sell it off to someone else than let us buy it?"

With a quick nod, he replied, "Pretty much."

An idea hit me as I smiled. "What if we put an offer in on it, but he didn't know it was us. Go in under another name."

Trying to hide his smile, he answered, "That's deceitful."

"How? He's being a dick about it when he knows damn well that ranch would thrive under our control. We could even work it into the deal that they would retain a certain amount of land, for Destiny. Word it differently though."

Leaning back in his chair, he rested his chin on his index fingers. "It could work."

"Then I say we give it a try, but only if he doesn't come around."

With a firm nod of his head, he dropped his hands. "All right. Let's give him some time to come to his senses, then we take this approach."

My cell rang in my back pocket with Ava's ring tone. With a smile, I reached for it and excused myself as I walked out of my father's office.

"Hello?"

"Ugh."

"I'm glad to know my voice turns you on so much."

"I told them. It didn't go very well."

Swallowing hard, I felt my stomach drop. "How bad?"

"Well, considering I tried to kind of throw it into the conversation at dinner, it could have gone worse. My father is currently debating if he wants to fly up there and kick your ass."

"What?"

With a chuckle, she sighed. "Oh man … not really. But they both think we're rushing."

"Do you? Do you think we're moving too fast?"

The silence scared me until she blew out a deep breath. "I called my manager at the boutique and told her I wouldn't be coming back. It's kind of a good thing you asked me to marry you, because she really loves my replacement."

With a chuckle, I breathed a sigh of relief. "Tomorrow I'm going to see if Liza will take me in to Austin. I'll need to pack up my apartment and all of that."

My cheeks were beginning to ache from the huge smile I had on my face. "I still have to go back and take care of my place. We can do it together."

"I like the sound of that. I don't think it will be too hard to sublease my apartment. I have the ideal location for downtown Austin."

"What about Maurice?" I asked while my mother motioned for me to help her with getting the dishes on the table.

"That's not a problem. I can work anywhere for him."

The sound of her voice stirred the craziest emotions in me. I longed to see her and this feeling of missing someone was totally new.

"I can't wait to see you, Ava."

"You have no idea how much I want to cut my visit short and come back to you." She paused for a few moments and said, "Um … Ryder this is something I've been meaning to talk to you about."

My heart stopped while I held my breath. "Oh?"

"Nothing bad! It's about Kate though."

My shoulders dropped. Ava had decided to merge the wedding dress she was designing with the one Kate was since they were so similar. She had spoken to my mother and father about it and they gave her their blessings for Ava to do what she wanted with Kate's designs. They did ask that if she was to do anything such as sell them, to give credit to Kate as well which Ava totally agreed should be done. Yet, at the same time, it felt as if she was getting lost in my sister as well as with Robert and Lizzy's story. She had read over half of the letters in the shoebox we found at the house in Helena.

"Okay. But Ava, maybe you should take a step back from this whole Kate and Lizzy thing."

"Kate and Lizzy thing? What's that supposed to mean?"

Taking in a deep breath, I slowly blew it out. "Maybe you're bored in the stone house. We could move into the main house if you want. Get you away from these crazy ideas you have about feeling a connection with Kate and that you feel a presence in the house. I'm sure Mom could find something for you to do with volunteer work or even learning about the cattle ranch."

When she didn't respond, I knew I had fucked up.

"Volunteer work?"

"Well, maybe that wasn't the word I was looking for."

"Oh, I'd certainly love to know what word you were looking for. 'Cause from the sounds of it, I heard I'm a bored, lonely, crazy person with nothing to do so I might as well put on the pants of a bored house wife who has nothing to do with her day other than go sit around and gossip with a bunch of women who are also bored and lonely crazy women. I have a job, asshole, that I do a good portion of the day. I'm not sure if you've been aware of it or not, but Maurice has been sending me ideas and asking me for more designs. He's loving what I've been sending him."

Shit.

"Ava, wait that's not what I meant."

I heard a door slam. "Maybe what you're looking for Ryder is someone like your old buddy, Vanessa. She fits the part of dutiful wife to the tee. By the way, dickhead, I happened to have been raised on a cattle farm and know a thing or two. I could probably repair a fence faster than you ... you ... you jerk."

"That's not what I meant and ..."

"You know what? I've decided to stay a few extra days here in Texas. Maybe I'll stay a week longer, possibly two."

Before I had a chance to say anything, the line went dead. I pulled it away from my ear and stared at it.

"What in the fuck just happened?"

Nate walked by and let out a snicker. "You were bound to fuck it up sooner or later. Hate to say it, bro."

Turning to look at him, I took my cell phone and threw it at him. Too bad I missed and it smashed against the wall and broke into pieces.

Twenty-Four

Ava

"Want to talk about it?"

I tried to plaster on a smile, but failed. "It's nothing."

"I know that look," Liza said with a warmness in her eyes. "That is a classic *I lost my shit on him* expression."

Giggling, I shook my head. "I don't know what's wrong with me Liza. At the same time I feel like he deserved it. I hung up on him though."

She shrugged. "So. I've hung up on Walker plenty of times when I've gotten mad."

With a glance out the window, I sighed. "Yeah well, ever since then when I call him it goes straight to voicemail. Like he's turned off his phone or worse yet … has me blocked."

"Nah, I don't see Ryder acting childish like that."

I huffed. "You didn't see him and his brother rolling around trying to shove handfuls of snow into each other's pants."

She chuckled. "Boys will be boys."

With a frustrated sigh, I dropped my head back against the seat. It was a beautiful day. In fact, we were driving with the windows down enjoying the fresh air. "Maybe he's right. I have been submerging myself into

Kate's journal and Lizzy and Robert's story. It's so beautiful, though. I mean he left everything to be with her. Walked away from a title to be with the woman he loved. Why aren't men like that now?"

"Wow. This from a girl who recently got engaged and is ready to build a new life with the man she loves. Ava … are you sure this is what you want?"

Snapping my head forward, I turned to Liza. "Yes. I've never been so sure of anything in my life. I can totally see myself living in Montana, being a wife to Ryder and helping him run his family's ranch. I want that. But, I also want to stay me. And this little adventure I've stumbled on has changed me … and maybe it's Ryder who's doubting."

Liza reached for my hand. "I seriously doubt it. I'm sure there is a reason why he isn't answering his phone."

She squeezed my hand and I fought like hell to hold my stupid tears back.

"Yeah. Maybe."

"Are you sure about this?"

Pushing the door open to my apartment, I smiled when I looked around. "Totally sure, Mom. I need to see what all I have that I need to pack up and get rid of, and what I'll want to take to Montana."

If I'm still moving to Montana.

It had been almost two days since I'd talked to Ryder. At first I was going out of my mind crazy. What if something had happened to him? I broke down and called Nate last night, asking if Ryder was okay. When he told me all was fine and asked if I wanted to talk to him, I said no and hung up.

It was then I decided to ask my mother to drive me into Austin so I could spend a few days at my apartment. I'd already called Jay, who was over being a new bride and ready for a night out on the town.

"Have you heard from Ryder?"

Oh hell. The last thing I wanted to give my parents was ammunition against my engagement.

"Not today. I think he had some meeting with his father."

"Ava, you know we're going to have to talk about when you'll be moving and all of that."

My heart hurt for lying to her. "I know. I'm probably going back up to get the cast off and coming right back down."

"You could get it off here, ya know."

I dropped my head. She was right. There was no real reason I needed to rush back to Montana. Clearly Ryder wasn't going to beg me to come back. Maybe we did move too fast.

"I'll make an appointment and see if they can get me in this afternoon. Lord knows I'm ready for this bitch to be off."

"Watch your mouth."

Rolling my eyes, I sighed. "Like you have an innocent mouth."

She reached for my hand. "Ava, something is bothering you. Please tell me what it is. You were so ready to leave and now you're coming back to your apartment for a few days."

Forcing a smile, I rested my hand over hers. "Mom, there is nothing wrong. I need to start getting everything in order. I just need some alone time, ya know? Get in some reading and clear my mind."

"You're so much like me, it is unreal."

My heart was full as I looked in her beautiful blue eyes. "That is a compliment I'll take any day."

Jay flopped down in the chair next to me in the orthopedic doctor's office. "You know, you up and leave me. Get engaged to a hot cowboy. Come home and the first thing you do is ask me to take you to the doctor. I should have said no."

With a grin, I looked her in the eyes. "The first thing I asked you was if you wanted to go out tonight, then I asked you to bring me here. Cut me some slack; they had an opening this afternoon."

"Ms. Moore?"

I got up and crossed my fingers. "Wish me luck!"

Jay lifted her hand dismissing me. "Yep. Good luck."

After taking a ton of x-rays, I was led into an examination room. "The doctor up in Montana was able to scan your x-rays over, so we have them for Dr. Russell."

"Oh good!" I said with probably too much excitement in my voice.

"He'll be a few minutes more."

I lifted my hand and gave her a thumbs up. *Jesus. What is wrong with me? Am I twelve?* "Um ... great thank you."

"Sorry about that wait, Ms. Moore."

I was pretty sure my jaw dropped to the ground when the doctor walked in.

"Are you ... um ... you're not the doctor are you?"

With a warm smile, he nodded. "I am."

I could not believe the sight in front of me. The guy couldn't have been older than me and not to mention he was easy on the eyes. Not nearly as good looking as Ryder ... but none the less he was pretty to look at. "Wow."

He stopped and turned to look at me. When he smiled that smile men do when they think you're interested, I quickly snapped out of it. "Wow? Is that wow a good thing or a bad thing."

I smiled politely as I felt my cheeks flush from embarrassment.

Sinking my teeth into my lip, I couldn't help but notice his eyes drop and his smile widened. Shit. No! No! No! Not flirting, Mr. Hot Doctor. Just nervous. "Um ... ahh ... good."

Clearing his throat, he put my x-rays up as I began to swing my legs. My cast felt heavy as hell but I didn't know what to do with my now nervous energy.

"Looks like everything has healed really well. You were scheduled to get your cast off in a few days so if you've got the time, I'd be *more* than happy to remove it for you ... myself."

I swallowed hard. How in the hell did he make that sound naughty?

Shit! I wanted my cast off and I needed to derail him. "Great!" Too excited sounding, Ava. Calm it down. "I mean, I'd love for you to take my cast off." *Dear lord. How did I make that sound naughty? Flippin' shit balls. Where is Jay when I need her?*

His eyes lit up. Derail Ava. Derail. I went to talk, but he cut me off.

"May I ask what brings you to Texas?"

"I live here. I was visiting Montana when I broke my leg and ankle."

"And you stayed up there for … work?"

With a nervous chuckle, I said. "No. I mean, I've been working up there but my fiancé lives in Montana. So, I guess you could say a little work and a little play."

Ugh. Why did I say that?"

"It's always good to play every now and then."

Oh God. He's flirting. What part of fiancé did you not hear?

"Yep. Keeps life exciting."

He seemed to zero in on my lips before he seemed to snap out of it.

"Well, let's get this cast off you."

By the time the good doctor got the cast off, I was ready to run out of the office.

Glancing down at my leg, I gasped. "Gross! That looks like … like … I don't even know what that looks like."

Dr. Russell laughed as did the nurse. "You're probably going to want to see about physical therapy at least for your ankle. You're moving around pretty good on it."

Excitement coursed through my body. Finally, I got that heavy bitch off! I was so happy I wanted to scream. "I am! Just in time for some salsa dancing at Volstead's tonight."

The nurse chuckled. "Well, don't get too crazy."

Not using my brains, I blurted out, "Oh I never get crazy, unless I'm dancing with a hot guy."

Dr. Russell stared at me and I swore his eyes darkened. "It was great meeting you, Ava. Please feel free to come back anytime."

Staring at him with a confused expression, I tried to figure out if he was really flirting or maybe it was just my imagination. After all, I was upset with Ryder and maybe I was reading into it. At any rate, I needed to get out of this office and quickly. "Well, if you'll pardon me being blunt, you're nice and all doc, but I pray I never have to come back and see you or any other doctor for a broken bone again."

"Touché. Let me walk you out, okay."

"Sure. Thank you so much again for working me in like this."

"Not a problem, Ava."

Jay lifted her eyebrow when she saw me walking out with Doctor

Hotty Pants. Standing, she let her eyes roam freely over him. "Well, I see you've been in good hands."

Dr. Russell laughed as he placed his hand on my lower back.

Holy shit balls. We have physical contact! That is not good!

"Well, you ladies enjoy yourself tonight."

With a polite nod, I grinned and said, "We will. Thanks again."

My leg and ankle were for sure sore and I was limping for fear of putting too much weight on it. We hadn't even made it to the elevator when Jay busted out laughing.

"You dirty slut!"

My eyes widen. "What the hell?"

"You were flirting with him … admit it! I could see it all over his face. He probably had to go back to his office and jack off."

"Oh my gosh … your mouth is filthy."

Stepping into the elevator, I pulled out my phone.

Nothing from Ryder.

My heart ached as I pushed the phone back into my purse.

"So, was that your way of paying back the fiancé for ignoring you?"

"Remind me why I tell you anything. And I was not flirting. I may have said something innocently that he took as flirting."

Jay busted out laughing again as we headed to her car. "You still in the mood to shake your ass?"

A feeling of dread washed over me. Was I really going to walk away from something as amazing as Ryder? No, of course I wouldn't. This whole silent treatment thing from him wasn't something he would do either.

With a frustrated sigh, I shrugged. "I don't know. I can't really move around on my ankle. Maybe I should pass."

"Pass? Why can't you sit your ass at the bar while I get my salsa on then? Why must we both be punished because you feel guilty for flirting with the hot doctor?"

"I don't feel guilty, because I was not flirting with him."

Jay shook her head. "Fine. Then I see no problems with going out tonight."

Dropping my head back, I moaned. "Fine. Just drop me off at home so I can stare at my stuff and wonder if I'm moving to Montana or not."

Jay dropped me off and called out, "I'll pick you up at eight!"

Once I got back into my apartment, I dug in my bag and pulled out Kate's journal. I sat on the sofa and quickly got lost in the pages of a young girl lost and confused.

Twenty-Five

Ryder

"You still haven't called her?" Nate asked.

"No. I want to surprise her."

"And you don't think by her calling you and it going to voice mail that she might think you're pissed at her?"

I stopped walking and stared at my brother. "Shit. I hadn't thought about that."

"She called last night."

"What?"

Nate smiled an evil smile. "She called my cell phone and asked if you were okay. I told her you were sitting right next to me."

Anger raced through my veins. "And you didn't think to let me talk to her?"

"Hey, it's not my fault you threw your phone and smashed it into a million pieces or the fact that you didn't want to call Layton or Reed and ask them for her number for fear Reed would think y'all were fighting and use that against you. You could have called Walker."

"I called him and left a message! He never got back with me! And again, why didn't you let me talk to her? Plus if she called you have her number on your phone asshole!"

"Huh. That sucks for you and she didn't want to talk to you. She only wanted to make sure you were okay and her number came up private asshole or I would have given it to you."

"Fucking hell. Why do I keep messing up with Ava?"

Nate walked out and took in a deep breath. "Feel that? That is beautiful Texas seventy-degree weather in December. Hell yes."

"Just get a damn taxi."

Nate chuckled as he held up his hand and a taxi came pulling up. "How do you know she's at her apartment?"

"I know Ava."

"So you think you do. Clearly you don't know how not to keep pissing her off."

"Fuck you, Nate. Let's hurry up so we can stop at the bank and I can get to Ava. The sooner I see her, the better."

When the taxi pulled up to Ava's apartment building, I jumped out. "Shall we wait?"

I glared at Nate. "I hope when you hook up with whoever you're hooking up with tonight, your dick goes limp and stays that way!"

Nate's eyes widened in horror. "Why would you say something so terrible like that?"

Rolling my eyes, I slammed the car door.

"Hey, Harry!" I said as I walked up to the doorman.

He lifted his brow. "Do I know you, sir?"

"I'm Ava Moore's fiancé. Ryder. Ryder Montgomery."

Harry looked me over. "Mr. Montgomery, I do remember you."

Smiling, I asked, "Is Ava home?"

"She is. She returned from her trip and was feeling rather happy with getting her cast off."

"Her cast off? She got her cast off?"

A woman walked up carrying a large amount of bags. "Harry! Please, will you help me with my shopping bags?"

I quickly reached for the door and held it open. Harry was so occupied with helping the woman that he forgot about me. I made my way over to the elevator and headed up to Ava's apartment.

My heart was racing in my chest. I knew Ava was going to be pissed at me and think I had been ignoring her. I only hope what I picked up at Nate's place would show her how sorry I was.

Taking in a deep breath, I reached my hand up and knocked on the door. It took a few seconds before the door opened and I saw her beautiful face.

Her mouth dropped open and her eyes lit up. "Ryder. I thought ... what are you doing here?"

"I missed you."

She shook her head and narrowed her eyes. "But ... you haven't been answering your phone."

Puffing my cheeks, I blew out a breath. "Yeah, about that. I didn't mean all the shit I said, Ava. I was so angry with myself for all of that I threw my phone and it broke into pieces. Then when I realized your number was in my phone and I couldn't remember it, I kind of freaked out."

Her eyebrows rose.

"I didn't want to call your family, then your father would ask why I hadn't taken the time to memorize his little girl's number if I asked her to marry me. He would know we argued and I didn't want that."

Her teeth sunk in her lip. "No, we don't want that."

"Baby, I'm so sorry. I don't care what you do or if you want to live in that little stone house for the rest of your life. All I care about is that you're by my side each night I close my eyes and every morning I wake up. You are my life. All that matters to me."

I dropped onto my knee and that's when I noticed.

"Oh my God," we both said at once.

Glancing up, her hands were covering her mouth. "Your cast is off and your leg ... looks ... so good. When did you get it off?"

She dropped her hands and looked at me. "Really, Ryder? Can that wait?"

"Oh ... shit. Yeah." I reached into my pocket and pulled out the jewelry box.

With a huge smile and my heart pounding in my chest, I opened the box. I knew the moment I bumped into Ava that day on the street that she was going to be my forever. "Ava Grace Moore, will you marry me?"

Tears rolled down her face as she nodded her head. Jumping up, I slipped the round antique diamond onto her finger.

"Ohmygawd," she mumbled while staring at the ring. "It's beautiful. It looks ... so elegant!"

Knowing I was about to make her very happy, I replied. "It's old. It was my great-great-I think one more great grandmother's."

Her head popped up. "Lizzy's?"

"Yep. It's been passed down to each first-born son."

Pinching her eyebrows together, she shook her head. "I thought Nate was older."

"He wanted you to have it and thought it would mean much more for you to wear it. He's had it in a safety deposit box here in Austin, so it was perfect timing."

Wiping her tears away, she stared at the ring. "It's ... I don't know what to say. It's perfect." Lifting her eyes to mine, she whispered, "You're perfect."

"I've missed you, Ava."

She pulled me into her apartment and we quickly got lost in a kiss. "Ryder, please make love to me."

My lips trailed lightly across her neck while she moaned softly. "It would be my pleasure."

Picking her up, I carried her to the bedroom where I gently set her on the floor.

We slowly undressed one another in silence. Nothing needed to be said because our love filled the entire room. My heart had never beat this hard before in my life. The idea of making love to her and knowing she would be mine forever was amazing.

Jumping back, Ava said, "Oh wait!" She reached down and began itching her leg like crazy. "It. Itches. So. Bad!"

I tried like hell not to laugh. There was no way I was going to say anything. She finally had that damn thing off and I was going to baby the hell out of her. "How about a nice hot bath?"

Her eyes lit up. "That sounds wonderful, but I'm supposed to be going Salsa dancing with Jay."

With a chuckle, I kissed the tip of her nose. "You got your cast off and you're ready to go."

"Well, not really. I planned it before I got the bright idea of getting the cast off. I made an appointment and it just so happened they were able to remove it. But, now that you're here, we have time to fool around and then go out."

"With, Jay? Your evil friend who left you drunk and alone? No thanks."

Ava hit my chest. "Stop it. She's my best friend, and I'm not sure when I'll get to go out with her again. Besides, I have a sexy little dress I've been wanting to wear."

She frowned. "That is if I can still fit into it with all the food your mother has been giving me."

Placing my hands on her hips, my chest felt tight. I loved this woman so much. "You look beautiful and I'd love to go dancing with my beautiful fiancée."

Slipping her panties down, she gave me a sexy smile that had my heart stopping. Licking her soft lips, she softly said, "I think we need to get back to the whole fooling around thing."

Twenty-Six

Ava

S tepping out of my bedroom, I waited for Ryder to turn around. The little silver cocktail dress I had bought a few months back fit like a glove. It hugged me in all the right places. The only thing that would make this better is if I had on my expensive-ass Michael Kors heels that I bought as a pick me up when Johnny dumped me. The last thing I wanted to do was break my ankle again.

I cleared my throat and waited for him to see me. When he did, I couldn't hide the smile that spread across my face. Even though we had just made the sweetest love to one another, Ryder was looking at me like he wanted more. Like he *needed* more. His face curved up into a smile that was so breathtaking I wanted to call Jay and tell her I wasn't interested in going out anymore.

"My god, you're the most beautiful woman I've ever seen."

I lifted my foot and wiggled my toes. "I can't wear my sexy heels though. I think I'll have to wear flats which won't really do anything for the dress."

He slowly sauntered my way. "Fuck the shoes. They couldn't do anything more if they tried."

Slipping his hand behind my neck, he pulled me closer. "If I kiss you, I'll smear your lipstick."

"I can always put it back on."

He kissed me ever so softly on the lips, causing my stomach to dance with excitement. Every time he kissed me, I was taken to a place I never wanted to leave. There was something so amazingly different about Ryder. He not only held my heart, he owned my soul.

The knock on the door had him pulling his lips away. I wanted to scream out for him to keep kissing me, but if I knew Jay, she would just walk in.

"That's probably Jay."

"Lucky me," Ryder mumbled before sitting down on the sofa.

I was still limping a bit on my leg. It felt weak, but I wasn't sure if it was in my head and I was just scared or it really was weak.

"Does she know I'm here?"

Pressing my lips together, I glanced over my shoulder. "No," I said scrunching my nose.

Ryder smiled. "This should be fun."

Opening the door, I smiled big. "Hey there!"

She whistled. "Damn girl. Are you hoping to get laid tonight?"

My face dropped. "Jesus, Jay. Really?"

Ryder wrapped his arms around my waist. Jay's expression went from happy to shocked. "She already did, so she's covered."

"Ryder!" I exclaimed as Jay rolled her eyes and acted like she was gagging.

"Please tell me he is *not* coming with us."

I put my hands up and looked between them both. "Now listen here. You both are special to me and I love you, y'all. But I can't have my fiancé and my best friend hating on each other."

Jay gasped and grabbed my hand.

"Holy shit! That diamond is huge." She peeked up at Ryder. "I will say, you know how to say you're sorry."

He smiled, turned, and walked toward the kitchen. "I need a quick beer before we leave for some fun Salsa dancing."

Following him, Jay pulled me to a stop. "Are you sure we can't ditch him on the way to the club?"

"Jay! I love him and if you can't get used to that we're going to have a serious problem on our hands."

She let out a frustrated moan. "Fine! If you *really* love him, I'll behave … kind of."

My face softened. "I really love him."

I knew she didn't want to do it, but she smiled. "I am happy for you and I'd never admit this to Ryder, but I think he's a great guy."

"Who's a great guy?" Ryder asked walking up to us with a beer in his hand. Jay took it from him and gulped it down in one drink. Ryder's eyes opened wide in shock.

"The guy I was trying to set Ava up with, but she insists she loves you so there goes that plan for tonight." She shrugged and handed him the empty beer bottle back.

Rolling my eyes, I reached up and kissed his lips. "Ignore her," I whispered.

Ryder winked and said, "Oh, don't worry. Ignoring Jay won't take too much effort."

Sighing, I turned and said, "I say we get the show on the road. Let me slip on my shoes and we are set."

Jay stared at the black flats I had on. "You're wearing … those?"

"Yes. I have to, Jay. I just got my cast off; I can't walk around in heels. I can barely walk around now in my bare feet."

She snarled her lip. Her eyes dropped back down to the flats. "You can't salsa dance in flats. That's not sexy."

"I think she looks sexy as fuck."

"You would," Jay bit back.

Lacing my fingers with Ryder's, I smiled. "Let's go before you two start at it again."

Ryder and I danced to a few slow songs. It felt so good to be back in his arms. Everything felt so right when we were together. I knew I needed to tell him about what I had read in Kate's journal. When to tell him was the question though.

The song ended so we made our way back to our table. Ryder guided us through the crowd with his hand on my back. It was such a simple gesture, but one that always made my heart drop and my stomach dance in delight.

Jay had been dancing with one guy practically all night. The way they were grinding on each other was a bit unsettling. Jay hadn't mentioned how things were with her husband, Phil. Her almost jet-black hair was pulled up in a slobby bun on the top of her head, but it still pulled out her blue eyes. She was the only person I knew who could get away with the brightest shade of red on her lips no matter if she was going out or going to the gym. She rocked it every single time.

Ryder leaned over and asked if I wanted another drink. "Yes! One more and then I'm done."

With that drop me over gorgeous smile of his, he winked and quickly kissed me on the lips before heading over to the bar. I watched him walk away and I couldn't seem to pull my eyes off of him. The way his ass looked in those jeans was almost sinful.

"God ... is it getting hot in here?" I said to myself as I waved my hand in front of my face in an attempt to cool off.

Ryder walked up to the bar and waited in line to order our drinks. Smiling, I shook my head. He came for me. And he brought diamonds with him. He was a keeper.

When I glanced to the right, my heart stopped. I sat up straighter and blinked my eyes a few times. When he lifted his hand in a wave, I looked over my shoulder before snapping my head back to him.

"Holy shit balls!"

Dr. Russell started to make his way toward me. I quickly looked back at Ryder. He was now at the bar ordering.

"Oh lord. Shit!"

Quickly getting up, I forced my way through the crowd to get to Jay. When I saw her rubbing up against her new friend, I pushed my way over to her.

"Jay!" I yelled out.

She was so focused on the guy she didn't hear me. Grabbing her arm, I pulled her. Turning to look at me, she grinned wide. "Did you come to join us? I've always wanted to try a threesome."

I pinched my eyebrows together and stared at her. "Okay, first off ... please tell me you're kidding because ... gross! No thank you. Second, Dr. Russell is here!"

Her smiled dropped. "What? Are you sure?"

I turned around and looked directly at him as he stood by the table waiting for me to come back. Ryder was now walking up and looking for me.

Turning back to Jay, I yelled in a panic sounding voice, "What do I do?"

"Um ... well clearly he thought you were wanting him to meet you here so, I think you nip it in the bud."

"What? That's your advice?"

The guy Jay was dancing with yelled out. "I agree. If you try to ignore him it only makes it seem like you did something wrong."

My eyes snapped over to him. "Who are you?"

"Jay's massage therapist."

I looked back at Jay. She wasn't smiling and I knew by the look in her eyes I was going to have a conversation with her that I didn't want to have.

Rolling my eyes, I turned back and walked straight up to Dr. Russell. He was standing practically next to Ryder.

"Hey!" he shouted as Ryder looked at him and then me confused. I smiled at Ryder and walked up to him.

Moving my lips to his ear I said, "That's the doctor who took my cast off."

Ryder pulled back and looked at Dr. Russell and then back to me. "What is he doing here? Did you invite him?"

"No!" I replied.

Turning to face Dr. Russell, I politely smiled. "What are you doing here?"

He tried to give a smile that probably worked on other girls, but did nothing for me. "Well, you mentioned this place and I thought I'd take a chance and see if you wanted to work out that leg."

Oh dear lord. This guy knew he was good looking and I would guess he used it to his advantage a lot.

"Um ... well ... that was nice of you, Dr. Russell, but do you not re-member me mentioning I have a fiancé?"

He smirked. "I thought he was in Montana?"

I could see Ryder getting pissed, but he never moved.

"Regardless, Dr. Russell, I think you somehow got the wrong idea. I'm not interested in you in any way. I love Ryder."

Dr. Russell stared at me. "You're saying no to me?"

My eyes widened in disbelief. Was this guy for real?

"I don't even know how to respond to that? Are you really that stuck on yourself that you think any woman would just fall at your feet?"

"They usually do."

Slowly shaking my head, I let out a gruff laugh. "You seriously need to be kicked in the balls. You have three seconds to turn and leave before my fiancé decides he's had enough."

His smile dropped as Ryder stood up and wrapped his arms around my waist. "I'm the fiancé."

Dr. Russell lifted his hand up and took a step back. "Sorry. I'll just be um …"

"Leaving?" Ryder said with anger laced in his voice.

With a nod of his head, the good doctor turned and left.

Turning in his arms, I looked up at Ryder. "I swear I didn't invite him, and any flirting he thought I was doing was done unintentionally."

Ryder's lips crashed to mine. Our tongues danced in perfect harmony. My arms wrapped around his neck while I let myself get lost in the man I loved.

When we both needed air, we pulled away just enough for Ryder to rest his head against mine. "I'm ready to go home," I said.

"Let's get a taxi and head back to your place."

Shaking my head, I gazed into his eyes. "No. I want to go home … to Montana."

The way his eyes lit up had my heart skipping a beat. He pushed a piece of my hair behind my ear while he searched my face. "Ava Moore, do you have any idea how happy you make me?"

My stomach fluttered as butterflies swarmed inside. "I think I do, because you make me just as happy."

Twenty-Seven

Ryder

Ava and I stayed in Austin for another two weeks while we got both of our places packed up and ready to move to Montana. We spent half our time in Austin, and the other half in Llano. I was glad though as it gave me a chance to get to know her family more. And I was pretty sure I was winning the approval of Reed.

"I wish you weren't leaving," Courtney said as she set two glasses of tea in front of us.

Ava tilted her head and smiled at her mother. "I know, Mom. But now that we've gotten everything settled, it's time."

She chewed on her lip. "But I thought you weren't going to be moving back to Montana until a few months into the new year. Why are you both rushing up there?"

I cleared my throat and glanced over to Reed who smiled and replied, "It just makes sense to make the move now so we can get settled in."

"And y'all will be living in Helena? Not on the ranch?"

"No, we'll be at the ranch for a few months. Ryder and I haven't really decided on where we'll live. The focus is on the wedding."

Reed pushed a breath out. "And you're sure you both want to do this? You don't think it's too soon?"

Ava reached for my hand and laced her fingers with mine. "Dad, when you first realized Mom was the one, didn't you want to start your life right then and there? If I remember correctly, your wedding was kind of last minute."

"We had our reasons," Reed said.

"And we have ours."

"I know, but why not make it for next year?" Reed said with a hopeful expression.

"Ugh, Daddy! Are we really going to argue about this when I'm fixin' to leave for the airport?"

He pushed off the counter and held his hand out for her. "No. You're right. This is your wedding and you do it how you want."

Ava threw her arms around her father and hugged him. "I love you so much."

Courtney smiled sweetly as she watched the scene play out along with me. "Will the dress be ready in time?"

"Yes! Lucy has a seamstress in Helena who promised she can have the dress done by Valentine's Day."

"My baby is getting married!" Courtney cried out as both her and Ava hugged for what seemed like forever.

We spent the entire drive to Austin talking about everything from our wedding to cattle ranching.

Ava and I had decided we wanted the wedding to be simple. It would just be the two of us in a simple ceremony on a beach in the Bahama's. The only real thing we had planned was her dress and the honeymoon.

"Call me the moment you land," Courtney said as she kissed Ava goodbye on the cheek.

With tears in her eyes, Ava nodded. "I promise I will."

Reed reached out and shook my hand. "Tell your parents I said hi. We're looking forward to coming and visiting when y'all get settled."

"Will do, sir. And thank you for giving us your blessings."

He smiled, and for the first time since Reed found out about Ava and I, I saw something in his eyes. Happiness. "The only thing I ask you to do is love her and take care of her, Ryder."

"That will be easy to do, Reed. She is the only reason my heart beats."

He rolled his eyes. "Save that shit for her, not me."

With a laugh, I nodded. "Will do."

Ava and Courtney hugged one last time at security. Ava started crying, so I wrapped my arm around her waist and led her to the line. Resting her head on my shoulder, she sniffled.

"I'm sad and I'm happy. Please don't mistake my tears for sadness," she softly said.

My finger went to her chin as I brought her eyes to mine. "It's okay to be sad. You're leaving your family and moving to a new state. I don't blame you for feeling sad, Ava. I was sad when I moved to Texas."

She nodded. "Ryder, when we get back to Montana, can we spend tonight in the stone house?"

"Of course, I figured we would."

She wiped her nose and looked into my eyes. Those baby blues looked lost. "Is everything okay, baby?"

Swallowing hard. "I read something in Kate's diary that I need to talk to you about."

My heart leapt to my throat. "O-okay. I promised my parents we'd have dinner with them, but then we can say we're tired and head to the house right after."

She chewed on her lip and I couldn't ignore the sick feeling that was settling into my stomach. I had no idea what it was she wanted to talk to me about. I knew it had something to do with Kate and she was clearly worried about it. It had me wondering if I really wanted to know.

Sometimes it was best to leave things left unknown.

"Dinner was amazing," Ava said with a huge smile. I knew she was happy to be back in Montana. I could almost see the change in her when we walked out of the airport. It warmed my heart knowing she loved it here as much as I did.

"I'm glad to have you back and to see you walking without that dreadful cast," my mother said as she and Ava cleared the table.

"We've got this if you two would like to talk business," my mother said. She motioned to my father and he gave her a knowing look.

Once they were both in the kitchen he stood.

"So, I heard from my lawyer. Once your marriage with Ava is final, the house in Helena gets put into both your names."

I stood and walked over to him and gave him a light slap on the arm. With a wide grin, I said, "Thanks, Dad, for getting all of that taken care of."

"You know it's going to be a pain in the ass if you two decide you want to live there. That forty-minute drive will get old really fast."

Lifting my eyebrows in agreement, I followed him into his office. He sighed and sat down behind his giant mahogany desk. "But, I know what we will do to make the woman we love happy, so I can't fault you on if you do move into the house."

I sat down in the leather chair and chuckled. "I do love her, Dad. It's crazy."

He lifted his eyes. "What is?"

With a shake of my head, I looked out the giant window that overlooked the snow-covered mountains. "This feeling. I've never before felt it with any other woman." Turning my attention back to him, he was grinning from ear to ear.

"It's like the moment she walks into the room I sense her. I can actually feel her there before I even see her. She looks my way and I literally have to catch my breath."

He leaned back in his chair and seemed to get lost for a moment before he laughed. "I remember the first time I asked your mother out."

You could see the love on my father's face and it warmed my heart. I knew my love with Ava was just as strong.

"She turn you down?" I asked laughing.

"Yes!" he said. "She turned me down flat. Told me there was no way she would get mixed up with a cowboy."

"Wow. I never knew that."

"Oh, she made me work for that first date. I can't tell you how many times I went into the little bank in Helena she worked at part time. Your grandmother was so angry with me. She told me I was wasting my time chasing after a city girl. That even if I did manage to make her marry me, she'd get bored of living on the ranch and leave me."

My smile faded. The same thought had crossed my mind a few times with Ava. Even though she grew up on a ranch, she loved her place in Austin. It was one of the main reasons I wanted to move into the house in Helena. Granted it wasn't Austin, but it was still the city.

"Did Mom ever feel that way?" I asked.

He shrugged. "If she did, she never told me and never gave me any indication she felt that way. The first time I brought her to the ranch I remember her eyes lighting up as we brought in some new cattle. The whole time she sat on the fence and took it all in. When we were finished and I walked up to her and I'll never forget the smile on her face. Then she said, 'I could watch you do that every single day for the rest of my life.' It was right at that moment I knew this was the girl. The one I would spend the rest of my life with."

"I only hope that Ava and I are as blessed as you and Mom."

"You are. I see it in the way that girl looks at you. Hell, the very first time the two of you were together in a room I'm positive everyone saw it."

The light knock on the door caused us both to turn and look. Ava grinned and said, "Hey, I don't mean to interrupt, but I'm feeling rather tired and was going to excuse myself."

I jumped up. "Thanks again, Dad. I'll see you in the morning?"

"Sounds good. I've got that meeting in town I'd like for you to be there for."

With a nod, I replied, "Sure. I'll be there."

"Good," was all he said as he glanced over to Ava. "Rest up, sweetheart. Glad to have you home."

"It's good to be home," Ava said with bright eyes.

By the time we got to the stone house, Ava was a basket of nerves. I was tempted to tell her I didn't want to know anything that came out of Kate's journal, but my curiosity was getting the better of me.

She sat down on the sofa and wringed her hands together.

"Jesus, Ava. You're kind of starting to freak me out. Did my sister do something illegal?"

Her eyes snapped up to mine. "What?" Frowning, she said, "No. God no, it's nothing like that."

I pulled a seat from the dining room table over and sat down facing her. "Then tell me what it is."

"Okay well, I wasn't sure if I should keep this to myself but I can't. I need to tell you and the only way I know how to do it is to just say it."

My heart was pounding so hard in my chest it felt like it was going to jump out. "All right."

"Kate was pregnant when she died."

I sat there for a few seconds letting her words sink in.

"What did you say?"

She sighed, "Oh gesh, don't make me say it again, Ryder."

Staring at her, I felt my chest squeezing tighter, like someone had a damn vise grip on it.

The only thing I could do was stare at her. My sister was pregnant. *Oh God. We not only lost her, but we lost her child as well.*

"Do you need me to really say it again?"

I shook my head. "No," I barely spoke.

Scraping my hands down my face, I let out a frustrated sigh. "What in the hell?" Dropping my hands back down, I hit Ava with question after question.

"How far along was she? Why didn't she tell anyone? Did Jackson know?"

Ava took in a deep breath and slowly let it out. "I don't think she was that far along, I'm not sure why she hadn't told y'all yet other than she thought she had time to figure things out first and then tell everyone. Yes, Jackson knew and he had asked her to marry him."

"What?" I stood up. "She was only a senior in high school! What in the fuck did she think she was going to do with a baby?"

Ava stood. "Ryder, getting mad about it is not going to make you understand anymore. Your sister was in love with Jackson; they made love in this house more than once and they were going to have a child. The only person who can really answer your questions is Jackson himself."

I shot my head in her direction as my heart sank. "What? Have you talked to him?"

Her eyes widened in surprise. "No! Of course not."

I walked back and forth not knowing how I should be feeling. My sister was pregnant. *Oh my God. Why did you take them from us?*

My throat was burning from the tears I was trying to hold back. I'd never really allowed myself to cry over my sister's death.

Jumping when I felt Ava's hand on my arm, I pulled her to me and wrapped her up in my arms. Not being able to hold back my emotions, I let my tears fall as I whispered, "Why did he take them from us, Ava? Why?"

Twenty-Eight

Ava

I sat on the sofa in the little stone house and stared down at Ryder. He had completely lost it. I'd never seen him so emotional before, and a part of me wondered if I had made a mistake in telling him about Kate's baby.

Then I realized what was happening. Ryder was finally allowing himself the chance to cry. It was as if the reality of his sister's death hit him in that moment and he decided to stop pretending Kate had gone away, and accepted the fact that she was gone forever.

My phone buzzed. Picking it up, it was from an unknown number.

Swiping it, I softly said, "Hello?"

"Ms. Moore?"

"Yes, this is Ava Moore."

"This is Parker, the caretaker of the house in Helena."

This was strange. Why was he calling me?

"Yes, hello. How are you doing?"

"I'm doing well. Ms. Moore, I know the last time you were at the house we chatted about its history. You had asked me if Kate ever came to the house alone and I couldn't remember."

My heart dropped to my stomach. "Yes. I was wondering that. You know she was so intrigued by Lizzy and Robert's love story as am I."

Ryder moved about some, but didn't wake up.

"Yes, she was. Well, I remembered something. I'm not sure why I had forgotten it, maybe because Kate's death was just a couple days after."

"What!" I practically screamed.

Parker cleared his throat. "Kate had come to the house. She called and said she was doing a family research paper and would be staying the night in the house. I remember thinking nothing of it. I didn't normally call Mrs. Montgomery to ask if the kids could stay, because they often did. They are such good kids, you know."

I tried to keep my voice steady. "Yes I know they are. So, Kate came and stayed at the house. Was she alone?"

"To the best of my memory, yes. She was alone. I do know that was the first time young Kate had stayed at the house alone, but she mentioned her beau would be stopping by later for dinner."

Why would Kate and Jackson stay the night at the house in Helena? It's not like they needed a place to be together.

"One more question, Parker. Do you remember what room she stayed in?"

"Oh yes, the master bedroom. Why?"

Lizzy and Robert's.

"Just curious. Thank you so much, Parker."

"Your welcome. Did you and Mrs. Montgomery enjoy the old letters from Lizzy and Robert?"

My mind was spinning. There was something missing to all of this. I had felt like there was something Kate was hiding the moment I started reading her diary. At first I thought it was a long-lost secret of Lizzy's. When I found out she was pregnant, I thought that was it, but it wasn't. There was something else and I could tell by how conflicted her words were in her diary. I needed to find out what it was.

"Um … oh yes, the letters. They are amazing! We have a few left to read. Did you say that Kate had come to the house before? Was it with her sisters or brothers?"

"Yes, they would come together. Young Kate loved exploring the old house."

That much I had figured out. Kate must have stumbled upon the letters while exploring. She wrote about some of the things that were in the letters in her own diary.

"Well, it's an amazing house to say the least. The letters have helped a lot in getting to know Lizzy and Robert."

"Wonderful! Wonderful. Okay, well that was all I needed to say. Just let me know when you'll be coming to the house again."

"Tomorrow."

"Tomorrow?"

I bumped Ryder to wake him up. "Yes, Ryder and I will be heading there tomorrow. He has a business meeting in town, so I think we'll stay the night."

"Sounds good. I'll be sure the heat is turned up for you then."

Ryder sat up and looked at me with a dazed look. "Thanks, Parker. Have a nice night."

I hung up the phone and stood. "I think there was something else Kate was hiding. I've felt it from the very moment I found her diary. I thought the pregnancy was it, but I can't shake this feeling there was something else."

"Oh God," Ryder moaned. "I don't know if I can take anymore secrets being found out."

"I'm going with y'all tomorrow to Helena. Can we stay the night at the house?"

Ryder lifted his eyebrow. "Yes. Why?"

My face curved with a smile. "We're going exploring."

"Don't explore without me."

My jaw dropped. "That's like asking me to never eat chocolate again!"

Ryder furrowed his brows. "Really? I'm just asking that you don't try to find anything until I get back."

"What am I supposed to do until you get back?"

He shrugged. "See if Jennifer wants to meet for lunch. Or Dani and the baby."

Dani had a little girl a few days after Christmas she named Lindsay. She was adorable and the moment I held her in my arms, something weird happened. I wanted a baby. Not that I would *ever* admit that to anyone.

"I guess I could do that," I somberly said.

Pulling me closer to him, Ryder held my eyes with his. "I want to be here if you find something."

His eyes looked so sad. There was no way I would ever go against his wishes. "I'll call Jennifer and Dani. Maybe they can both sneak away for lunch."

His hand came up to my face where I leaned into it. "Thank you."

Smiling, I closed my eyes and let the moment between us settle in my heart.

"One more thing."

Opening my eyes, I looked at him skeptically. "What?"

"I called Jackson."

Gasping, I replied, "When?"

"This morning. I asked him if he would join us for dinner. I didn't ask him to come to the house. Not really knowing what happened here between them, I wasn't sure how he would feel."

"That was sweet of you to think that way. What are you planning on saying to him?"

I couldn't imagine how Ryder was feeling or what he was even thinking. Even more so, I couldn't imagine what information he thought he would get from Jackson.

"I'm not sure. I guess I want to ask him about the baby. Was Kate scared? Was she happy? What in the hell were they thinking?"

With a slight frown, I placed my hands on his chest. "Will you do me one favor?"

His face softened. "Of course."

"Remember he suffered a loss as well and he had to hide part of that loss. Put yourself in his shoes, Ryder. He lost the girl he loved and his child."

His eyes fought back the tears that were welling up. "I know. I promise I'll remember that."

Reaching up on my toes, I gently kissed him. "You better go before you're late."

With a nod, he replied, "I'll call you when the meetings over."

Following him back out to his truck, I watched him drive off. Out of the corner of my eye, I saw Vanessa. Peeking over, I watched her wave and smile as Ryder drove off.

Ugh.

Before she could see me, I quickly turned and headed back into the house.

"Ava? Ava wait!"

Shit. Put on your happy face, Ava.

Plastering on a fake ass smile, I turned to face her.

"I thought that was you. I see you got your cast off."

The way she made her breasts bounce when she walked turned my stomach. She was the last person I wanted to see and probably the only reason I would not ever move into this house permanently. "Yep, I got it off about two weeks ago."

She let out a fake chuckle. "I bet you're happy to get it off."

I wiggled my eyebrows and replied, "I am. It makes everything so much easier. Even Ryder agrees."

Her smile faltered for a moment. "What brings you and Ryder here?"

I could tell her Ryder was here for a lunch meeting, but I thought I would put this bitch in her place once and for all. "Lucy has a friend who is making my wedding dress."

Her mouth dropped open. "Your what?" Shaking her head, she let out a dry laugh as she said, "I swear you said wedding dress."

Holding up my left hand, I smiled as big as I possibly could. I could have let out my old cheerleader personality with an *Oh my gawd, Ryder asked me to marry him! Ahh!* Instead, I simply said, "You heard right. Ryder and I are getting married on Valentine's Day."

I don't know why, but her deer-in-the-headlights look made me want to do a little dance. *I wonder if I asked her to give me a tour of my future home again if she would be down for it?*

"Vanessa? Are you okay? You seem a little ... stunned."

Her eyes flicked between the ring, the house, and me. Clearing her throat, she forced a smile. "I'm fine. I was just taken aback I guess. I didn't realize he was that serious about you."

You. Did. Not. You. Bitch.

Narrowing my eyes at her, I stated, "I didn't realize you were that close to him to make that assumption."

With a look that honestly should have had me falling over dead, she screwed her face and shot daggers at me. "We're not. I just didn't picture Ryder settling."

"You mean settling down."

"No, I meant settling."

Oh, hell no.

Walking toward her, I stopped just short. "Listen here, Vanessa. I've got your number. I grew up with a brother and a best friend who taught me how to throw a right hook, and trust me when I say I am not afraid to use it."

Her mouth fell open. "Are you threatening to hit me?"

"I'm just telling you that if you think you can fuck around with me, I'm here to tell you you cannot. I love Ryder and he loves me. I'm wearing his ring on my finger and if we're going to be neighbors someday I suggest you get it through your damn head now that you will never get your greedy little paws on this house or my fiancé. Am I making myself clear?"

Vanessa took a step back. "I've never."

"And you never will." Lifting my hand, I waved my fingers and said, "Bye, neighbor."

Spinning on my heels, I couldn't help but do an internal jump and fist pump. I've always wanted to tell someone off. Damn, it felt good; she was the first one I tried it out on.

Glancing back to where she had been standing, I smiled when I saw her walking away. Looking forward, I made a mental note to tell Walker his baby sister was a bad ass!

Twenty-Nine

Ryder

I stared at the middle of the table as my father spoke about the use of vaccines on the cattle being raised on organic farms.

My head was going off in a million different directions as I tried to focus on what my father was saying. It's not like I could afford to be daydreaming. If I planned on running the ranch someday, I needed to stay focused.

The next thing I knew, Dad was standing and thanking everyone for taking the time out of their busy day.

When the last person left, he turned and looked at me. "Where in the hell where you during that?"

I pulled my head back and looked at him like I had no clue what he was talking about. "Don't pull that look with me Ryder. I'm not your mother. You were a million miles away."

Pushing my fingers through my hair, I blew out a breath. "Dad, if I tell you something, will you swear not to share it with Mom?"

He lifted a brow. "It depends. If I deem it something she doesn't need to know, then yes."

"Well, how do I know if you will deem it something she needs to know or not before I tell you?"

He shrugged. "Don't know. Guess you'll have to tell me to find out."

Letting out a frustrated sigh, I shook my head. "Never mind. I'll deal with it."

The papers he had been looking at dropped to the desk. "Would it make you feel better if I promised not to tell her?"

"Yes. It really would. I'm not even sure I should be telling you."

He leaned back in the chair and rested his chin on his fingers like he always does when he is intrigued. "Well hell, now I want to know."

I shook my head. "I'm not sure you do, but I feel like I need to tell you."

He dropped his hands. "Ryder, is everything okay? You look a bit lost."

Swallowing hard, I took in a deep breath. Was this right of me to be telling my father Kate was pregnant when she died? I'd hardly slept a wink last night thinking about it. If it would have been my daughter, I think I would have wanted to know. My mother on the other hand, I didn't think she should know. It would only make the loss that much more.

"I am, Dad. I'm so conflicted on if I should say anything or keep this to myself."

"Only you can decide."

I nodded. "Ava found a diary hidden in a secret compartment of the desk in the old stone house."

"Who's diary was it?"

Swallowing hard, I barely spoke the word, "Kate's."

He sat forward. "Kate's? She found a diary that was Kate's?"

I nodded.

"When?"

"The same day she found the family Bible."

He constricted his face. "Why didn't she tell anyone?"

"She did. She told me and Jennifer and we both agreed because of the very private things written in the diary, and the fact that Kate hid it so well, that she would not want Mom of all people reading it."

He looked out the window for a moment before agreeing. "I agree. I don't think your mother should know about it. Has Ava read it?"

"Yes. It's weird that she even found it, Dad. Ever since the first day we stayed in that cabin, Ava's been saying she feels a presence there and she swears it's Kate."

My father smiled warmly. "They are so much alike. Even down to the designing. It's as if fate brought her into your life."

"I know. But Ava told me something last night that she herself has been debating about."

His eyes filled with worry. "Ryder, is this something Kate would want me to know?"

My heart ached. It would have been something she would have wanted all of us to know … but on her terms.

"I think so … eventually. She'd want us to know in her own little way. Her terms."

With a chuckle, he closed his eyes. "I miss her. There is not a day that goes by that I don't think of her. Sometimes I think I see her in a crowd and I have to catch my breath."

I knew exactly what he meant. "There was this one time, at a concert I was at with Nate and Jennifer, and I swear I saw her. I even walked up to the girl, took her by the arm and turned her to face me. She looked exactly like Kate."

We sat for a few moments, lost in our own memories of her. "Back to what Ava found out. Um … well … shit I don't know how to say this so I'll just say it like Ava did. Dad, Kate was pregnant when she died."

His face turned white immediately. "What did you say?"

Jesus, I really am just like my father. "Kate, was pregnant. Jackson was the father. She wasn't that far along, and from what Ava said, Kate had planned on telling the family but thought she had time to get things settled. Whatever she meant by that."

He sat there staring at me. "Dad? You're not having a heart attack or anything are you because I totally didn't pay attention to a damn thing you said in that meeting just now."

He blinked a few times and looked at me. "No … I'm not having a heart attack. I'm in shock. Let it sink in please before you start cracking jokes."

"Sorry. I'm just unsure myself how to process this and it's been over twenty-four hours since I found out."

My father stood. "I agree, your mother shouldn't know about this …

at least not right now. Let me think about this. Have you told anyone else?"

"No. Ava's only told me and we are having dinner with Jackson tonight."

His eyes widened in horror. "What? Why?"

"I want answers."

He frowned. "What kind of answers? Your sister was pregnant. Do you want Jackson to describe what they did?"

My stomach turned. "Ugh. Really, Dad? No, I want to know how she felt about it. Was she happy? Did they tell Jackson's parents? What in the hell was she going to do being pregnant at seventeen and in high school?"

Shaking his head slowly, he walked up to me. "Ryder, what does any of that matter?"

The lump in my throat made it hard to talk. "I don't know how to explain it, Dad, but I have to know."

Standing, he walked over to me and put his hand on my shoulder. "I don't know if Jackson is going to be able to tell you anything that is going to help."

"I know."

"All right, I don't want you hanging on to some false hope that he can give you the answers you're looking for."

I nodded.

With a sigh, he said, "I'm heading back home. Kiss that beautiful fiancée of yours."

He reached out his hand for mine. With a quick shake, he turned and grabbed his stuff and was out the door.

Walking over to the window, I looked out over the city. Helena was nothing compared to Austin, yet it was home and I loved it. What would life had been like for Kate had she lived? Would she have stayed here and gotten married?

I closed my eyes and tried to ignore the empty spot in my heart. "Damn it, Kate. Why did you leave us?"

Thirty

Ava

I sat across the table from Dani and Jennifer and listened to the two sisters go about some local event happening. Dani lived about an hour or so from Helena, so her coming in was not something she did often, but today she was thrilled to bring Lindsay in. Jennifer was currently holding the sleeping baby I couldn't stop staring at.

The ache in my chest was strong as I started daydreaming about what a baby with Ryder would look like.

Light-brown hair. For sure her hair would be curly. Yes … she would have curly light-brown hair and blue eyes.

"Ava? You seem a million miles away," Dani said with a concerned look.

Looking up from Lindsay, I forced a smile.

"Yep, totally fine. Sorry, I was just looking at Lindsay. She's so beautiful."

Something moved across Dani's face. Looking at Lindsay, she looked back at me. "Ava. Are you pregnant?"

She asked exactly as I was taking a drink of Diet Coke. I started choking as she jumped up. "Are you okay?"

After I finally got done hacking up my right lung, I looked at her. "Why would you ask me that?"

Jennifer started laughing. "I was about to ask the same thing, truth be told. The way you've been eyeing Lindsay, and you have that look."

I swear my voice raised in pitch. "I don't have a look!"

Dani sat back down. "Oh yes you do, Ava Moore. I know that look, I've seen it on my own face."

A heavy feeling settled in my stomach while my eyes darted back and forth between the two of them. "You're both crazy. That's like saying Nate is going to settle down and get married."

Both of them started laughing. "Yeah, that's not happening any time soon," Jennifer said.

"Neither is a baby. Let me get through marrying your brother and trying not to beat Vanessa's ass."

Dani's eyes darkened. "Vanessa, huh. She has been after Ryder for as long as I can remember."

"Well, I'm pretty sure after today she knows that is not going to happen. Or she put a restraining order out against me."

Both girls chuckled. "Why, what happened?"

I shook my head and took a sip of soda. "She rubbed me the wrong way and I may have gone off on her while flashing my engagement ring in her face."

"God, I knew I liked you the moment we first met. I've always wanted to just walk up to Vanessa and punch her right in the mouth," Dani said while motioning with her hands like she was punching someone.

"Holy shit balls, Dani. What did the girl ever do to you?"

She rolled her eyes. "That little bitch cut off my Barbie's hair and then said Ken would never love my Barbie like he did her Barbie 'cause her bitch Barbie had hair. That … that … C-word!"

I forced myself not to start laughing. Holding up my hands I said, "Whoa, bring it back in, Rocky. Deep breath in and blow it out."

Jennifer shook her head. "Do you remember when that little boy, Tommy, moved in across the street and every time we came into town he would come over to play. I had the biggest crush on him. He even tried to kiss me once. He told me I was the prettiest girl in the world. Problem was he said it in front of Vanessa. The next day she told him I was actually a boy and he stopped talking to me. Still to this day, if I run into him he will totally cross the street to avoid talking to me."

Dani gasped. "Is that why he stopped coming over?"

"Yep. Sucks too, because he is drop dead handsome now. And single!"

With a giggle, I said, "Man she is a cu—"

"No!" Dani and Jennifer yelled out. I wasn't sure how Lindsay slept through that outburst but she did.

Jennifer frantically shook her head. "Don't use that word. I hate that word."

My phone buzzed. Pulling it out of my purse, I saw Ryder's name.

Ryder: Heading home, buttercup.

Ugh. I was feeling so many different emotions today. The pull to have a baby, the excitement of what I might find in the house that Kate left behind, the nervousness of meeting Jackson for dinner, guilt for not telling Jennifer and Dani about their sister Kate's pregnancy, and to top it off, planning a wedding that was just a couple weeks away.

"Ryder is on his way back to the house. This was so much fun. Dani, thank you for driving in."

I pulled enough money out of my purse to cover lunch. Standing, I walked over and kissed them both on the cheek and then kissed the baby on top of her head. I took in a long deep breath.

Oh lord ... she smells so good.

"Tell Ryder we said hi," Jennifer said.

With a smile, I nodded and replied, "I sure will. Bye, girls."

As I walked off, Dani called out, "Don't think I didn't notice you smelling her! You've got the baby bug, admit it!"

Without turning around, I lifted my hand and waved.

I did have the damn baby bug, but I would never admit it. At least not right now.

Walking into the house, Ryder was sitting on the sofa in the front living room reading something. He looked completely focused on it.

Oh. My. God. He started looking and found something without me! I'm going to kill him!

"Hey, what are you reading?"

He looked up and frowned. "Did you threaten Vanessa today with bodily harm?"

Placing my hand on my hip, I narrowed my eyes as anger swept up to my face, heating my cheeks. "I knew it. I knew that little bitch would do something." Walking up to him, I asked, "What is it? A restraining order or something?"

Ryder laughed. "What? Why would she do that? Jesus, Ava. What did you say to her?"

"Wait. How do you know?"

"She practically attacked me when I pulled up. She said she was innocently standing outside when you walked up to her and threatened to punch her if she ever talked to me again."

My mouth dropped open. If he took her side I was taking this diamond and chucking it in his face.

"I can't believe this. You're actually going to sit there and tell me you believe I would ever do something like that?"

Ryder stood up and smiled. "No, I don't believe her, but I do believe she got you so mad you probably did threaten her."

"I did, but she started it. When she found out we were getting married, she said she couldn't believe you would settle for someone like me."

He pinched his eyebrows. "Damn, baby, please don't let anything she says get to you. She doesn't matter and what comes out of her mouth really doesn't matter either."

Grinning, I glanced down at the paper. "What were you reading?"

He quickly picked up the paper and folded it. "Nothing."

Lifting my eyebrows, I lowered my head and looked at him. "Really? Cause you were very focused on that piece of paper when I walked in."

The cutest damn smile spread over his face. Pulling me to him, he kissed me softly and then whispered, "They're my vows."

Plunk. That was my heart dropping. Just like that, I was swept off my feet. "Your vows?"

"Yeah, I wrote them last night when I couldn't sleep. I need to polish it up a bit. Actually a lot. I can't make heads or tails of the whole second half. I must have been dozing off."

I melted right there on the spot. "If I didn't want to search this house so badly, I'd totally push you down and rip your clothes off."

His face lit up. "I like the sound of that."

I slapped him on the chest. "Later! Let's go exploring."

Thirty minutes later we were standing in the middle of the master bedroom looking around. "Okay, so we checked all the drawers in the dressers. The closet is empty, and the desk doesn't have any secret doors. Now what?" Ryder asked.

"I guess we could ask Jackson if he knows if Kate left anything in the house." I sat down on the bed and looked around. I had this overwhelming feeling there was something in this room and Kate wanted us to find it.

Shaking my head, I closed my eyes. *Show me, Kate. You have to show me.*

Opening my eyes again, I got up and started walking around the room. I walked over to a painting and stopped in front of it.

"Who painted this?" I asked leaning in and seeing the initials LM.

"Lizzy, I believe. She painted a lot of the pictures in the house."

My breath caught. "Can we take it down?"

Ryder walked over and grabbed it. "Sure."

He took it down and turned just enough for me to see the manila envelope taped to the back. My hands came up to my mouth.

"Ryder," I whispered.

He turned the painting and saw it. "Holy shit."

Carefully, Ryder set the picture down on the bed. We stood there and stared at the envelope. I knew the writing the moment I saw it. It was Kate's.

My chest rose and fell with each labored breath. I had no idea what we would find in that envelope. Ryder reached for my hand and whispered, "It's Kate's handwriting." He turned and looked at me. I could see the fear in his eyes, but something told me this was nothing to fear. At least I prayed like hell it wasn't.

I smiled and squeezed his hand.

"I can't do it, Ava. You have to see what's in there."

I nodded as my pulse raced. My voice was caught in my throat. "O-okay."

With shaking hands, I gently pulled the envelope off the back of the painting. Ryder took the painting and hung it back up. Sitting down in the chair, I pulled in a deep breath while Ryder walked across the room and stared out the window.

I reached in and pulled out a stack of papers. It was legal papers ... a contract.

Oh my God. Smiling, I covered my mouth with my hand as it hit me what I was looking at. It was a contract between *Amour Des Lettres* and Kate. My heart was pounding so loudly I was surprised Ryder couldn't hear it.

Scanning the contract, I felt the tears building in my eyes. I had never even met Kate, but it was as if she was my own sister. The pride I was feeling was beyond anything I'd ever felt before. My goodness. She was only seventeen.

Amour Des Lettres was a design company in France. They were the one design company everyone dreamed of being in with. Even me. I interviewed for a position with them when I was in France. It was there I ran into Maurice and ended up working for him.

They wanted four of Kate's designs. What must she had felt when she got this contract in her hands and at such a young age.

I looked up and felt the tears falling down my face. "Ryder. It's not bad at all. It's the most amazing thing ever."

He spun around and his face fell when he saw me crying. "Why are you crying? And smiling?"

Pressing my lips together, I tried to contain the sobs I wanted to let out. My heart was happy and so sad at the same time. Kate had the brightest future in front of her, and in one moment it was taken from her.

Once I felt like I could talk, I handed him the contract. He took it and looked at it with a confused expression.

"What is this? Who is Amour Des Lettres?"

I wiped the tears away. "They are a design company in France. One of the best. They're known for their wedding dresses mostly. They sell for over thirty thousand a piece. They wanted four of Kate's designs."

His eyes lifted to mine. "W-what?"

Nodding my head, I smiled and let out a sob. "Ryder, this was huge. I can't even imagine how over the moon Kate must have been," I said with a giggle.

Ryder shook his head while slowing sitting down. "Kate had an opportunity to design for this company?"

I nodded my head. "It looks like she had submitted a few designs that they wanted, but here, on this page they are offering her a full time designer position. In France."

"Holy shit," Ryder whispered. "She didn't sign it." He snapped his head up and looked at me.

I shrugged my shoulders. "The baby maybe?"

Ryder bent over and took a few deep breaths. Then I saw his body begin to shake and I knew he was upset. Jumping up, I fell to the floor in front of him.

"She had her whole life ahead of her. Her whole damn life. I don't fucking understand why this happened. Fuck!" he yelled out and my heart broke even more.

I took the contract from his hand and crawled onto his lap. He buried his face into my neck and held me like he was going to lose me.

Nothing was said for the longest time as we just sat there. I peeked over to the clock and cleared my throat. "We need to get going if we want to be on time for dinner with Jackson."

Ryder nodded. The look in his eyes was empty.

"Maybe Jackson will be able to help answer some questions."

Standing, he made his way to toward the door. "Maybe."

Thirty-One

Ryder

A va grabbed my leg and squeezed it. "Stop bouncing your leg. You're shaking the table."

      I had no idea why I was so nervous. No, that was a lie. I did. Just the thought of seeing Jackson made me feel sick. He was the one reminder I always tried to avoid. Maybe even the whole reason Nate and I left Montana. I ran into Jackson six months after Kate died. The pain of seeing him was almost too much to stand. He must have felt the same, because I saw it in his eyes.

"Tell me what you're thinking right now," Ava asked in a low voice.

I looked around the restaurant. "That we should have done this at the house. Because even though my sister is gone, I still want to kick his ass for getting her pregnant."

"Ryder."

Ava's voice was laced with concern. I rolled my eyes. "Don't worry. I won't kick his ass."

Every time the door to the place opened, we both looked over, each holding our breath. Ava had no clue what he looked like, but when I released my breath, she would release hers.

Her phone buzzed as she picked it up and typed something back. It was her boss, Maurice. He had been keeping her busy the last few weeks. Before he would send her designs to clean up, now she was doing her own designs. I was so proud of her. If only he would put her stuff in a show. My chest felt light as I thought back to earlier when Ava was so proud of Kate. She never even knew her, but there was something there. Some kind of weird connection I didn't want to admit at first, but now I saw it. The way she stood up and walked to that picture was almost as if Kate whispered it in her ear.

The door opened and Ava asked, "Is that him?"

I nodded and stood. Jackson scanned the restaurant before our eyes met. He looked the same, just a bit older. His sandy-brown hair was cut short and he was dressed in a suit.

"Yes, that's him."

"Go, Kate. He's a looker." I quickly shot a look to Ava. "What? I'm just saying she had good taste."

With a huff, I forced a smile when Jackson walked up. Reaching my hand out, I somehow managed to talk. "Hey, Jackson. It's good seeing you." Motioning to Ava, I said, "This is my fiancée, Ava."

Jackson, shook my hand and then Ava's. "It's good seeing you again, Ryder." He smiled at Ava. "It's a pleasure meeting you, Ava."

"The pleasure is all mine."

I pointed for him to sit. "Please, sit down. Would you like a drink?"

He laughed and said, "Yes, something strong."

It seemed we were both a little nervous about meeting.

After the waitress took his order, he looked directly at me. "I have to say getting a call from you out of the blue has me a bit out of sorts."

With a nod, I replied, "I know. It's just ... well ..." I turned to Ava and she placed her hand on my leg and took control of the conversation.

"Jackson, I found Kate's diary a few months back in the old stone house."

His brows raised. "Really? Just now someone found it?"

Okay, so he knew she kept a diary.

"Well, she had hidden it in a place that really not many people would look to find it. I kind of had a few clues."

Jackson looked at me and barely grinned. The last thing I wanted to tell him was my fiancée felt a connection with his dead girlfriend.

"Anyway, I started reading and it was soon clear to me that Kate would not have wanted anyone, like her mother, to read the diary. I talked to Ryder and Jennifer about it and they both agreed that Lucy should not find out about it only because there are some rather ... personal and graphic memories."

Jackson's face turned red and his eyes looked sad. "Kate was amazing. I truly loved her with all my heart."

I looked away. It felt like someone was trying to rip my heart out and stomp on it.

"I know you did. I can tell by the way she writes about you. But, in reading the diary, I found out she was pregnant and I told Ryder."

Jackson moved about in his seat and cracked his neck. "Oh. That explains the phone call."

I cleared the lump in my throat. "It's nothing like that. For my own sanity, I just needed to know how she felt about the pregnancy. Why didn't you guys say anything? What were your plans?"

Jackson picked up his drink and downed it in one gulp. Lifting his hand, he pointed for another.

"Please forgive me, I don't normally drink, but it's been awhile since I've talked about Kate and the baby. Well, actually I've never talked to anyone about it. I've kept the secret like she asked me to."

In that moment, my heart broke for the guy. He had to hide the fact that he had a child with the love his life. I wouldn't even try to understand how that must feel.

"It's okay, believe me I understand. Totally understand and I'm sure this is selfish on my part," I said, glancing over to Ava.

"No. I want to talk about it. I think it will actually do me good." His hand pushed through his hair as the waitress dropped off his drink. He picked it up and took only a sip this time.

"When Kate told me she was pregnant, I was stunned. We were always careful. None of that really matters now. The fact was we were going to have a baby. We had both gotten our acceptance letters for the University of Montana. As soon as she told me about the baby, I asked her to marry me and she said yes."

"What in the hell where you going to do? Go to college with an infant?"

Ava kicked me under the table. I needed to keep my emotions in check.

Jackson took in a deep breath and pushed it out. "That's what we were trying to figure out. We thought we had it all figured out. She was going to tell your family and I'd tell mine. She was due in March and she figured she would go to school up until she had the baby. She had talked to the principle who agreed to let her homeschool after she had the baby to finish her degree."

Holy shit. The fucking principle of the high school knew our sister was pregnant?

"She knew Kate was pregnant?"

Jackson shook his head. "No. Kate told her that her father was going out of the country and taking the family."

I pulled my head back in disbelief. "And she believed it?"

Jackson smiled. "I don't think she did. I think she put two and two together, but never said anything."

"Okay, so then what were you going to do?"

He looked at Ava. "Wait. Your name."

"What about it?" Ava asked.

Jackson smiled. "Ava. That was one of the names Kate had picked out if the baby was a girl."

My head turned to look at Ava. Her face turned white. "W-what?" I could see her chest moving up and down.

"Yeah, she met someone who worked at the movie theater who had that name, and I remember she wrote it down with the other baby names. I think I still have the list at home in a box of things I saved."

Ava reached for my hand. *Jesus. Maybe my sister was in that damn house. I'm never sleeping there again.*

Jackson saw the reaction of what he had just said on Ava's face. She had been trying to keep it in, but a single tear slipped and rolled down her face. "Sorry, Ava, your name just clicked."

She wiped a tear away. "S-okay."

"Anyway, I thought we had it somewhat planned. We knew it would be hard, but I was pretty sure we could do it. I was going to take a full load one year; Kate would take a couple classes since we'd have the baby. Then we'd switch the next year. I'd take a light class load and she would take more." He looked away and I saw the tears building in his eyes.

"Then everything changed. Two days before she … before she died, she called and asked me to meet her at your family house in Helena. She said she wanted to spend the night with me and we had something important to talk about."

His voice cracked and he took a few moments to get his emotions in check.

Ava reached for his hand and held it. "It's okay, Jackson. Take your time; I know this has to be hard."

He nodded. All I could think about was what Kate was about to tell Jackson. You could almost still feel the pain pouring off of him.

"Kate told her parents she was spending the night with a friend or something. We had the house to ourselves." He smiled as a tear rolled down his face. "She made us dinner and then we went for a walk and I dared to let myself believe that someday we'd be a family and walking our own—"

He closed his eyes. When he opened them he smiled.

Ava and I exchanged looks as Jackson cleared his throat.

"Anyway, after we had … well … spent some time together," Jackson looked at me and then looked away. "She told me she had gotten a job offer. I remember laughing and thinking it was probably working for your family's ranch. When she showed me the contract, I was so happy for her. I felt like I was going to burst at the seams I was so damn happy. Then she told me she would have to move to France. At first I thought she was kidding, but I could see the look in her eyes. I remember getting angry. I told her I couldn't believe she was going to just up and leave me. Take our child and move to another country. I said some pretty hurtful things to her … things that haunt me every fucking night in my dreams."

I couldn't imagine what Jackson must have been going through. If Ava told me she was pregnant and leaving for France, I'd blow a fucking gasket too.

Ava held onto Jackson's hand as she said, "Jackson, you can't beat yourself up over all of that. Never mind the fact that y'all were so young in the first place."

He let out a gruff laugh. "Yeah. It sucked. She had to wait until she was eighteen before she could actually go to France and work as a designer, but they wanted four of her dresses. They told her they would easily bring in over twenty thousand and the demand for more of her work would be something they could see. After I calmed down, I told her I'd go with her. That when the time came, I'd move to France with her."

"What?" I whispered. I was stunned. Beyond stunned. Here I wanted to knock the hell out of this kid this whole time and now he is sitting here saying he would have given up his own dreams so she could follow hers.

"Oh, Jackson. What did Kate say?" Ava asked.

"At first she said no. She took the contract and taped it behind a picture in the master bedroom."

"That's where we found it today," Ava said.

Jackson looked stunned. "You found it? Today? How did you know to look there?"

Ava waved her hand and replied, "It's kind of hard to explain, but we did find the contract. She hadn't signed them though."

Jackson wiped at his eyes again. "No. She didn't because she said we needed to think things through. She wasn't ready to let me walk away from my dreams and there was no way she would ever take the baby away from me. So, we decided we would decide in two days."

The lump in my throat was growing. I needed a break. Standing, I quickly said, "I need a second. Excuse me."

Turning, I quickly headed outside and dragged in one deep breath after another until if felt like I was able to breathe.

Dropping my head, I whispered, "Oh, Kate. My sweet sweet, Kate."

Thirty-Two

Ava

Jackson had excused himself right after Ryder did, except he went to the men's restroom. I checked my phone and smiled when I saw I had a voice message from Renee. After listening to it, I hit her number.

"Bonjour."

"Bonjour, Renee, It's Ava Moore."

"Ava! What in the hell! You have this whole damn office in an uproar right now, can I tell you that?"

I quickly peeked between the men's room and the front door.

"Listen, I don't have a lot of time to talk."

"Well, you better make time. He wants to talk to you."

My breath caught. "Does he remember Kate?"

"By the smile on his face, I'd say he does. He rattled off something about her young life ending too soon. My French is good, but when that man rattles that shit off fast I can barely understand him."

"Yeah, I'll have to catch you up on that."

"Oh, Ava, there is one condition. He wants you to fly here … to Paris."

Ryder walked back in through the front door.

"Holy flippin' shit balls. Why? When?"

"What are you doing on the second week of February?"

My heart started racing. *This is not happening.* "Getting married in the Bahama's."

Renee busted out laughing. "Better make that Paris."

"I gotta go. I'll call you back in a few."

"Don't you dare show those designs to Maurice. Amour Des Lettres has first dibs!"

"Right. Later."

I hit End and stood when Ryder walked up. "Sorry about that. It's just all so much hearing this. Knowing my sister had this whole other world planned out that none of us knew about."

Kissing his cheek, I replied, "I know. It had to have been so overwhelming for both of them."

Jackson appeared before us and apologized. "I guess we both needed a moment."

"I guess so," Ryder said.

After they both ordered another drink, Jackson started back up where he left off. "The day Kate died, we left school early and hiked up River Mountain. We sat for a few hours and talked about what we both wanted. For me, there was only one option, and that was for Kate to follow her dreams. If she hadn't, I would forever doubt her happiness. All I cared about was her and the baby. We had decided to tell your parents first and tell them about Amour Des Lettres offer to her. She was going to take it. We decided to stick with the plan of finishing high school, and then after we graduated, we'd move to France. She had called and spoke with some guy in France ..."

I cleared my throat and softly said, "Michael Blancet?"

Looking at me with a surprised look, he replied, "Yeah. That's the guy. She called and told him what our plan was and about the baby. He was more than understanding. So much so, I remember Kate saying she had to be dreaming. He agreed to wait, but he told her he wanted her designs. It was all coming together ... or so we thought."

His jaw began to tremble. "We agreed to meet at the stone house and then tell her parents. When I walked in she was ... she ..." He dropped his head while his body jerked with sobs. I quickly got up and went over to him.

My heart ached. It ached for Jackson and what he lost; it ached for Ryder's family and what they lost, it ached for Kate and the future that she had that was taken from her. So many broken dreams. I was going to do everything in my power to give Kate those dreams. I could feel it in my heart she knew and she wanted this.

After Jackson regained his composure, I sat back down. My phone buzzed on the table. Ryder and Jackson were now talking about Jackson's family. It gave me a chance to read the email that just came in.

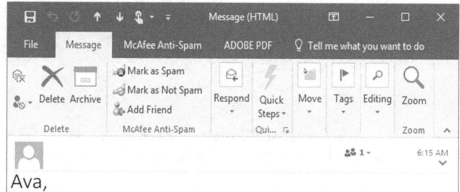

Ava,
I told Michael you were getting married in a few weeks. He said if you will leave it up to him, he will take care of the wedding details, but he wants you and Kate's designs in Paris by February twelfth when he gets back from the Milan show. I told him you said yes.
See you soon!
P.S. I can't wait to meet your cowboy.

"Oh my God."

I wanted to kiss and kill Renee.

"Is everything okay?"

My head jerked up. Ryder was looking at me with a concerned expression. "Um … yes?"

He laughed. "Is that a question to my question?"

I swallowed hard. "Well, you see there is this friend of mine who I went to college with. She works in France. At Amour Des Lettres. As Michael Blancet's assistant."

Jackson leaned forward with his full attention on me.

"I kind of sent her a text and asked her to ask her boss if he knew the name Kate Montgomery from Montana."

"And?" Ryder asked with a confused expression on his face.

"It looks like we aren't getting married in the Bahamas after all," I said with a lighthearted chuckle.

Ryder frowned and shook his head. "Why not?"

Pressing my lips together, I replied, "Cause we're getting married in the city of love instead."

The Saint James Paris hotel Michael had put us up in was beyond crazy beautiful. Ryder and I hadn't stopped pointing and gasping since we walked in.

"Okay, let's act like we're supposed to be staying at this hotel and stop acting like a damn tourist," I said as we made our way up to our suite. The two grand staircases where beyond beautiful. It was like nothing I'd ever seen.

"We are tourists," Ryder said.

The moment we opened the door to our room, I knew I was never going to stay at another hotel like this again in my lifetime.

"Oh my."

Ryder and I walked in and looked around. "It has two floors!" Ryder called out as he ran up the steps. "There is a baby-grand piano up here!" he yelled in excitement.

I tried to hold back my giggles, but failed. I was just as excited. Paris was where I originally thought I would be living. Where I dreamed of designing clothes and wedding dresses people would be begging for.

Ryder came back downstairs holding his phone up. "What are you doing?"

"Rubbing this shit in Nate's face."

I rolled my eyes and smiled.

"We have our own balcony. I'm having naughty thoughts!" Ryder said from outside.

"I like the sound of that!" I replied.

Glancing around the room, I took in the beauty. It was classic French décor all the way. The furniture itself looked like it was taken from a palace. I walked up and looked out to see the most breath taking garden I'd ever seen. Even in the winter it was filled with flowers.

This was like a dream come true. Not only were Kate's dreams about to come true, but mine were as well.

Two hours later, Ryder and I were getting out of a taxi and walking into Amour Des Lettres main office. Michael greeted us as we walked in. His English was almost perfect as he spoke to Ryder about how much he adored Kate and how he had never seen such talent until yesterday.

I pinched my eyebrows together at his comment. What an odd thing to say.

Michael turned to me and looked me over and then slowly shook his head. "Kate has blessed me ten-fold."

I peeked over to Renee who stood there with a huge-ass grin on her face. "Now, come to my office. We have much to talk about it."

Following Michael to his office. Ryder stopped every now and then and took a selfie with random girl walking down the hall and fired it off to Nate. He laughed every time he got a response. They were all the same.

I hate you.

When we walked into Michael's office, I stopped dead in my tracks. "My dress!"

Turning quickly, I placed my hands on Ryder's chest and pushed him as hard as I could. He went tumbling backwards and fell right on his ass.

"You can't see my dress!"

He looked up at me with a stunned expression. "Why not? I've seen it on paper. What difference does it make?"

My heart was beating like a wild horse running in an open field. "You can't see it."

Stepping in Michael's office, I slammed the door shut and made my way over to the dress.

Covering my mouth, I held back the waterworks show. It was beautiful. How Lucy's friend managed to do this in the short amount of time she had was amazing. No wonder it cost me a small fortune!

"I don't think I've ever seen a more beautiful wedding gown, Ava," Michael said while we both gazed at it.

"The end product is breathtaking," I said with a huge smile. Never mind the fact that Michael Blancet just said my wedding dress was beautiful.

"It is. Now, let me have Renee put this back in the bag so that your poor Ryder can join us."

My face turned red. "Well, I really don't want him seeing it until I'm in it."

He nodded and motioned for me to let Ryder back in now that Renee had zipped up the bag. Ryder walked in and shot me a dirty look. I mouthed, *sorry*, to him and blew him a kiss.

"Sit, both of you please. We have much to talk about."

We each took a seat and sat there stunned while Michael said he wanted the original designs that Kate had sent them. He also wanted the five other designs of Kate's that I sent a few weeks back that were not finished.

Ryder took my hand and squeezed it. Kate's dreams of becoming a fashion designer were going to happen.

"We already decided the money will go into a scholarship account for young girls in Montana to follow their own dreams," Ryder said when Michael started talking money.

"I do have one question though," Ryder said. "Who will be finishing my sister's other designs?"

My heart sank. I'd have given anything to have been able to finish them.

Michael sat back in his chair. "Oh, that will be done by our latest designer. She lives in America and is *very* familiar with Kate's work."

Ryder and I both looked at each other. *What in the hell is he talking about?*

"Who?" I asked a little too hard.

With a wide smile, Michael said, "You, Ava. You will finish Kate's designs. The moment I saw your dress I knew that my sweet Kate brought you to me to finish the work she had begun, and so much more."

I was positive I had just peed my pants. "Wait. What?"

Everything from that point on was nothing but a blur.

Thirty-Three

Ryder

After filling my parents in on everything that had happened since we got to Paris, I was exhausted. Ava and I had been going non-stop since we landed in France. Between finishing up the deal for Kate's designs, and then Michael offering Ava a position, things were insane.

Ava had called Jackson to let him know also. We had talked one other time since dinner that first night. I had asked him why he was still single and the only thing he said was no one had moved his heart like Kate enough to make him fall again. Ava was hell bent on making sure Jackson moved on and found happiness again. So much so, she and my mother planned a dinner where they invited a shit load of people, many whom were young and single. Jackson wasn't interested though. He spent most of the night talking to Jennifer.

The water in the bathroom turned off as I made my way in. Ava was soaking in the tub. She had never looked so beautiful.

"So? What did Maurice say?"

She kept her eyes closed. "Well, after he called me a bitch about six times, he told me he was proud of me and that his little secret weapon would have gotten noticed sooner or later."

I smiled and made my way over to her and sat on the edge of the giant tub. "You look tense."

"I'm getting married tomorrow. I am tense."

Moving my eyes to the faucet, I couldn't help but notice the shower head was a hand held.

"Then I think it's time to relax you."

Her eyes opened as a smile slowly grew across her face.

"What did you have in mind?"

I stood and quickly got undressed and joined her. Lifting the shower head, I turned it on and adjusted the temperature.

"Spread your legs apart, Ava."

Her mouth parted open as she did what I said. Placing the jetted water up to her clit, she gasped.

"Touch your breasts."

She quickly did what I said. My dick was so hard it was throbbing as I watched her pull and twist each nipple.

"Ryder! Oh God!"

Her body trembled as she came. It was the most beautiful thing I'd ever seen. Turning off the water, I watched her come down from her orgasm.

"Shit," she mumbled.

"Feel relaxed now?"

Her eyes moved down to my rock hard cock. When she gave me a wicked smile, I knew my day was about to get even better as we made our way to the bed.

Crawling on me, she slowly sank down until I was balls deep inside of her. Our lips pressed together as she slowly moved up and down.

"Faster, Ava."

It didn't take long before she called out my name and I did the same, pouring myself into her felt better than ever.

She stayed on me while we both caught our breaths.

"Is it just me, or is sex in Paris better?" Ava asked, still sitting on me with my dick jumping inside of her.

"Sex with you is better each time no matter where we are, baby."

Rubbing her nose against mine, she giggled. "Good answer."

"How about we spend the rest of the day taking in the sites?" I asked.

With a huge smile, Ava nodded and jumped up. "Yes! Let's get dressed. There is so much I want to show you!"

We spent the rest of the afternoon exploring Paris. Ava showed me all of her favorite shops and we went to one that had the most amazing dresses in Paris. *Ava's words not mine.* "Kate's designs will be in this store."

I shook my head. "It's bittersweet."

Lacing her fingers with mine, she smiled weakly. "I know, but it's also amazing at the same time to know your sister's dreams are coming true. And that a scholarship is being made in her honor. Her life lives on and y'all should be so proud of her."

Choking back tears, I nodded. "I am. I still wish she was here to see it all."

Ava reached up and gently kissed me. "She sees it, Ryder."

I cupped her face within my hands. "Thank you. Thank you for making this all happen, buttercup."

A tear fell from her eye and slowly made a path down her beautiful face. Wiping it away with my thumb, I stared into those baby blues of hers.

"I wish I had known her. I think we would have been good friends."

"She would have loved you and you would have loved her."

Ava smiled bigger. "So … you sure you want to marry me?"

Throwing my head back, I laughed. "I've debated it all day today."

Hitting me on the chest, we made our way back to the hotel. Ava ordered room service and we spent the rest of the evening wrapped up in each other's arms.

I stood and stared at myself in the mirror.

I'm in Paris.

I'm getting married.

I'm freaking out.

My cell rang on the side table. Quickly walking over to grab it, I saw his name and debated answering.

Nate.

"Hello?"

"Are you sure about this, bro? The whole ball and chain thing? It's not too late to back out."

Rolling my eyes, I let out a frustrated sigh. "What in the hell are you calling me for? It's like three in the morning there."

"I've been at your bachelor party! It was fucking amazing! The stripper we hired ... holy shit, dude. She fucked me until I swear she broke my dick."

Pinching my eyebrows together, I replied, "Wait. You had a bachelor party for me ... without me there?"

"Yeah, well it's not my fault you ran off to France to get married."

"Asshole, I would have been in the Bahamas today so I still would have not been there."

The line was silent. "All right, well whatever; we celebrated your dick being owned by one woman for the rest of your life. How does it feel knowing that? God ... my body just trembled thinking about it."

"Someday, Nate, there is going to be a girl who is going to change you."

He let out a roar of laughter. "Fuck. No. I like the way my life is, thank you very much."

"What was her name?"

"Who?"

"The stripper."

A loud crash came from the background as Nate mumbled something about not being able to find the lights. "Hell, I don't know. Candy. Misty. Rock my world. I have no clue what her name was. All I know is she could fuck."

I shook my head. I knew this was not the life Nate wanted. He just hadn't met the right girl to tame his wild ways.

"Listen, I've got to go. Nate? Are you okay?"

"Me? Hell yeah. Drunk as hell from that awesome as fuck bachelor party I threw you."

With a moan, I replied, "Well, glad it was fun. I'll talk to you when we land in the US."

"Tell Ava I said hi. And Ryder, I really am happy for you. Ava is a great woman and what she has done for Kate … well, just tell her I said thank you."

My heart warmed. I knew deep down inside my brother wasn't a total asshole. "I will, bro. Talk soon."

After getting off the phone with him, I took one last look at myself and made my way downstairs. The wedding was being held here in the hotel in one of the private ball rooms. When I walked in, I smiled. The room was filled with white and pink roses. Ava would love it.

Straight ahead was a balcony that overlooked the garden. Making my way out I noticed Karen, the wedding consultant Michael had hired, making some last minute touches. She turned to me and spoke in French.

I had no clue what she rattled off. "It looks beautiful. Very beautiful."

She smiled and gave me a pat on the arm before heading back into the room.

Looking out over the garden I took in a deep breath and slowly blew it out. *"I'm getting married. Holy shit I'm getting married," I mumbled.*

A young girl was walking through the gardens that caught my eye. I didn't pay too much attention to her until she turned and looked up. My heart stopped and my chest grew tight. Wrapping her coat tightly around her body, she stared up at me.

She looked exactly like … Kate.

I closed my eyes tightly and re-opened them. Lifting her hand, she waved. I mindlessly did the same as I tried to get a better look at her.

"Are you ready?" Renee asked as she stepped up next to me.

There was no way I could pull my eyes away from the girl. She stood there looking up at me while I tried to figure out how I could see her face … yet I couldn't make it out.

"Ryder? Are you okay?" Waving her hand in front of me to drop my gaze, I turned to her.

"Yeah. Um … that girl down in the gardens. She looks so familiar to me."

Renee turned and looked out over the gardens and frowned. "What girl?"

Snapping my head back forward, my heart dropped.

She was gone.

"She was right there," I said pointing.

Renee shook her head. "Did you drink too much last night? There was no one standing there when I walked out here. Are you sure you saw someone?"

I continued to stare in the spot I saw the girl. Turning around, I fought to regain my composure.

"I'm fine. Must be nerves."

With a bright smile, Renee nodded. "Must be. At any rate, Michael is upstairs fussing over Ava's gown. I think we'll be ready to start in the next few minutes. Do you need anything?"

"A drink. Something strong."

She laced her arm in mine as we headed out of the room and made our way to the small bar in the hotel. Even though Renee was from Texas, she spoke perfect French ... at least it sounded to me like she did. Speaking to the bartender, he looked at me and chuckled.

Before I knew it, two glasses of ice water were placed in front of us.

"If there is one thing I've learned in my life, the only thing to calm a person down is deep breaths and a nice chat."

With a chuckle, I took the water and drank it. "That's good advice; I'll have to remember it."

"Ryder, I'm glad I had a chance to speak with you in private. I wanted to take a moment to just tell you your sister was amazingly talented. I've only ever met one other person who had crazy talent like that and you happen to be marrying her."

My heart slammed against my chest. The different emotions I felt were like a tornado in my body. I was happy ... sad ... scared ... excited. All of it balled up into one.

"I'm a lucky guy, believe me I know."

Renee looked at her phone and then over to me. "So, are you ready to get hitched? Ava's about to come down."

Swallowing hard, I finished off my ice water and stood. "Never been more ready."

Thirty-Four

Ava

Michael Blancet ... one of the most famous designers of my time ... was standing behind me gazing at me in the mirror.

"This has to be one of the most stunning gowns I've ever seen. I cannot believe it was made in Montana! I must hire the seamstress and make her mine!"

Giggling, I let my eyes roam over the gown I had designed. The beaded Queen Anne neckline added the perfect amount of elegance. The sheer V-back bodice gave the gown that sexy look I was going for. The scalloped hem lace was breathtaking and came just short of my ass I swear.

Michael lifted the lace-trimmed chapel-length train and let it free fall. "Gorgeous. Simply gorgeous. The use of the misty tulle, diamond tulle, and this delicate allover lace just screams elegance. We will have to lift poor Ryder's tongue off the ground when he sees you in this."

With a wide smile, I took another look at myself in the mirror. The gown fit my body like a glove. I wasn't sure how she was able to get this dress made in time, but I was going to have to give her a bonus for the exquisite job she did.

Lifting my eyes, I softly blew out a breath. My blonde hair was pulled up into a French twist. My grandmother's pearl-drop earrings dangled from my ears adding the perfect touch. I opted for a simple pearl necklace that had been my mother's. It added a simple touch and didn't take away from the neckline of the gown.

"Your blue eyes are dancing with excitement, Ava."

Peeking over to Michael, I laughed. "Do you have any idea what you being here fussing over my dress is doing to me?"

He winked. "I hope it is making you piss your lace thong you better have on under this beauty. And it better be one of my designs."

Feeling my face heat, I shook my head. "Ah, the French."

The light knock on the door had my stomach dropping. "Oh God. This is it."

"Let's get this thing going. I can't wait to get you photographed in this gown."

Rolling my eyes, I took the pink peony bouquet Karen handed me. They were Kate's favorite flower and I thought appropriate for the occasion. "Merci, Karen. Will Ryder get to be in any of the photos?"

Michael stopped. Turning to Karen, he fired off in French and I'm pretty sure he asked her if Ryder was wearing the Armani suit.

"Oui," she quickly replied.

Holding out his arm, I took it and let him lead the way. "Yes, he can. Thank God you're marrying a handsome man or your wedding pictures would only be of you and the gown."

"So, why no big wedding? You designed such a beautiful dress?" Michael asked. "I would think you would want to show it off."

With a shrug, I replied, "Ryder and I talked about it. I was engaged before and was planning a huge wedding. It was a pain and I hated the whole process. When Ryder asked me to marry him, I knew I wanted something intimate. Something just the two of us shared together. We'll have a reception in both Montana and Texas, but this part ... this part is just for us."

He smiled. "Fair enough. Love doesn't need to be celebrated in front of huge crowds for two people to know they love one another. The focus is clearly on the two of you. I like it."

I chucked and concentrated on each step I took.

By the time I made it down the staircase, I was sweating from being a nervous wreck walking in the damn heels I had on. I was still worried about my ankle being weak.

We stopped outside the giant double doors of the banquet room. My chest was rising and falling so quickly, I was sure Michael thought I was going to pass out.

"Telle une belle mariée."

With a smile, I leaned over and kissed Michael on the cheek. "Merci beaucoup, Michael. For everything. I'm pretty sure you're the best boss a girl could ever ask for. I am for sure very lucky."

He tossed his head back and laughed. "I'm the lucky one," he whispered as he stepped back and they opened the double doors. My eyes scanned the room and I couldn't help but smile when I saw the white and pink roses.

The music started and I had to be prompted by Karen to start walking. I felt his eyes on me before I even saw him. My heart was racing as I looked straight ahead. Sucking in a breath of air, I was overcome with the sight before me. I'd never seen Ryder look so handsome. His face curved into the most delicious grin I'd ever seen. I could see his bright eyes as he swept them over my body.

The closer I got, the more my heart raced. I imagined Ryder must have been pushing his hand through his hair in a nervous manner because it was the perfect amount of messy. Nothing else in this world mattered to me except for the man standing in front of me.

Dear Lord ... he looked sexy as hell.

Stopping in front of him, he looked me in the eyes and said, "You take my breath away, Ava. I can't even begin to tell you how beautiful you look."

Swallowing hard, I pressed my lips together in an attempt to hold my tears at bay. When I finally felt like I could speak, I barely got the words out.

"You look ... handsome. I can't breathe."

He chuckled and kissed me on the cheek. I was taken by surprise when he placed his lips near my ear and said, "I can't wait to slowly take that dress off and make love to my gorgeous wife."

My knees wobbled and I was pretty sure I let out a moan. When we turned toward the pastor, I tried like hell to focus on him, but all I heard were Ryder's whispered words playing over and over in my head. Then add in the beautiful backdrop of the garden and I was all kinds of not paying attention.

When it came time for our vows, my heart raced. *Holy flippin' shit balls. I can't remember my vows!* Ryder had been rubbing his thumb over my hand the entire time, causing tingles to race across my body. I was ready to tell Michael the hell with his photos, I wanted to go right to our room.

When the pastor told Ryder to recite his vows, Ryder opened his mouth and nothing came out.

"Oh shit."

I really tried to hold back, but I lost it laughing. Ryder looked at me like I had lost my damn mind.

Dabbing my eyes carefully so I didn't ruin my makeup, I finally got myself under control.

"I forgot mine too."

The corner of Ryder's mouth rose into a sexy as hell smirk. "You did?"

Nodding, I replied, "All I need to know is that you love me."

He cupped my face. "I love you so damn much, I can't even think straight. Do you love me?"

I lifted my eyes as if thinking hard about his question.

"Ava!"

"Yes, I love you, Ryder, and all I want is to be your wife and wake up every morning in your arms."

"Good enough for me," he whispered with an even bigger grin on his face, crushing his lips to mine.

The preacher tapped on our shoulders and said, "Um ... I pronounce you man and wife. You're already kissing, so keep at it!"

We both laughed as Ryder deepened the kiss while dipping me back. Renee and Michael broke out in cheer.

"Don't ruin her makeup," the photographer said in a thick French accent.

Ryder pulled his lips back and looked into my eyes. I could see my whole future in them and all I saw was happiness.

"Are you ready, Mrs. Montgomery?"

"Oh I'm more than ready, Mr. Montgomery."

I stopped at the bottom of the staircase and moaned. "I'm too tired to walk up these stupid steps."

Ryder laughed and the next thing I knew, I was in his arms as he walked up them.

"You're going to carry me the whole way?"

"I am."

Smiling, I sunk my teeth into my lip and took in his handsome face. I wasn't sure how I got so lucky to score such a catch. He caught me staring at him.

"What are you thinking?" he asked.

"How lucky I am. How this seems like a dream. I'm praying I don't wake up in my apartment with Jay passed out on my couch."

His laughter rippled through my body warming it up even more.

"I promise this is no dream."

When we finally made it to our room, Ryder carried me and slowly let me down until my feet hit the floor.

"Have I told you how breathtaking you look?"

My stomach fluttered while his eyes danced with desire. "A few times."

Placing his hand on the side of my face, I leaned into it. "So beautiful."

I covered his hand with mine and looked into his eyes. My heart was racing and my breathing picked up. I felt like I had just run a race.

"I can't believe I'm your wife. It seems like it was yesterday you bumped into me."

He slowly shook his head while his eyes searched across my face. "Do you have any idea how happy I am right now?"

My cheeks were beginning to hurt from smiling so much. "I have an idea, but why don't you show me."

"Oh Mrs. Montgomery, it would be my pleasure."

Licking my lips, I asked, "What are you going to do first?"

"Turn around."

I did as he said. The moment his fingers touched my bare back, I felt my body tremble. His touch did amazing things to me and I couldn't wait for more.

"Your skin is so soft," he whispered as he ran his fingers down my back. "When you first turned around and I saw how far down your dress dipped, I wanted to rip it off you and bury myself deep inside of you."

"Oh God," I panted out.

The moment I felt him begin to unzip my gown, my panties got even wetter. I jumped when he placed his hands on my shoulders. "Are you ready for me to make love to you?"

Glancing over my shoulder to him, I forced the words out. "Y-yes."

With one move of his hands, my gown pooled at my feet.

"Holy fuck," he whispered and I couldn't help but smile. I was safely guessing my baby-blue lace thong and matching bra were the reason for his reaction.

Turning around to face him, his eyes widened and it was as if he were gazing on me for the very first time. I loved how my bra practically pushed my breasts up to my chin. Ryder's eyes fell right to them.

"I can't ... even ... form words."

Smiling, I chewed on my lip nervously. "Then use your hands," I softly spoke.

And use his hands he did. Reaching behind my back, he expertly unclasped my bra and let it fall. Cupping my breasts with his hands, I dropped my head and let out a low moan.

His mouth claimed my nipple as he worked the other with his fingers.

Placing soft kissing on my chest, he spoke against my skin. "You smell so goddamn good. I want to lick every inch of your body."

I shuddered at the thought. His nose softly made a trail across my neck until he was whispering in my ear. "I'm going to make love to my wife all ... night ... long."

"Yes," I gasped.

His lips captured mine in a kiss that was so powerful, I felt as if I was lost in it. Ryder lifted and carried me over to the bed where he gently placed me. His fingertips slowly traced down between my breasts, down my stomach, and along my panties.

"Lift your hips, baby."

Doing as he said, Ryder slipped my panties down and off. Pushing my legs apart, he crawled over my body and kissed me gently on the lips. His hand moved lightly over my body as I pushed up my hips. I needed him to touch more before I combusted.

"Ryder, please touch me."

He pulled up and looked into my eyes. His crooked smile had my heart skipping a beat and desire building between my legs. "I am touching you, baby."

Frantically shaking my head, "Please. Touch. Me."

My voice sounded needy, but I didn't care.

"I'll do anything for you, Ava. Anything."

My body felt as if it was on fire. The need to feel him inside of me was beyond insane.

When he pushed his fingers inside of me, I gasped.

"Fucking hell. You're so wet."

"I want you. God, Ryder, I want you like never before."

His mouth was on mine while his fingers worked my body up into a frenzy. I could feel my orgasm building as he deepened the kiss. It hit me hard and fast as I moaned into his mouth. Trembling as my body pulsed with desire, Ryder pulled his mouth away.

"Son-of-a-bitch, I love it when you fall apart."

He teased my entrance with his tip while I tried to focus. The mind-blowing orgasm felt like it was still rippling through my body. The only thing I could think about was how much I wanted him inside of me.

"Ryder! Please!"

He slowly slid inside of me and our worlds instantly became one.

"Oh, Ava. You feel so good. I want to be inside you forever."

"Yes," I gasped. "God, yes!"

Ryder made the sweetest love to me, taking his time as he explored my body with his hands and mouth.

When neither one of us could take it anymore, he grabbed my hips and gave me what I needed. When we came together, it was the most amazing moment ever. One I would never forget.

My body was exhausted as Ryder pulled me up and led me into the shower. He pampered me with the most sensual shower I'd ever had where there was no sex involved at all. He washed every inch of my body in the most tender and caring way. At one point I started to cry I was so overcome with love.

"Baby, are you tired?" he asked as my tears mixed with the water.

I shook my head. "No. I'm just so happy, Ryder. I can't even begin to tell you how happy I am."

His smile made my knees weak. "You make me so happy too. Come on, let's dry off."

"And snuggle?" I asked.

With a chuckle, he replied, "Yes. And snuggle."

We talked well into the night about the ranch, the house in Helena, and our future together. We had so many dreams and I couldn't wait to start making each and every one come true.

My eyes grew heavy as I began to fall asleep.

"I swear I saw Kate today."

Forcing them back up, I lifted my head and rested my chin on my hands over his chest. "When?"

He stared up at the ceiling. I could see the tears building and my heart ached for him. "Right before the wedding. The young girl was standing in the garden and she looked up at me. Her face was hard to see. She waved though, which I thought was kind of weird, but at the same time I had the overwhelming feeling it as Kate. Renee walked up and I turned to look at her for one second. When I looked back … the girl was gone."

Goose bumps covered my body. "Maybe it was Kate."

He smiled. "Maybe it was."

"I can't wait until her designs are being walked down the runway. I just wish she was here."

Ryder's arm pulled me closer as he gazed down at me. "I know, but knowing you had such a huge part in this, and will continue to, is more than amazing."

"It was Kate's name and work that caught Michael's eye … not mine."

He shook his head. "You are amazing, do you know that?"

I snuggled back down into Ryder's side. "This whole day has been amazing."

"Yes, it has."

We both settled in while my body began to relax.

I swore I heard a little girl's voice calling out Ryder's name as sleep started to claim me. Smiling, I whispered, "Kate," before drifting into a dream where Ryder carried a little girl with light-brown curly hair and bright blue eyes on his shoulders.

And her name was ... Kate.

Epilogue

One Year Later

My mother sighed. "Ava, you need to slow down. You're making me a nervous wreck with how you're rushing all over the place."

"We're late."

Hearing her sigh only made me sigh … again. "Ava, I'm just saying I think you need to slow down. I mean, you're building a house on the ranch, you've just remodeled part of the house in Helena, and now you're rushing around Paris. You *need* to slow down!"

Ryder and I had decided to move into Lizzy and Robert's house while having a house built on the ranch. Once the ranch house was completed, we would live there full time, but spend time in Helena as well. As much as I loved the old house in Helena, I was still a country girl at heart and I wanted to raise my child in the country.

I laughed. "Mom, we're late and I have to be there early."

"Sweetheart, you're pregnant!"

"So? Why is me being pregnant have anything to do with this?"

I knew I wasn't being fair to my mother. It had to be hard for her with me living in Montana. Then throw in I was expecting my first child in a few months. My parents, Walker, Liza, and Nickolas had flown into Paris yesterday and it had been nothing but rushing ever since we picked them up from the airport.

"It doesn't, I'm your mother and it's my job to worry. Anyway, change of subject." Turning to Lucy and Nate Sr., my mother asked, "Are you both just so excited?"

"Yes. Beyond excited!" Lucy exclaimed.

Nate walked in and got everyone's attention. "We really need to head down to the limo now if we want to be there early."

"Ava, do you need to use the restroom before we leave?" my mother asked as Nate laughed.

"Yeah, Ava. Do you need to use the potty?" Nate teased as his father smacked him across the back of the head.

Rolling my eyes, I placed my hand on my six-month pregnant belly. "I'm good, Mom."

My father came up and walked next to me. "Cut your mom some slack. She is jet lagged and hasn't seen you in months. Let her baby you some."

Smiling, I stopped, reached up, and kissed him on the cheek. "I'm so glad y'all are here. I really am. I've missed you both so much."

He kissed my forehead softly. "We've missed you too, sweetheart. We are both so proud of you. I know tonight the main focus is on Kate's work, but I want you to know that when they preview your spring line, I'm going to be yelling out that you're my daughter."

Laughing, I felt the tears build up in my eyes. "I love you, Daddy."

"I love you too."

My eyes filled with tears as I blinked rapidly to keep them back. Ryder took my hand and kissed the back of it. "You ready?"

Taking in a deep breath, I replied, "As I'm ever going to be."

Ryder held the limo door open and helped me as I crawled in. Lucy, Nate Sr., Jennifer, Jackson, Dani, and Nate, as well as my parents, all followed in behind me. Ryder slid in last and sat next to me. My heart started to pound in my chest as I looked at Kate's family. This was it. This was the moment they had been waiting for.

My mother snuggled up next to my father and smiled when he whispered something in her ear. I was so happy my family was here. Walker and Liza would be taking a separate car since they had Nickolas and didn't want to arrive as early as we had to.

I couldn't help the smile on my face as I watched Jackson and Jennifer. The two of them had grown close over the last year. Both insisting they were only friends, but I could see the way they looked at each other. I knew Jennifer struggled with the fact that Jackson was so in love with her sister. If only she would try to open her heart to the idea. I could see Jackson was tearing himself up by fighting his feelings for Jennifer.

Turning to look out the window, I decided to do something about the two of them once we got back to the states.

Turning to ask Ryder if he remembered my Tic Tacs, my latest pregnancy craving, I noticed Lucy. She was staring at me.

"Are you okay, Lucy?"

She smiled sweetly. "Very much okay. I just want to say one thing while everyone is in the car."

I squeezed Ryder's hand.

Nate threw up his hands and said, "I swear it wasn't me who had sex with that model in the bar last night."

Everyone turned to look at Nate. "Oh, was that not what you were going to talk about?"

Nate Sr. shook his head, "Jesus H. Christ. And this is what I spawned."

Covering my mouth to hide my smile, I peeked up at Ryder who was shooting Nate a dirty look.

Lucy cleared her throat. "No, but thank you for clearing that up for us, darling."

Nate smiled and nodded his head as Jennifer punched him in the arm while Jackson and Dani laughed.

"What I wanted to say was thank you to Ava. Since you came into our world in a whirlwind flash, nothing has been the same. Because of you, we are about to see our beloved Kate's dreams come true. But I don't want this to just be about Kate, because you, my sweet girl, should be so proud to have two of your own designs in this show. I can't express enough how proud we all are of you, Ava. It warms my heart to see you be able to follow your dreams, and I know if Kate was here she'd be saying the same thing."

Oh dear. I promised myself I wouldn't cry. Dani handed me a tissue and I dabbed the corner of each eye while my mother reached over and took my hand.

"Thank you, Lucy, so much."

Ryder reached over and rubbed my stomach. "Kate is here. Tucked away and enjoying every moment."

"She is!" Jennifer said with a huge smile.

When we found out I was having a girl, there wasn't a second thought to what her name would be.

Kate.

"We're here," Ryder said.

While Ryder and everyone went to their seats, I made my way backstage. Any last minute adjustments, I wanted to be a part of.

"There she is!" Renee said as she walked up and hugged me. "How are you feeling?"

"Amazing! Tired! Nervous ... scared ... I may puke."

"You can blame that all on the little one," Renee said with a laugh while rubbing my stomach.

By the time the show started, something kicked in and I was running on adrenaline and excitement.

I cried when each of Kate's designs went out. Peeking out, I watched Ryder and his family do the same. I even saw Nate quickly wipe a tear away. Jackson sat with a huge smile on his face. I couldn't help but notice when he reached for Jennifer's hand and held it.

Kate's wedding gowns would be in the Barcelona wedding show along with three of my own. I wasn't sure if I would be able to fly in for that because it was a week before my due date. I was holding out hope though. Even though Ryder had already said no.

Michael was introduced after the show and walked out on stage. Renee came up and stood next to me as I looked over the two models in front of me. "You both look beautiful," I said with a huge smile.

They both wore dresses I had designed that were a throwback to the early nineteen thirties. One was called the Lizzy and the other Kathleen. Named after the two women who inspired the designs.

I reached up and adjusted the pin holding the pill cap hat on the one model. "The black lace looks amazing up against your blue eyes," I told the model.

"Thank you, Ms. Montgomery."

"Ava, please call me Ava."

"This is it!" Renee called out.

Michael was introducing a sneak preview of the spring line of *Ava Grace*. My heart raced as the first model walked out. Renee took my hand and squeezed it and said, "Welcome to the party!"

Laughing, I adjusted the hat one more time before ushering the next model out. Taking a few deep breaths, I turned to Renee. "What if I fall?"

Shaking her head, she simply said, "Don't. A pregnant woman falling on a runway will not look sexy at all."

Michael introduced me as I said a quick prayer I wouldn't trip, slip, or puke. When I walked out, the only person I saw was Ryder standing there with a huge bouquet of white and pink roses. I focused on him at first as I started walking. Looking around, I smiled and said thank you before kissing Michael on each cheek. Turning to my parents, I almost started crying. My father and Walker were both wiping tears away. Liza and my mother were wearing huge smiles on their faces while clapping like crazy.

I brought my attention back to my handsome husband. Taking the flowers, I kissed him on the lips. "Thank you." I said as I wiped my tears quickly away.

"I'm so proud of you, Ava."

"Thank you, but do you know what I want more than anything?" I asked.

He shook his head. "What?"

"A peanut butter and strawberry sandwich on sourdough toast."

With a wink, he replied, "I'll get right on that."

When he placed his hand on my stomach, Kate kicked. We both looked down at his hand and then back up at each other.

Closing my eyes, I smiled. Life had never been so utterly perfect.
Thank you, Kate.

The End

Other Titles

Broken Series

Broken
Broken Dreams
Broken Promises
Broken Love

First three books on Audiobook

Journey of Love Series

Unconditional Love
Undeniable Love
Unforgettable Love

Entire series on Audiobook

Speed Series

Ignite
Adrenaline

With Me Series

Stay With Me
Only With Me (coming 1.31.17)

Boston Love Series

Searching For Harmony
Fighting for Love (coming 4.4.17)

Stand Alones

The Journey Home
Who We Were (Available on audio book)
The Playbook (Available on Audiobook
Made for You

Coming Soon

Fated Hearts Series

Heart in Motion (Coming 6.27.17)
Guarded Hearts (Coming 7.25.17)

Seduced Series

Seduced (Coming 9.12.17)

Joint Projects

Finding Forever (Co-written with Kristin Mayer)
Stories for Amanda

Young Adult – writing as Ella Bordeaux

Beautiful
Forever Beautiful (coming March 2017